# Work Like You Don't Need The Money

Pete and Holly – Summer Lake Book Two

## SJ McCoy

A Sweet N Steamy Romance

Published by Xenion, Inc

Work Like You Don't Need The Money Copyright © SJ McCoy 2013

Published by Xenion, Inc.
First Paperback edition 2017
www.sjmccoy.com

This book is a work of fiction. Names, characters, places, and events are figments of the author's imagination, fictitious, or are used fictitiously. Any resemblance to actual events, locales or persons living or dead is coincidental.

Cover Design by Dana Lamothe of Designs by Dana
Editor: Kristi Cramer of Kristi Cramer Books
Proofreader: Aileen Blomberg

ISBN 978-1-946220-08-0

# Dedication

*For Sam. Sometimes life really is too short. Few xxx*

# Chapter One

Holly stared out of the truck window, trying to make out the shape of the mountains beyond the rain that was belting against the glass. It had been quite a weekend.

"Are you doing okay over there?" asked Pete.

"Me? I'm fine. I'm more concerned about you driving in this." Holly didn't like to spend time on the road and she hated that Pete had to drive through what had become a torrential downpour. She stole a glance at him. He didn't seem concerned in the slightest. He emanated waves of warmth and confidence, drawing her in. She took in his dark blond hair, deep blue eyes, and chiseled features. He should look quite imposing, but a tiny dimple on his chin and an air of friendliness softened the edges of a powerful persona.

He was powerfully attractive. She knew that much. The looks were one thing, one very distracting thing. But the looks combined with the magnetic personality made her feel he was like a flame—and she was the moth.

"I'm fine to drive," he said, peering through the windshield as the wipers worked double time in a losing battle with the rain. "And we don't have much choice if we want to get you back to LA tonight."

They'd spent the weekend up at Summer Lake, where Holly's best friend Emma, and Pete's partner, Jack, had just got engaged. Holly couldn't believe that she'd only met Pete yesterday morning, when Emma had arranged for him to drive her up to the lake from LA. He was one of those rare men who put you right at ease and made you feel like you'd known him forever.

Holly jumped as thunder exploded, seemingly right above them. Lightning streaked across the sky.

"Are you okay?" asked Pete, not taking his eyes off the road, or even the rain battered windshield through which he was focusing to try to stay on the road.

"I think so," Holly replied. "I hate this weather."

"We'll be fine," Pete assured her. "It should ease up soon."

Holly hoped so. She was beginning to question her need to get back to the city tonight. She had to open the store in the morning, but they could probably still get there by ten if they stopped somewhere for the night. If not, Roberto, Erin, and Anna all had keys and were quite capable of opening the place themselves. Heck, they could run the place for weeks if she could back off enough to let them. She couldn't though. Her fashion boutique was her life. Her great achievement. She hated to admit it, but she needed it more than it needed her. Though the way this storm was developing, she was just about ready to accept that it could survive without her...for a morning.

Thunder boomed again just overhead and she jumped up in her seat. Still without taking his eyes off the road, Pete reached over to touch her arm. With his attention focused on driving, his fingers grazed her breast before settling on her arm. Tingles of desire flooded her body at his touch. She was glad his eyes were fixed on the road so he couldn't see the way her body reacted. Her nipples pushed at her shirt, seeking more of his attention. He'd had this effect on her all weekend.

Emma had threatened to set the two of them up, but Holly knew now that would never work. Pete was big time. In a big way. While she herself was small time and knew it only too well. Pete had a huge corporation, a fancy oceanfront home, and was building another home up at the lake—he even talked about his plane! A light jet apparently. That was a different world from the one Holly lived in. Yes, she owned the boutique and did very well for herself. She had her own home—a modest townhouse, and for her that was huge success. It may not be much compared to Pete, but she was the only woman in the Hayes family who worked at all. Her parents still lived in the same small house where she'd grown up. Her two older sisters lived in the same neighborhood, both housewives with kids of their own.

Her body didn't seem to care about the difference in their statuses though. The warmth of his fingers on her arm sent heat spreading though her, awakening butterflies in her stomach that she thought had long since migrated. She could see the corner of his mouth lift in a small smile as he withdrew his hand.

"Don't worry," he said, "I've got you covered."

The images that filled her mind at those words didn't have anything to do with driving in the rain.

"I'm sorry I'm such a wuss," she said. "But can we just find somewhere and stop for the night after all? I don't think my nerves can take much more of this."

"Are you sure? I can get us there if you need to get back tonight."

"I don't need to get there that badly, and you're only doing it for me, right?"

"I don't have anything to be back for until tomorrow afternoon. So yeah, I'm in no hurry myself."

Holly was sure she could see that little smile going again. Was she imagining it or did he like the idea of the two of them spending the night someplace? The little smile grew into a huge grin, the one she'd seen so often over the weekend. She realized he was only doing what came naturally and taking charge when he said, "You have impeccable timing, Holly. We're about ten miles from a great little B&B. We'll be there in no time. And, there's a wonderful Spanish restaurant next door. Dinner is on me. How does that sound?"

"Sounds perfect." She stole another glance at him. He always seemed to have everything covered. She'd heard Jack call him Peter the Great a few times over the weekend and she could see why. She felt sure that if Pete snapped his fingers and commanded it, the whole universe would rearrange itself according to his bidding. Well, she may not be in the same league as him, financially or socially, but she could certainly enjoy an evening with him before they returned to their own worlds.

Pete pulled off the highway and drove through a quaint little town, the main street mostly deserted in the pouring rain. At the end of the street, he pulled in to the parking lot of the B&B. To Holly it looked like something out of a picture book. A white picket fence surrounded a beautiful garden, all overlooked by a two story, white house. The wraparound porch was full of overflowing planters and dripping hanging baskets.

She looked at Pete. "Did you just magic this place up?"

He laughed. "I'm just a guy who knows his way around, not some evil wizard!"

"Oh, I wasn't thinking evil. Just too good to be anything but magic."

He laughed again. "Why has Emma kept you hidden away all these years? Flattery will get you everywhere with me. We definitely need to hang out more."

Though she loved the idea, Holly couldn't see that happening. The two of them moved in such different circles.

"Why don't you make a run for the porch, and I'll bring our bags. No point in us both getting drenched."

As Holly made a dash up the path to the shelter of the porch, she couldn't help but smile to herself. He really was from a different world. Most guys she knew would have made a run for it themselves and left her to struggle with her own bag. She stood dripping on the porch as Pete sauntered up, a bag in each hand, not caring that he was getting more drenched with every step. Once he reached the porch, he shook himself like a big dog, then opened the door for her with that big grin.

"Shall we, my lady?"

She stepped inside. A small dark haired woman came scurrying out from the back to greet them.

"Glad you found us. This is no weather for anyone to be out in, and you're in luck, we've just got the one room left. It's small, but it's dry. Anyone after you will have another hundred miles to drive before they find a place tonight."

Holly's heart raced. Just one, small, room?

Pete gave her a mischievous grin and said, "Well, aren't we the lucky ones? We'll take it. Didn't I tell you that you have perfect timing?"

Holly nodded and swallowed, hard. This wasn't exactly her style, but Pete seemed think it was perfectly normal. She watched him silently as he filled out the paperwork and chatted with the owner. Surely he wasn't thinking that they would sleep together, just like that? He was obviously used to things falling into place for him, but did he really expect her to fall into his bed? And did she really think she'd be able to resist if he did?

She watched him lift their bags and followed him up the stairs. When he reached the bedroom door, he put down the bags and dug out the key.

He turned to her with a smile. "Don't look so scared, I'll take the sofa."

He swung the door open and ushered her to enter ahead of him. Holly looked around. The room was cute, chintzy, and very small—and there was no sofa. She looked at Pete.

"So, I'll take the floor."

She looked around again. There wasn't enough clear floor space anywhere that a man Pete's size could lay down.

He grinned. "Okay then, the tub."

They peeked inside the bathroom. Holly wasn't surprised to see a closet sized space with a shower stall and no tub.

He shrugged. "I can sleep in the truck. No problem."

"Oh, no. You mustn't," said Holly. "You can take the top." She burst out laughing at the delighted grin on his face. "Not like that! What kind of girl do you think I am?"

"The kind I would like to take the top with?" He didn't miss a beat. He was laughing, but he sounded like he meant it, too.

"Well, you'll be happy then, because I'll let you," she teased. "You can take the far side and stay on top of the covers and I'll sleep over here." She patted the pillow closest to the door.

"Aww. Okay then," he smiled. "Thank you. I can assure you I will be a gentleman."

Holly had no doubt. He'd been the perfect gentleman since she'd met him yesterday morning. For a moment she hoped that he wouldn't be. That was crazy thinking though. It wouldn't ever go anywhere between them, and she wasn't into one night stands. Still, a girl could easily forget her usual standards around Pete. Apart from being drop dead gorgeous, there was something so commanding about him. If he really wanted to take the top, there was no way she would be able to say no. Being enclosed in this small room with him wasn't doing her any good.

"I'm going to take a quick shower," she said.

"Okay, I'll run next door, see if I can get us a table for later. Do you want to text me when you're done?"

Holly was relieved he was going to give her some space. She was about to ask for his number, then realized that she had it from when he'd called to arrange to pick her up to drive up to the lake. It seemed so strange that forty-eight hours ago he'd been nothing more than a name to her. A friend of a friend. Now here they were sharing a room. And later, a bed. She pulled herself together.

"Will do. I won't take too long."

"Take your time, there's no rush. We've got all night." His eyes met hers and though they still held a smile, there was something else there, too. A question? A challenge? She had to stop this!

"We sure do, sweetie, but you have no idea how long it can take a girl, so mind what you say." She picked up her bag. "Go on then, shoo! I'll text you when I'm done." She had to get him out of the room. It was like he cast some field around himself—magnetic, magical, whatever it was, the closer she was to him the more it drew her in. She was pretty sure it would draw them both onto that bed any minute now if she didn't break the spell.

~ ~ ~

Pete took his time walking through the parking lot to the restaurant. He was already drenched so he didn't see the point in making a run for it. Perhaps a good soaking was what he needed to cool himself off anyway. He'd never understood it when people used the term 'hot and bothered.' Never, that was, until yesterday morning when he'd first laid eyes on Holly. At his first glimpse of her standing outside her little townhouse waiting for him, he'd felt a rush of heat. He wasn't sure whether it had started or just settled in the front of his pants, but he was sure that particular region had not cooled off yet. He'd spent much of the weekend with his hands in his pockets, constantly trying to disguise the hard-on that sprang to life every time she came within three feet of him. Scratch that. Every time he saw her. In fact, scratch that too. Even now, when she wasn't in sight and he was standing in a parking lot in the pouring rain, the thought of her, in the shower, had the heat boiling again.

He definitely needed to cool off. Despite the fact that she was beautiful, tall and slender with shiny chocolate colored hair and eyes he could only describe as amber. Despite the fact that she made him laugh so much with her down to Earth and sometimes downright coarse sense of humor. Despite the fact that he felt an almost overwhelming desire to undress her every time he saw her—to uncover her pert breasts and get his hands on that perky backside that seemed to taunt him with every step she took. Despite all of that, he really needed to leave her alone. She was Emma's best friend!

She would be Emma's Maid of Honor when he himself was Jack's Best Man. He couldn't afford to act on his desire for her, because their lives were going to be entangled for the next few months, at least. He couldn't risk sleeping with the bridesmaid before the wedding...could he? He pursed his lips. No! Damn you, Pete, no! That's not part of the plan.

He lived his life according to his plan. Always had. His plan was the driving force behind Phoenix, the construction company he and Jack had founded ten years ago. His plan gave shape to everything he did, everything he was. He didn't deviate from it, certainly wouldn't do so for a woman. There was no room for the complication of someone who interested him as much as Holly did. The plan was to work for four more years the way he had been doing. For now, Phoenix was his life—his wife, his child and his purpose. In four more years he would have everything in place, whereby he could work more normal hours and have the time and the energy to devote to finding the right woman, building a family and making *them* his life and his purpose.

In the meantime, he dated some, of course, but he didn't see the point in getting involved with anyone who really interested him. It didn't fit the plan yet. It was better not to start something he couldn't finish. Holly interested him way too much. He had to let it go before it started.

He pushed open the door to the restaurant and went inside. He stood on the welcome mat for a few moments to drip while his eyes adjusted to the dark interior.

"Mr. Pete!" The owner of the restaurant came out from behind the bar to greet him.

"Alonso!" Pete shook the hand the Spaniard offered him.

"Been too long, Mr. Pete. No Emma this time?"

"Not this time."

Pete and Emma had discovered this place years ago. They'd grown up together in Summer Lake and were still close friends. Until recently, when Emma had moved back to the lake, they had often shared the drive up from LA. The first time they'd stopped here had been a night like tonight. Rained off the road, they'd found the B&B and eaten here. Over the past few years, they'd made it a point to stop in every so often and visit with Alonso and his family.

"Emma's staying up at the lake this summer. But I do have a friend with me. I came to see if you'd have a table for us later?"

"Of course, my friend. Tonight you can have your pick of many tables. The rain makes the people stay at home."

Pete looked around. The place was almost deserted. "Well, at least I can bring you a little business."

"It is always good to see you. I think of you as my family, not as my business. You have sent me so many people, so much business. I am appreciate so very, very, much. You spread my name and now I have diners come here from LA thanks to you."

Pete had done his best to spread word of Alonso's restaurant. He liked the little Spaniard and respected his hard work and wonderful cuisine. Pete liked to do whatever he could to support those who were striving for excellence.

"I'm glad to help," he smiled. "But, please let me buy dinner? I feel better about recommending what I paid for."

Alonso nodded. "Okay, Mr. Pete, but you will have a drink with me, as my friend, no?"

"I'd love to." Pete sat on a stool as Alonso went back behind the bar.

"A Chivas, with me, my friend?"

Pete grinned. "Perfect. Thank you."

Even as he sipped the whiskey and chatted with Alonso, Pete couldn't keep his mind from wandering back to Holly. To what he'd be doing right now if he were in that shower with her. He smiled and nodded as Alonso chatted about his family and the restaurant, but he couldn't shake the images of Holly soaping herself.

His phone buzzed in his pocket as if the straining in his pants had set off an alarm. A text from Holly.

> *I'm ready.*

He drummed his fingers on the bar, lips quirking upwards. Wishing that her being ready involved her being *un*dressed instead of dressed.

"I have to go," he told Alonso. "I'll be back in a little while with my friend."

"Okay, Mr. Pete, I'll be waiting. We will make you a beautiful dinner."

"I have no doubt. Thanks again for the Chivas."

Pete knocked on the bedroom door and waited. When Holly opened it he felt the air rush out of his lungs and the heat surge through his veins. She wore a floor length simple summer dress. Nothing fancy, but boy did it show off her figure. It clung to her slender body, seeming to highlight the breasts he couldn't get out of his mind. As she turned away to let him in, he noticed it did the same for her pert little backside too. He was grateful she had her back turned while she collected her purse from the nightstand. He hurriedly adjusted his jeans to hide the effect she was having on him.

"I thought I'd return the favor and get out of your way for a while."

She smiled as she turned to face him. Pete simply nodded. He didn't trust himself to say anything. The only words he could imagine speaking were, *Take the dress off!* His mind was screaming them. Either she had to get out of the room or get out of the dress. One or the other had to happen in the next few seconds.

"I'll see you down there, then."

Pete allowed himself to breathe again as she closed the door behind her.

Oh, boy. He was going to have to sleep in the truck. No two ways about it. There was no way in hell he'd be able to sleep next to that woman and not sleep *with* her.

# Chapter Two

Holly ran across the parking lot and stepped inside the restaurant. She immediately felt at home. The neighborhood where she'd grown up had a large Spanish community, and she still loved to visit the *bodegas* and *tapas* bars around her parents' home.

"Good evening, Miss." A handsome man in his late thirties, maybe, came around the bar to greet her. "A table for one?"

"No, thank you. I'd like to sit at the bar for now. A friend will be joining me to eat."

"Ah, you are the friend of Mr. Pete?"

Holly smiled, "Yes, that would be me."

The man offered his hand with a big smile. "*Bienvenido*, any friend of Mr. Pete is a friend and family here. I am Alonso, welcome."

"*Encantada.* Thank you, Alonso. I'm Holly."

"*Encantado* to meet you too, Holly. Please, what can I get you?"

Holly settled herself at the bar. "What's your favorite wine from home?"

Alonso grinned, "You like the Spanish wines? I have a wonderful Rioja. You want to try?"

"Yes, please."

Alonso disappeared into the back. Holly could hear a conversation in Spanish, then he returned with a beautiful dark haired woman, about Holly's age, a bottle and three glasses.

"Holly, I'd like you to meet my wife, Elena."

Elena smiled and came around the bar to kiss Holly on both cheeks. Accustomed to this greeting, Holly smiled. "*Encantada, Señora* Elena."

"*Dios mío!* You speak Spanish?"

"*Un poquito,* only a little."

Alonso beamed and poured the Rioja. Holly tasted it and smiled. "This is wonderful!"

"I am happy you like it. It is my brother's wine. Here in California it seems people only want the local wines. I understand, but I am sad that they miss out on other flavors."

"They're seriously missing out big time if they don't try this," said Holly. "Do you ever offer tastings or use it as a special house wine?"

Alonso and Elena exchanged a look. "No," said Alonso, "I never thought to try that."

"Oh, you must. The easy way would be simply to offer the Rioja as a special house red and have your staff tell its story whenever someone orders it. Or, if you wanted to invest some time and energy, you could offer a tasting evening or even a pairing menu. Promote your brother's wines and your own menu at the same time. I'll bet you could organize trips up here, a coach from the city for an evening, or even work with the B&B to make it a weekend thing." Holly stopped herself, realizing that Alonso and his wife were staring at her.

"Sorry. I tend to see marketing ideas and get carried away with them," she smiled.

"These are brilliant ideas," smiled Alonso.

"They are," added Elena. "Please, will you teach me more on these things?"

"I'd love to. I don't know that I'm good enough to teach, but I'll gladly share my ideas with you."

Elena looked around the restaurant. It was practically empty. "Alonso, would you check on the children, please?"

Alonso disappeared into the back and Elena ushered Holly over to a table, collecting a notepad and pen on the way. Holly was excited to share her ideas and Elena seemed eager for any suggestions she could get.

As Holly was telling Elena about one of the restaurants she knew that offered a *'Tapas* and Tastings' happy hour, three small children came out from behind the bar. They solemnly lined up beside the table. All three were made up of dark hair, olive skin and great big smiles. They stood quietly, smiling at her, but Holly could sense pent up laughter and energy just waiting to be unleashed.

"Holly, these are our children, Alonso Jr., Carlos, and Isabel. *Niños*, this is *Señorita* Holly."

"*Hola, Señorita* Holly," chorused the children who, Holly guessed, ranged from six to ten years old, the little girl being the youngest.

"*Hola*," she replied and smiled at them.

The little girl stepped forward to kiss Holly's cheeks. When Holly bent down to her, she wrapped her arms around Holly's neck and climbed into her lap.

Elena smiled. "Isabel tells us who we can trust. Mostly she hides from strangers, but when she finds a true and gentle soul she loves them out loud. It seems that you are such a soul, just as I thought."

Holly was touched by the gesture of the dark haired little beauty smiling up at her. "Why, thank you, Isabel. I am honored."

The oldest boy stepped forward. "You want to see our garden?"

Isabel slid to the floor and tugged on Holly's hand. Seeing Elena was smiling and nodding her agreement, Holly allowed herself to be led out to a covered patio where the children were growing herbs and potted plants. In no time she was laughing and chasing with the three of them. They were delightful children. They made her think again how much she wanted kids of her own. Carlos wanted to pick a flower to give to her so she would remember him. Alonso, older and wiser, was telling him that if he did, she wouldn't be able to keep it because flowers curl up and die when they are picked. Seeing how disappointed Carlos looked, she decided to show them how they could press flowers and keep them.

They trooped back inside, each carrying a flower. Holly had noticed some big heavy books on the shelves around the fireplace at the far end of the bar. She asked Elena if they could use them, then settled back at the table. Once she sat down, Isabel crawled into her lap again and the two boys stood on either side of her. Alonso Jr. placed an arm around her shoulder as he leaned in to watch her placing the first flower carefully between the pages of the book. Not to be outdone, Carlos moved closer and put his hand on her other shoulder. Holly smiled, thrilled to be in the company of these affectionate little people.

~ ~ ~

Pete stopped and caught his breath as he stepped inside the restaurant. He'd been imagining that perfect body, sitting on a bar stool waiting for him. Having visions of how she really looked and felt underneath that dress. Now, instead, he saw her sitting at a table, surrounded by three of his favorite children. Her fairer head was encircled by three dark ones, little smiles and hands clamoring for her attention.

He stood transfixed, watching her with the kids, laughing and doing something with an old book. Instead of dousing his attraction for her, as he might have expected, the sight of her laughing and obviously being so good with them only intensified his desire for her. He clenched his fist. He'd have to knock that on the head—and quick!

Alonso greeted him from behind the bar, "Hey, Mr. Pete, didn't I tell you? More like family!" He smiled over to where Holly was sitting. "*Chicos*, you must leave *Señorita* Holly to have dinner now."

Pete watched the children edge closer to her as Holly looked up and smiled at him.

"Hey, Pete."

"Hey, yourself." He cleared his throat, surprised by how hoarse his voice sounded. She was scrambling his senses, those amber eyes shining at him, looking so damn happy!

"Would you mind if we finish up here first?"

"Of course not."

Isabel slid down from Holly's lap and came over to him. She slipped her tiny hand into his and led him over to the table. Alonso Sr. shot Pete a questioning look, he smiled and nodded. Isabel was just too cute, smiling up at him and she was, after all, taking him over to Holly.

Holly smiled at him as he sat down, "We're nearly finished, sorry. We're pressing flowers."

Pete grinned. Whatever he might have guessed they were doing, he would never have thought of that.

Alonso Jr. looked a little put out to be discovered in such a girly pursuit. He liked to talk 'business' with Pete whenever he stopped by. "I am only watching," he stated.

Pete grinned at him. "Then you, sir, are a very smart young man. As a man, you need to watch and listen when a lady shows you how to do the things she likes. If you learn about those little things, then maybe someday you will be able to please her, by doing them for her."

Alonso Jr. smiled back, "Do you know how to please *Señorita* Holly?"

Pete's lips quirked at the possible interpretations of that question. He held Holly's eyes with his own and was pleased to see them widen as he replied, "Not yet, Alonso, but I'd like to learn."

Elena appeared at his elbow, "So good to see you, Mr. Pete!"

"And you, Elena. How are you?"

"I am well, thank you. If you will excuse me, I must get the children to bed now. *Vamonos, hijos.* Let's go."

Pete watched as they gathered around Holly, reaching for hugs and kisses.

"Good night, *Señorita* Holly," said Isabel.

"We will keep the flowers safe until you come back," said Alonso Jr.

"Please come back soon," said Carlos as he hugged her waist.

"Goodnight, children." Holly smiled as Elena shooed them into the back.

"Seems I'm not the only one you've got wrapped around your little finger," said Pete.

Holly raised an eyebrow, "I don't see you getting wrapped around anyone's finger, Mr. Bigshot! But yes, I think I did just make some new friends."

"Mr. Bigshot?" laughed Pete. "What the hell makes you say that?" He was surprised by the name and even more surprised that he liked her using it.

"Oh, come on," she smiled. "It's obvious that you're used to saying 'Jump' and having everyone ask 'How high?'"

Pete laughed. She was probably right, but he didn't like to think of it that way. He couldn't work out the look on her face. Was she dismissing him, or tempting him? He gave her a hard stare, remaining silent, watching the laughter fade from her face as she stared back at him. He held the silence a few moments longer than was comfortable, then said, "Jump!"

She laughed. "No way, Mr. Bigshot. You're not getting me like that."

Though she was laughing, the gleam in her eyes looked a lot like lust and that dress couldn't hide her taut nipples. She really did want him. Perhaps not as much as he wanted her, that might be impossible, but her body was giving her away. Would it really be such a bad idea to act on something they both wanted so badly?

"What way will I get you then?" He couldn't resist asking and was shocked when she met his eyes.

"Any way you want as long as it's just sex, no strings."

He wasn't used to a woman taking his breath away and leaving him speechless, but here she'd done it again. She stood before him, chin lifted, shoulders thrown back, lips slightly parted, looking so very kissable. But he shouldn't. They shouldn't. How could he not?! Or was she really just teasing?

Alonso rescued him. "We have your table now, my friends. The best in the house. Please, follow me."

Pete allowed Holly to walk ahead of him, watching her backside sway while considering her words, 'Any way you like.' What was that quote? Something about 'Let me count the ways'? It would take them quite a while to work through all the ways he wanted her! She couldn't be serious? And could he do it if she were? More like could he stop himself? He already knew the answer to that one.

Once they were seated and Alonso had left them with a bottle of the Rioja, he peered over his menu at her. "It's not fair to taunt a guy like that, you know. Especially to tease him with something you can see he wants so badly."

"I wasn't teasing. I was offering."

She looked up at him and he locked her eyes with his own. Needing to pin her down on what she was really saying. "Any way I like?"

He watched her swallow and press her lips together as she nodded slowly.

"Why, Holly?"

"Isn't it obvious?"

"It's obvious that I want you. Beyond that, I'm not sure I can think straight enough to make sense of anything!"

"Well, I think it's obvious that I want you too. It's also obvious that we shouldn't. We're from different worlds. We have no business being together, but we're going to be seeing a lot of each other until Emma and Jack's wedding. We can dance around it and make life difficult, or we can get it over with and out of the way."

"Get it over with?!" Pete was taken aback by her forthright explanation and pretty much insulted that any woman, especially one he wanted this badly, would consider sex with him something she had to 'get it over with.' He stared at her, eyebrows lowered. The waiter came to take their order, giving Pete a moment to calm down. Once the waiter had gone, he looked at Holly again.

She smiled sweetly at him, "What's up, Mr. Bigshot, like to think you're something special do you?"

He had to laugh, "I don't think it, sweetheart, I know it, and I'm going to show you just how special. All...Night...Long..."

He saw the bravado slip. She wasn't near as brazen as she was trying to make out. But she *had* offered herself to him on a plate. And her argument did have some merit; it would be torture to keep seeing her and wanting her over the next few months. This way, they could get it out of their system. As she put it, 'get it over with.' She'd given him reason to overcome his own self-discipline, he intended to make the most of it.

When the waiter returned with their food, Pete resisted the urge to wolf it down and get her back to the B&B as quickly as possible. For all the physical attraction, it was more than that too. He enjoyed just being around her. Talking to her, laughing with her. Looking at her now, she was nervous, a little unsure of what she'd done. If she wanted to back out, so be it, but he was determined to make it such an enjoyable evening that she wouldn't want to. That she'd be as wanting and willing as he was by the time they got back to the room.

~ ~ ~

Holly swallowed a forkful of paella and had to chase it with a sip of water. Her throat was dry. Her palms were sweating. What in hell had she just done? She looked up to find that intense blue gaze fixed on her. Was he trying to figure her out, or figure out what he was going to do to her? The butterflies in her stomach were swirling madly. Her body hummed in anticipation. When he looked at her like that she felt as though she was already naked before him.

Sex with Pete was inevitable. She'd known that for certain when he'd returned to the room after her shower. The way he'd looked at her, even when she'd turned away from him, she'd felt his eyes burning through her dress. The way her body responded to him. The way she was powerless to stop it. The currents of desire zinging between the two of them were undeniable. She had been feeling powerless, out of control, swept along toward the unavoidable truth that they were going to end up naked together. When he'd made his comment about learning to please her and then asked how he could get her, she'd had one of her impulsive moments. She'd spoken to take back the only little bit of control she could have. It was going to happen one way or another, at least this way she could pretend that she was in control of the when – and of the terms: no strings!

He was talking to her now, but she couldn't process what he was saying. She was too focused on watching his lips move. On the way they curled into that little smile. On what it would be like when they met hers, and how they would feel against her skin.... Apparently those lips had just asked a question, because he was looking at her now, waiting for her to speak, expecting an answer.

"I'm sorry?"

He smiled. "I asked how the paella was."

"Oh. It was wonderful."

"Dessert?" asked Pete as the waiter removed their plates.

Holly shook her head. "No. You?"

"I'm saving mine for later." There went that smile again as he ran his eyes over her.

"Pete, I...."

He reached across the table and took her hand in both of his own. The predatory look was gone.

"It's okay, Sweetheart. We don't have to do this if you don't want to."

The warmth from his hands and his eyes spread through her. Whatever hesitation she'd felt, this was only drawing her deeper in. Was that his plan? Trouble was, when he looked at her like that she wanted him to care about her, not just desire her. But that would never happen, she knew that. Gathering her strength, she smiled at him. The sex, at least, was inevitable, so they may as well have fun with it.

"We don't have to?" She'd meant to tease, but didn't enjoy the struggle on his face. She stroked her finger across the palm of his hand. "We could always try not to, but I believe we'll find we do have to if we're honest about it." She raised an eyebrow and gave her best temptress smile, or what she hoped looked like one...she'd never tried to be a temptress before. It worked. The hard lust returned to his eyes.

"I do value honesty, and I do believe you are right. I also believe it's time to get out of here." He called for the check.

"Can I get this?" asked Holly.

"Please, let me? It really is my pleasure."

"Then thank you." She liked that he hadn't dismissed her out of hand or made anything of the fact that the cost of a dinner like this was nothing to him, but was a big deal for her.

As they got ready to leave, Alonso called them over to the bar. The place had filled up a little now.

"Will you stay to have a drink with me?"

"Thanks," said Pete, "but it's been a long day and we need to get Holly to bed." As he spoke, he put his hand at the small of her back and she inhaled sharply.

"Then please wait, I will bring Elena to say goodbye."

As they waited, Pete ran his fingers up her back then slowly down again, finishing with his hand around her bottom, drawing her against his side. She looked up at him.

"I thought you were the one saying we didn't *have* to do this?"

He smiled down at her. "I was wrong. We do."

He held her tight against him and she felt his heat spreading through her. She knew he was right.

Alonso returned with Elena and they said their goodbyes, promising to come back soon to see the children.

# Chapter Three

Outside the restaurant Pete turned to face her. When he looked at her like that, Holly felt as though his eyes had her pinned down and there was nothing she could do to resist anything he wanted.

"C'mere."

She stepped toward him. He took her hand and pulled her out into the rain. She tried to make a dash for it, but he stood still and crushed her to his chest. The rain soaked through to her skin as they stood there.

"Relax and enjoy it, sweetheart. Once you're wet you won't care anymore. Then you'll really start to enjoy yourself." The corner of his mouth lifted and she knew he wasn't just talking about the rain. Then he surprised her. "Want to go for a walk?"

She laughed. He was right of course. She tended to forget the simple stuff like this, but now that she was drenched, the rain smelled good. It felt good running down her. She was with this gorgeous man. Why not go for a walk with him before they spent the night together?

"Where are we going?"

He put an arm around her waist and led her down a path at the side of the B&B. In a few hundred yards they rounded a corner and the path ran alongside a river.

She turned to Pete. "This is beautiful!"

"*You* are beautiful," he replied and pulled her to him.

Holly felt as though she might melt into him as he closed his arms around her. As though he might turn the rain to steam with the heat he radiated. She looked up to meet his intense eyes, inches from her own. One hand at the small of her back held her against him, the other came up to cup the back of her head.

"I wanted our first kiss to be a long, slow, wet one." He smiled.

She didn't have chance to return the smile before his lips came down on hers. His hand tangled in her hair, gently tugging her head back as she opened her lips to him. Her hands came up to his shoulders, and she clung to him as he kissed her deeply, commanding her response. She moaned through the kiss as he pressed his hardness against her, while his tongue explored her mouth. He was invading her, taking possession of every inch of her being. She had no resistance to offer.

Eventually his lips left hers. His hand, still tangled in her hair, drew her head back so she was looking up into his eyes, which were now a deep violet color.

"I knew kissing you would be something else. I didn't know it would be this good." He dropped his head and kissed her lips. Pulling her head back he kissed her neck. He trailed a finger down her throat and down between her breasts. His eyes darkened as he watched her nipples stiffen and push at the wet fabric of her dress, which was now clinging to her. He spoke urgently, "I have to have you, Holly, but not here."

She came to her senses. They were outside, by the river, in the rain. But had he wanted her naked right then and there she would have gladly obliged. He took her hand and led her back to the B&B. They slipped inside and ran up the stairs to their little room.

He'd let her enter the room ahead of him and now she felt a moment of panic as she turned to find him with his back against the door looking down at her. He was so much man. Well over six feet of him. All hard muscle and power. Suddenly the room seemed even smaller as his presence filled the tiny space. She shivered as he stepped toward her. His arms came around her and she could feel hot skin through wet fabric. He pulled his shirt off over his head. She swallowed hard at the sight of his broad, muscled chest. A hint of damp golden hair glistened above abs as chiseled as his features.

He held her face between his hands and kissed her. This time slow and gentle, before kissing his way down her neck. His hands closed around her breasts, and she moaned at the feel of his hot, hard fingers pressing through her cold, damp dress. He bent his head to mouth her nipple through the fabric. She let her head fall back and pushed her hips against him. Lost as she was in the sensations of his hands and mouth moving over her, his voice, low and commanding, came as a surprise.

"Take the dress off, Holly."

She straightened up.

"Take it off. I need to see you."

This was new to her. She'd only known guys to be all over her, pulling her clothes off themselves. Pete towered over her.

"It has to be you, Holly. Undress yourself for me. Give yourself to me."

She felt the heat mount between her legs at his words. She only knew how to be taken by a man. To give herself? He was unbuckling his belt. He let his jeans fall to his feet and stood before her.

"Take off the dress."

She had no choice; her body was obeying his command. She slipped the straps off her shoulders, unfastened the side zipper and let the dress fall to the floor. His eyes blazed as they rested on her breasts.

"The bra."

She unclasped it and took it off, feeling the tips harden under the heat of his gaze. She went to remove her panties.

"Not those."

As she looked up he was in front of her, kissing her, walking her backwards until her legs met the bed and he came down on top of her. She wrapped her arms around his back, arching up to press against his hot naked chest. Feeling the heat of his hardness pushing at her. He took her breast in his mouth, sucking then gently grazing with his teeth. As he did, he slid his hand inside her panties.

"So wet for me," he murmured as he stroked her. She moaned, arching her hips up to him. He slipped a finger inside her, then two. She moaned, unable to do anything except move with him. She felt herself tense as he slid a third finger inside her, stretching her.

"Give yourself to me," he spoke to her breast before his mouth closed around it again. He slid his fingers deeper and a touched a place she didn't know was there.

"Ooh," was all she managed as she floated away, hips bucking wildly as the he sent waves of pleasure coursing through her..

When she finally came back to Earth, he was smiling down at her.

"Maybe I was right. Maybe that was all we needed to do."

"What kind of Bigshot are you?" she asked. "Thinking you can get away with that when you've got this hidden away?" She slipped her hand inside his boxers and closed her fingers around his hot, hard shaft. She enjoyed the surprise in his eyes. Two could play at this commanding, she decided.

"Take them off, Mr. Bigshot, we're not done here."

He smiled, but didn't move. He obviously wasn't used to being told what to do. She stood up and took off her panties then, surprised at herself, she ran her fingers over her breasts and slowly down over her stomach until she was touching herself.

"If you want this, and don't pretend you don't, you're going to have to take them off for me. He took off his shorts and reached for the condom that he'd placed on the nightstand. Holly swallowed as she watched him roll it on. He was obviously ready for her. His speed surprised her as he stood up and grabbed her. Standing behind her, he turned her to face the mirror. Meeting her eyes as he looked over her shoulder, he closed one hand around her breast and slowly walked the other down over her stomach until his fingers disappeared between her legs. She moaned and leaned back against him.

"So, you want me?" he murmured into her neck.

She nodded, completely aroused, watching his hands caress her in the mirror.

"Tell me."

"I want you, Pete. I want to give myself to you."

He spun her around and walked her back to the bed. She didn't quite know how she found herself looking up into his eyes, but suddenly he was on top of her, her legs spread wide.

He was holding his weight off her, but she knew she was only seconds away from what she'd been wanting since the moment she met him.

"Please, Pete. I want you."

He thrust his hips and plunged deep. He felt so good. His hot body covering hers, his thick hard shaft filling her, deep and fast. She felt her inner muscles tighten when he found her eyes.

"Kiss me."

She obeyed, bringing her arms up around his neck and opening her lips to him. As his mouth covered hers, his tongue mirrored the movements of his body, hot and demanding. As before, she felt he was invading her entire being. She was giving him all that she was and he was taking it, owning her. As he took her to the point of no return, the heat he radiated ignited a spark in her belly that exploded into a raging fire as he reached his own climax, thrusting deep as he throbbed inside her. She came undone, moaning his name as he carried her along with the power of his orgasm.

She lay breathing hard, his head on her shoulder, still filling her. That was incredible! She would never claim to be inexperienced in the bedroom—or out of it for that matter, but sweet lord above. That was mind blowing! He lifted his head; she couldn't make out the look in his eyes as they burned into her own.

"Wow!" was all he said as he rolled to the side and wrapped her in his arms. Holly pressed closer, drawn to his warmth, needing to be close to him. They lay that way for a long, quiet time. He held her tight and stroked her hair, planted kisses on her forehead, her eyelids, her nose, then found her lips again in a deep gentle exploration. She clung to him, wanting to savor every moment of their one night, wishing it could last. Knowing that when tomorrow came, it would all be over. She wondered how she would stand to be around him over the next few months and not want to take off all her clothes and give herself to him every time she saw him.

He got up and disappeared into the bathroom, then returned, smiling down at her. "Time to clean up."

How very unromantic, she thought as she nodded.

He slapped her backside and grinned. "Come on then."

She'd thought he'd meant clean himself up, but he pulled her to her feet and into the bathroom. He opened the shower door, turned on the water, then stepped inside, beckoning with his finger for her to follow. She stepped inside and he closed the door behind her. She leaned against the wall and he stood over her, bracing his hands above her head. She watched the water run down over his broad shoulders and felt it run over her sensitized breasts. She realized that he'd pinned her down with his eyes again. Even if he moved his big body out of the way, there was no chance she'd ever be able to move away from him while he was looking at her like that.

"You seem to like getting me wet." She'd meant to break the spell, but her choice of words only intensified it. His eyes were violet again. She followed his gaze and watched her nipples harden, his eyes just as capable of touching her as his hands and his mouth.

"I love getting you wet." He stroked her inner thigh, working his way up until he found how wet she really was. He looked down. "See what you do to me?" Holly was shocked to see how hard he was again.

~ ~ ~

"Hold that thought." He stepped out of the shower and returned moments later with a fresh condom stretched over him. Pete couldn't believe how quickly he was ready to take her again, but something about this woman made him want her in a way he wasn't used to. He didn't want to take it, he wanted her to offer it, willingly. As she had said in the restaurant, 'Any way you want.' The words echoed in his mind. He sat back against the stone bench that formed one wall of the shower, drawing her to him so that she straddled him as she stood before him, water running down over her. He squeezed some soap into his hands and soaped her all over, concentrating on her breasts and that great little ass, gently teasing between her legs. When she let her head fall back, he lifted her so she was kneeling on the bench, facing him, breasts at mouth level. He nipped and sucked while she moaned, then he let her slide down until her legs were spread, her opening just above his throbbing cock. He held her eyes as she lowered herself to receive him. At this angle he was even deeper inside her. Her eyes told him how good it felt as she moaned with each thrust. She bucked her hips as she rode him desperately, her wetness clenching around him, taking him close to the edge. He leaned back so he was supporting all her weight, deepening their connection. He grasped her ass and pulled her down to receive his thrusts, knowing he was reaching that spot inside her. He felt her begin to tighten around him. He let himself go, feeling the blood surge in his veins, taking her with him as they came together, wet bodies heaving as one, waves of pleasure sweeping through them.

As he regained his senses he held her close, feeling her heart pound in her chest as her lithe body pressed against his, warm water still running over them. If this was supposed to be getting her out of his system, it wasn't working. He was already dreaming up all the ways he wanted her, and it would take a hell of a lot longer than this one night to get through them all. She lifted herself off him and stood, letting the water run over her. She was so damned hot! He felt himself begin to stir again, what the...? But he didn't want more sex, not yet. He just wanted to hold her, be close to her, to learn the contours of her body. He stepped out of the shower and when she followed, he folded her into a towel and began to dry her. Her eyes were full of questions, but she didn't speak as he gently worked the towel over her, not caring that he himself was still naked and dripping. Once he'd finished, he wrapped a fresh towel around her and quickly dried himself off, tying the towel around his waist. She sat on the bed and smiled at him, still silent.

"Would Madam care for a glass of wine?" he asked.

She raised an eyebrow. "And where would we get one of those? It must be past midnight."

He rummaged in his bag and pulled out a bottle of Cabernet Sauvignon, then found his keys which had a Swiss army type key ring, complete with corkscrew.

Her eyes held amusement and something else, he wasn't quite sure what, as she said, "You really do have everything covered don't you, Bigshot?"

"I try," he grinned. "It's good to plan for every eventuality. I don't carry wine glasses, but if you're happy to drink from plastic cups then we're good to go."

The sound of her laughter did something to him that he couldn't quite put a finger on.

Once they had their wine, he sat on the bed, leaning back against the wall and patted his lap. "Want the best seat in the house?"

She walked over and sat between his legs. He curled an arm around her waist as she leaned back against him. He nuzzled his lips to her neck and felt her body tremor.

"You've got until morning to stop that," she laughed.

"But you said I could have you any way I wanted, and we've only just gotten started." He tightened his arm around her waist, surprised by how much he hated the thought of letting her go. He ran his hand up her thigh and slipped his fingers between her legs, caressing her nub as he whispered in her ear, "Don't try telling me you don't want more."

"I...I...Ohhh...."

Pete smiled to himself as her words melted into a moan of pleasure. Using both hands now, he slid two fingers into her wetness while he continued to work the little nub that was giving her so much pleasure. As he felt her begin to tense, he kissed her neck and whispered, "Come for me, Holly."

And she did. She leaned back into him, moving her hips in time with his fingers, moaning and writhing. Once she lay still, he pressed his lips into her hair.

"So, you're not going to tell me I have to stop that in the morning?"

He was surprised when she turned her head and held his eyes.

"'Fraid so, Mr. Bigshot. Even you can't have everything you want."

Pete stared at her. "Seriously?"

She smiled, "Seriously. We've done what we needed to do here. Dealt with the inevitable. Now we can move on."

Pete was stunned. "So this is it? You're just going to use me for this one night, then cast me aside?" He tried to say it jokingly, but it was how he felt and he didn't like it.

Holly laughed. "We're both grownups, Pete. We wanted each other. We got what we wanted. We'd be crazy to complicate things by trying to pretend it's anything else."

Pete took a sharp breath. "I guess you're right." He wasn't used to this; he was used to women wanting more from him, wanting his time, wanting his attention. Hell, wanting more sex. He knew how to please them! Now he wanted more from Holly and *she* wasn't interested. Hell, she was right, what was he thinking? He'd be crazy to pretend it was anything else. She was hot, that was all. He didn't have room for a woman in his life anyway, she was doing him a favor by reminding him he didn't need to complicate matters.

She wriggled around so she was facing him, straddling him. She dropped her head down, bringing her sweet tasting lips to his. He tangled his fists in her hair, pressing her to him as he explored her mouth. When they came up for air, her amber eyes shone down at him.

"I didn't say we're done here, did I? I just said we've only got until morning, so we'd better make the most of it."

Pete sure wasn't going to argue with that. He rolled them over so she was underneath him and set about making sure that if this was to be their only night together, it would be one she'd never forget.

# Chapter Four

Holly lay awake watching the sky slowly fade from dark to gray. Pete slept on beside her, his face relaxed, his arm flung above his head, his features still intense and achingly beautiful, with long lashes closed over his piercing blue eyes. What the hell had she been thinking? Insisting that this was a one-off, not to be repeated night? She wanted this man more than she wanted her next breath. But that was the point, wasn't it? The more of him she got, the more she wanted. She could so easily become addicted to the feel of his arms around her, the taste of his lips, his deep laugh and easy smile, the heat between her legs when he so much as looked at her. Oh yes, she could so easily become addicted. But she knew it could never go anywhere. He was out of her league. Sure, physically they connected perfectly. But socially and financially they were from different worlds. She knew that as she would begin to want more and more from Pete, he would want less and less from her. She was a realist, if nothing else. Although they'd started out hot and heavy, when the novelty of the sex wore off, Pete would see that there were so many other ways in which they really weren't compatible and would lose interest. This way was best, even though it didn't feel like it.

She looked at his sleeping face, trying to imprint it onto her memory. She ran her hands across his hard chest, wanting some more of him before this little bubble they had created had to burst and they returned to the real world. He opened his eyes and a smile spread across his face. Catching her hand, he drew it beneath the covers and she felt how hot and hard he was.

"I was dreaming about you. Look what you've done to me again." His voice was deep and gravelly, still full of sleep. His smile was sexy as sin as he closed her hand around him and began to move his hips slowly. "Since you caused this, do you think you could help me find somewhere to put it? Somewhere wet and warm?"

Holly gasped as his hand slipped between her legs. Holding her eyes, he slipped a finger inside her.

"Somewhere like this?"

She nodded dumbly, eyes still locked with his as he withdrew his hand. He pulled her on top of him. He held her hips and looked at her legs, spread and ready for him to plunge into her. She tried to lower herself, wanting to feel him inside, but he held her up. She questioned him with her eyes.

"Touch us first." He again brought her hand to close around him and began to move it in long slow strokes. "Touch yourself too, Holly. Let me watch you."

She hesitated, but once more her body obeyed the command from his eyes. Her hand slipped between her legs and she stroked herself for him. She moaned as the heat intensified in her belly. She felt him grow harder in her hand, his eyes fixed on her fingers stroking the little nub between her legs. She guided his glistening head toward her opening, moving him against her rhythmically. She gasped as she slid the very tip of him inside her then out again.

Pete breathed hard as he watched her. He let her go for a moment as he reached for a condom, quickly rolling it on. Then he grabbed her hips to hold her in place as he thrust up inside her. Holly went from having total control over both their bodies to being completely at his mercy as he pounded into her, pulling her down to receive each thrust of his hips. She felt him tense and they both gasped as she tightened around him until he exploded, taking them both over the edge. Eventually they lay still, still connected, breathing hard. Pete ran a hand down her back then grasped her ass cheek.

"Good morning, sexy lady!"

"Good morning, Mr. Bigshot," she smiled as she rolled off him. "And after that performance, you can't deny that's your name."

Pete laughed and drew her towards him, "I guess not. But since you made it so clear that this was a one shot deal, I had to make it a big one."

Holly's heart fell. She'd been so lost in the moment, she'd forgotten that this was it. That now they would get up, get dressed and go back to real life. That her time with Pete was over, not just beginning.

"Well, you certainly did that, but now it's time to head back to reality, don't you think? If we leave soon, I can still get back in time to open the store up myself."

"Or," Pete held her closer to him, "You could let your people open up, I could cancel my meeting and we could see where this day takes us?"

Holly looked into his eyes, inches from her own. How she would love to see where this day might take them, but no, she knew where it would ultimately end. There was no point. She pecked his lips with a quick kiss.

"Much as I would love to, I'm no Bigshot like you. I'm just a small time, small business owner who needs to get back to work. You may get away with ordering the world to stop to suit your whims, but I don't play in the big leagues. That's why we need to accept that this night was our one and only night. Nothing else would work." There. She'd said it. Spelled out that she knew and understood how different they were, that he was out of her league.

Pete just stared at her. She could see his mind working. She hoped that he would come up with something to persuade her that she was wrong, that she could, in fact, play hooky with him.

"But, sweetheart...." His eyes were back to that beautiful intense violet color. They burned into her own. She held her breath. He smiled. "Whatever you say. I'd never be one to keep a woman from her work. So, I guess it *is* time to go. You want the first shower?"

Holly let out the breath. What had she expected? Everything she'd said made sense. She knew it. He was only agreeing with her. Still, she felt the disappointment settle in the pit of her stomach.

"Sure." She sprang from the bed, eager to be away from him now that she could no longer be close to him.

~ ~ ~

Pete watched her rounded naked little ass disappear into the bathroom. If he hadn't just come so hard he wouldn't have been able to stop himself from following her in there. But she seemed determined that this was it. He had to respect that. She was right; it really was for the best, wasn't it? She'd already gotten under his skin after only one weekend. All he wanted was more of her. Every time he had her he wanted her more. It was best to stop now. Be glad they'd had this one night and leave it at that. Besides, he really didn't need to be canceling this afternoon's meeting with Bowers.

~ ~ ~

By five o'clock, Pete was leaning back in his chair, feet on his desk, fingers steepled together under his chin as he stared out the window at the LA skyline. Bowers had been in a great mood. The meeting had gone well and they'd managed to get past the last few stumbling blocks. Yet his mind kept straying back to Holly. He'd dropped her off at her little store just before ten. She'd left him with another of her sweet kisses and a smile.

"See you around, Bigshot," she'd said, eyes dancing. She'd been laughing at him, but he'd laughed with her. She was real, not just beautiful. She was hot, smart, and strong, the kind of woman he would want in his life. And, as she had pointed out, trying to pursue anything further would be crazy. He wasn't ready to make room for someone special in his life yet. Holly was nothing if not special. Yeah, the sex was awesome, but she stirred something deep inside him. Deep inside his being, not just in his pants. He smiled as he felt the beginnings of life down there now.

His cell phone buzzed. It was Jack.

"S'up, partner?"

"Yo, bro! Wanted to see how it went with Bowers."

"Yeah, it went great, he signed off on pretty much everything. He's meeting with his board tomorrow and we'll talk again Wednesday. It looks like we should be ready to roll early next month."

"Great, we can go over it this weekend. You are coming up Friday, right?"

"I am. Just 'cause you've got a wedding to organize, doesn't mean I don't still have a house to build."

"No worries there. I've been talking to Meyers this morning. I'm meeting with the crew tomorrow and we're ahead of schedule all around. We'll be killing two birds with one stone this weekend though."

"How so?"

"Em wants to get everyone together to talk wedding stuff. You're going to be here, Dan's coming too, and he's bringing Laura again. Since we'll have the whole wedding party together, Em wants to talk details and organize us."

Pete laughed. "You ready for all this, bro?" He was still surprised, though pleased at how hard and fast his partner had fallen for his childhood friend, Emma.

Jack laughed too. "I am. I still can't quite believe it myself. Seriously though, you know I'd do anything to see her happy and she's dreamed of this wedding at her Gramps' place since she was a little kid. I'm going to make damned sure she gets what she wants. If anything, it'll probably be me marching around with a clipboard, taking care of details."

"Ha! You know, when she was still in scared little mouse mode, wondering whether she dared take a chance on you, I told her you were a detail guy when it comes to the things you care about."

"Well, you got that right, and there is a detail I want your help with this weekend."

"Fire away. You know I'll help if I can."

"You know how I said the whole wedding party is coming up here? The only one missing is Holly. Em said she was going to drive to the city and pick her up, but that seems crazy to me since you're coming anyway. Would you mind bringing her with you?"

Pete felt himself grin. "It'd be my pleasure."

Jack paused—a moment filled with expectation. "You want to elaborate on that?"

"Not particularly."

"Hmm. You two seemed to be getting along well last weekend. Anything I should know?'

"She is a fascinating woman."

Jack laughed. "So, you're telling me you're fascinated?"

"I'm telling you nothing, Benson. Other than, yes, I will do you a favor and bring her up there with me on Friday."

"Are you sure it's *you* that's doing *me* the favor?"

Pete laughed. "Whatever. I was going to come up Friday morning, but I don't know if Holly will leave before Saturday, is that going to work?"

"Let me talk to Em. She really wanted everyone here Friday night. And I suspect you may be able to use your considerable powers of persuasion to get Holly to do as you say?"

Pete smiled to himself, thinking of ways he might do just that. "I'll call her."

"Okay, I'll let you know what Em's thinking."

Pete laughed.

"What's so funny?"

"This conversation. You and me arranging our weekend around what a couple of women want."

Jack laughed too, "Yeah, it would've seemed pretty farfetched not so long ago, huh?"

"Still seems it now," said Pete. His intercom buzzed, "I gotta go, bro. Judy's after me."

"Later."

~ ~ ~

Jack pulled into Emma's driveway and sat for a moment, staring out at the lake. He still found it hard to believe how much his life had changed in the last couple of months—how happy he was now. Phoenix, the construction company he and Pete had built up over the last ten years, had been the main focus of his life. He'd spent most of that time traveling, overseeing projects around the country. Driving himself into the ground if he was honest. The last year had been different. Pete had effectively grounded him in LA. Although that brotherly attempt at making him slow down had no doubt saved him from complete burnout, Jack had never been happy in the city. LA was too harsh, too superficial, too fast and too brittle for his taste.

Then he'd met Emma. She'd changed everything. She was such a contradiction, this beautiful, self-assured woman, who was also so playful, goofing around with Pete, and so scared, as he'd discovered when he'd begun to pursue her. Jack was pretty sure now that, for him at least, it had been love at first sight. Especially since his first sight of her had been seeing her wiggling her backside at Pete before she'd barreled into Jack himself and literally knocked him off his feet!

Now...now they were getting married.

They'd stayed up most of the night talking, making plans for their future, making love, and more plans. Jack watched the late afternoon sun dance on the lake and sighed a happy sigh. Life was good. As he climbed out of the old truck Emma's Gramps had loaned him, he thought of his conversation with Pete. He was grateful Em wouldn't have to drive down to the city to pick up her friend. He was curious too about Pete's reaction. Pete and Holly had seemed to be getting along well over the weekend and Pete wasn't normally coy about the women he liked. This could be interesting.

Emma appeared on the front deck. Jack's heart expanded in his chest at the sight of her.

"Hey, Mr. Benson! I was starting to wonder if you were going to sit out there all night."

Jack bounded up the steps and wrapped her in his arms. "Hey, yourself, Mrs. Benson-to-be. I was just taking a moment to think about what a lucky SOB I am and how much I love you."

"I love you too, Jack, so much. And now I'm over myself and my silly fears I can't wait to marry you."

Jack pressed her closer to him. "You have no idea how glad I am to hear you say that, Mousey. Part of me still thinks you're going to get scared again and change your mind."

"No such luck, Mr. B, You're stuck with me now. Nothing could stop me from marrying you. And I'm so excited to plan this wedding. You really don't mind getting into all the details with me? I'm not going to drive you nuts and scare *you* off?"

"Baby, you know I'm a detail guy and there is nothing more important to me than making you happy and making you my wife. In fact, I took care of one little detail myself today."

"What's that?"

"I asked Pete to bring Holly with him this weekend. I didn't want you to drive down there when you don't have to."

"Oh."

"Is that okay?"

"Of course. It's great with me, I just don't know what Holly will think. I didn't really get chance to talk with her before they left." She gave Jack a mischievous little smile. "I have to confess that I had been threatening to play match-maker for those two for a while. I don't know what they thought of each other."

Jack grinned. "You had, huh? Well, I don't know about Holly, but I'd guess Pete is more than interested."

Emma gave a little squeal of delight. "You would? Why? What did he say? Don't you think they'd be great together?"

"Slow down, Em. Don't get too excited. You know a relationship isn't part of Pete's plan yet and he never deviates from the plan. But he was definitely interested in Holly. Normally he'd tell me all about a woman he likes, but he was real cagey about her. Let's just watch and see, yeah?"

"Okay, I suppose so," grumbled Emma, "But at least I'm going to call Holly and see what she has to say about it."

Jack raised an eyebrow sternly.

"Oh, come on," she laughed, "I *have* to call my best friend and Maid of Honor, and Pete's name is bound to come up since he's your Best Man!"

Jack shook his head, smiling.

~ ~ ~

Holly poured some more of her favorite bubbles under the running water as she waited for the tub to fill. A long hot bubble bath was one of her favorite ways to relax, and tonight she *really* needed to relax. She'd been distracted all day at the store. So much so, that Roberto, her visual merchandising manager, had shown concern. Roberto was an absolute darling and a dear friend, but he was much more given to displays of camp effervescence than genuine concern. For him to react that way, she knew she must have seemed completely unhinged. She couldn't help it though. She just couldn't get thoughts of Pete and images of their lovemaking out of her mind. No matter how much or how often she tried to correct herself. They were images of sex, that's all it was. Hot, toe curling, but strings-free sex. Nothing more. So why did she also keep smiling to herself, remembering things he'd said over the weekend? Laughing about little comments he'd made? Remembering the feel of his lips on her hair as he murmured to her?

She undressed and checked she had everything she needed before she stepped into the steaming bubbles. Glass of wine, definitely needed tonight, a big bold cabernet. Book, not that she thought she would be able to focus on it, but she had to try. Cell phone, she wasn't expecting any calls, was she? She certainly didn't want to talk to anyone, but it was force of habit.

She sank gratefully up to her nose in gardenia scented bubbles and closed her eyes. Maybe now she'd able to rerun the memories of her time with Pete, then store them in a dark corner of her mind. She would put them safely out of everyday reach, yet leave them accessible to indulge in on the nights she felt alone, wondering if she would ever find the happiness her sisters seemed to have. The happiness which, for that matter, her friend Emma had found with the gorgeous Jack. Holly sighed. Jack, Pete's partner. All the roads in her mind led back to Pete. She ran her hands down her body, wishing they were Pete's hands as she closed her eyes and remembered his touch. At that moment her phone rang, startling her hands out from between her legs. She quickly dried them and picked up the phone. Seeing Emma's name on the display, she answered.

"Hey, Sweetie. How's the future Mrs. Benson this evening?"

"Hey, Holly. I am wonderful, thank you. How about you?"

"I'm good, thanks. What's up?"

"What's up? Why does anything have to be up for me to call my Maid of Honor?" Emma's laugh had just a hint of teasing to it.

"Sorry, Em. It's been a long day, and I suppose 'What's up' is a polite way of asking what you want."

"Oh. Is everything okay? I can call another time if you like?"

Emma didn't sound as though she had any intention of getting off the phone any time soon. Holly smiled, realizing that talking to her friend was probably a much more realistic way to get her mind off Pete than what she had been about to do.

"Everything's fine," she said, "And of course I want to talk to you, silly. I want to hear all about your plans. And we *are* going to talk dresses, right?"

"You know we are! You have to help me find or design the perfect dress. You know that's not my thing. I'm depending on you."

"Don't worry. I already started browsing a few catalogs this afternoon."

"Ooh, thank you! Will you bring some with you this weekend? We can talk dresses, and flowers, and hair, and cake while the guys are working on Pete's house."

Holly caught her breath at the mention of his name.

"I'm planning to bring them, but you know I'm not going to get up there until mid-morning on Saturday. Much as I love you, I am not going to drive up there in the dark."

"But you're coming with Pete aren't you?"

"I am?" She closed her eyes against the images those words conjured in her mind.

"I was going to come get you on Friday. I wanted to spring you from work early so we can all have dinner together on Friday night. Jack asked Pete if he would bring you instead."

"First I've heard of it." Holly's mind was racing now. How had she managed to forget that she would no doubt have to spend some alone time with him in the lead up to the wedding? How had she thought that their one night would 'get it out of their system' as she had so crudely put it? This was going to be torture!

Emma didn't seem to notice her discomfort. "Jack only asked him this afternoon and knowing Pete, he's probably still at the office. This way at least I got to you before he calls. Please say yes when he offers you a ride? Please? For me?"

Holly shook her head. "Okay, just for you."

"And besides, I want to hear how the two of you got along this weekend. You looked quite cozy together every time I saw you."

For once, Holly didn't know what to say. She shared almost everything with Emma, but this? This was complicated. Pete was Emma's oldest and dearest friend. Emma had been hoping to get them together. She wasn't going to be easily deterred.

"I'm waiting..." teased Emma.

"Oh, screw it," declared Holly. "I don't know how to be anything but up front. We 'got along' incredibly well. You were right, okay? He is gorgeous, a wonderful person, a great guy. He is smoking hot and the chemistry between us is overwhelming. We got along so well.... We got each other off even better! We stopped on the way back to the city, spent the night together and screwed each other senseless!" She laughed. "Does that answer your questions?"

"Well! Err, I suppose so, but only because I'm stunned! Once my brain absorbs this I'm sure I will have a million questions."

"Whenever you're ready, ask away. In the meantime, I should warn you that we agreed it was a one-off. While we were very, VERY attracted to one another, we both agree that we are not in a position to explore anything further. We wanted each other and we're consenting adults, so we took what we wanted. End of story, okay?"

"Um, no," said Emma. "Not okay. I mean, I want to know the whole story, and I want to know why you can't explore anything further. You two are PERFECT for each other. Why just a one-nighter? It doesn't make sense. It's not even something either of you would do!"

"Em, Sweetie, you're such a little romantic, that's why you don't see it. We're from different worlds. Pete is a big time Bigshot, I am not. He has a huge corporation, mega-bucks homes, cars and money. Dammit, Em, he even has a plane! I'm not from that world. I have to work. I work hard every day in my small business. He would never be interested in someone like me for anything more than sex. I understand that and I opted to go for the sex, because I wanted him. And, by the way? Yes! It was awesome!" she finished with a laugh.

"Too much information, Holly. Remember Pete is like my big brother."

"I can vouch for the big part!"

"Shut up!" laughed Emma. "And on the serious side, your reasons why there can't be anything more than sex between you are ridiculous!"

"Excuse me?"

"You are not from different worlds at all. Pete is just like us. He and I grew up together, remember? Same little school, same small town, hicksville, California. Yes, he's got lots of money and stuff now, and he has quite a name and some influence in the city, but that doesn't make him any different from you."

"Ha! Tell my accountant that, would you?"

"Holly! You and Pete are really quite similar. You're both go-getters. I think you would make a lovely couple."

"Like I said, Em, you, my friend, are a hopeless romantic. I live and work in the real world, where men like Pete don't want anything but sex from women like me. I'm fine with it. I'm glad we did it and we got it out of the way so there won't be any weirdness going on between the two of us in the build up to your wedding."

"Okay. Whatever you say. I am not going to argue with you at this point."

"No?" Holly had expected more of an inquisition.

"No," said Emma, in what Holly recognized as her sweetest voice.

"Okay, so what does 'at this point' mean then?"

Emma laughed. "You know me too well. I'm simply going to wait until I see you together this weekend. Then I'll have a much better idea of what's really going on and will be able to bug you much more effectively because I'll be armed with facts and not just intuition!"

"Whatever. Just because you're living your 'Happily Ever After' doesn't mean you need to go around trying to orchestrate one for me."

"We'll see."

"Yes we will, but for now I'm going. You caught me in a steaming bubble bath and now it's not steaming anymore."

"Okay, but we'll talk soon, yes? And you will come with Pete on Friday?"

"Apparently," sighed Holly.

# Chapter Five

Holly sat staring at her screen. She was no more relaxed this morning than she had been last night. If anything, she was even more agitated. After talking to Emma, she'd given up on the tub and instead had tried to watch a movie. Trouble was, she'd spent more time looking at her phone than at the T.V. She'd been on edge, waiting for Pete to call to make arrangements for the weekend. What would he say? Would he be sticking to their agreement, or wanting more? She certainly wanted more. But she'd been clear. They'd had their one night: that was it, no more. After she'd taken her shower at the B&B, it had seemed he was good with the arrangement. He hadn't pushed or even asked for anything else. He'd even laughed when she'd left him with the stupid 'See you around, Bigshot,' which she'd blurted out in order to stop herself from asking when they could do it again.

He hadn't called last night though. Of course, now she was convinced that he didn't want to. Jack had landed him in a difficult position. He'd had what he wanted, he didn't want to be stuck driving her up to the lake. That was why he hadn't called.

She hadn't been able to face the customers this morning, or, for that matter, her cheery staff. Roberto had been in great form, relating gossip from a celebrity bash he and his partner, John, had been invited to the night before. Erin and Anna were hanging on his words, wanting descriptions of the stars, their clothes, and makeup. Usually she enjoyed the happy banter with her staff. This morning, she'd retreated to her office in the back of the store, claiming paperwork.

She sipped her coffee and tried to concentrate on the stock spreadsheet before her, but the numbers stared back unsympathetically, refusing to make sense. The door to the office burst open and Roberto bounded through.

"Flowers! Look, Holly. Beautiful, big, blooming flowers!"

Behind him a delivery guy held a huge bouquet of oriental lilies. Holly simply stared.

"Come on!" cried Roberto, snatching the flowers and handing them to her. "Sign for them and read us the card. We need to know already!"

Erin and Anna peeped around the door behind him, eyes wide and big grins.

"Sign for them?"

"Please," said the delivery man. "We don't normally need it, but the guy insisted. He held out a clipboard.

Holly scribbled her name as she asked, "What guy?"

"Oh, open the card and find out!" exclaimed Roberto.

Holly took the little envelope and opened it.

> *Come with me on Friday?*
> *Bigshot*
> *x*

She tried to suppress a huge smile, but failed.

"Ooh, la la! Lookit that smile. Mona Lisa's got nothing on you, *chica*! *Please*, we need all the details! My, how you've been keeping this one quiet!"

The delivery guy smiled and backed out of the door, leaving them to it.

"Berto, you are incorrigible," she laughed.

"No newsflash there darling," he batted his eyelids at her as he rested his elbows on the desk and his chin on his hands. "Now. Details!"

"Okay. Nothing exciting, I'm afraid. He's a friend of Emma's. He very kindly gave me a ride up to Summer Lake last weekend. As you know, Emma and Jack got engaged and now he's offering to let me ride up with him again on Friday, since we all need to be there."

Berto snatched the little card from her hand. He read it and then fanned himself with it as she tried to snatch it back.

"Oh, *Dios mio*! He wants you to *cum* with him?!"

"Berto!" she laughed.

Erin and Anna giggled in the doorway.

"And you say he gave you a *ride* last weekend?" Berto continued to fan himself. "Are the flowers enough to convince you to do it again?" He waggled his eyebrows suggestively. "Was he a *good* ride? Does he have a large *vehicle*?"

Erin and Anna collapsed in a fit of giggles. Holly herself threw her hands up in amused exasperation.

"Give it up, Berto," she laughed.

"No way, darling. I need details. What's he like? How hot is he? What's his name? Do we know him? Will I need to steal him from you?"

"His name is Pete. Yes he is hot. Hotter than hell, actually. And yes, sweetie, you probably will want to steal him, but you don't have a shot. He's one of those powerful masculine men and he'd probably be scared of you!"

"Oh, I have my powers of persuasion," said Roberto, nodding with a knowing smile.

"Yes, you do, but for now can we get back to work? This place will fall apart if we all spend our time back here gossiping about hot men!"

Erin and Anna scurried back out into the store. Roberto lingered in the doorway, his face serious now.

"Is this what's been bothering you?" he asked.

"Yes, sweetie, it is. He put me in a spin, but it's not going anywhere so I just need to get over it. I'm fine though, thank you."

"Okay, Holls, if you say so. But never forget, I'm here for you, me and John. Anything. Ever. You know you have us, right?"

"I do, Berto, and I'm so grateful. I love you guys."

"We love you too, Holls. Now, I'm going to get back to work so you can get back to staring at your screen and trying to work it out, okay?"

Holly smiled, "Okay, smart ass. I'll be out in a little while."

When Holly did step out onto the floor it was almost lunchtime. She'd sat and smiled at the note and the flowers for a while. She still didn't know where this was headed, but she knew from the flowers and from Pete's choice of words, that it was going somewhere. The butterflies in her stomach had taken flight once more.

She stood with Roberto, listening as he explained his arrangement of the new jewelry display. He had such a great eye. She was convinced that much of the store's success was owed to him. She was admiring a beautiful pair of emerald teardrop earrings when she heard him say, "Oh, sweet lord above, lookit this! Now that is what I call an M-A-N, man!"

She laughed as he started to fan himself again and followed his gaze to where—Pete! He was striding through the store towards them! Holly felt her throat go dry. What was he doing here? She'd thought he was gorgeous over the weekend; even in jeans and a T-shirt he had emanated power. Now, in a *very* expensively cut navy-blue suit, dazzling white shirt, and light blue tie, he was stunning. It seemed he commanded the attention of every person in the store as he made his way to where she stood.

When he stopped in front of her, he held her eyes and a dozen questions passed between them, unspoken.

Roberto broke the silence. "I promise I shall exit stage left in two shakes and let you continue this intense conversation, darling, but Holls, first you have to introduce me to this beautiful man so that I can hold, I mean shake, his hand."

Pete burst out laughing at that. Holly said, "Sorry Roberto, this is Pete Hemming. Pete, meet Roberto, my dear friend and visual merchandising manager."

Roberto made a big show of holding out his hand to shake. "Touch me if you dare, hottie!" he challenged.

Pete shook his hand firmly and leaned in to slap Roberto's back in that half handshake, half hug thing that men do to show affection.

Roberto hugged him back and said in a surprisingly serious tone, "Well played, sir." He turned to Holly. "He has my approval, darling. Now, you two play nicely. I have work to do." He left them both laughing as he sauntered away.

"So?" Pete was pinning her down with his eyes. He was such an imposing presence, filling the space around them with his maleness. Was that even a word, she wondered? Either way, that's how she felt. The blue gaze demanded an answer.

"Yes." She saw the corner of his lips lift in that half smile.

"Good," he said, wrapping her in a hug. She felt herself melt against his hard chest, breathing in his spicy cologne and his warmth.

"Have lunch with me?" he asked as she stepped back, suddenly aware that Erin and Anna were openly gawking at them.

"Now?"

"It is lunch time."

Holly tried to gather her wits. "Okay, just let me get my purse. I'll meet you out front."

He nodded. She could feel his eyes on her backside all the way to the office door. Once inside, she quickly applied fresh lipstick and eyeliner, cursing her trembling hands. She was grateful she'd worn this dress today, an empire line maxi that skimmed her feet; she felt good because she knew she looked good.

She hurried back out, and found Pete waiting at the front of the store with Roberto. The two of them were deep in conversation, for all the world looking like old friends. She was pleased to have been wrong about Pete's reaction to Roberto.

"Run along and have fun now, children," said Roberto, "And Holls, you know we can take care of the place if you want to call it a day."

Pete grinned at him, while Holly shot him a dark look. "I'm going for lunch, Berto. I'll be back in an hour."

"Yes, dear. Whatever you say, dear." He smiled after them as Pete held the door for her.

"He's quite a character," said Pete as they emerged onto the street.

"You can say that again!" Holly laughed. "You handled him well. I'm impressed. A lot of folk don't know how to take him and it can get quite uncomfortable."

"He's a sweetheart and he obviously adores you. Sexual orientation doesn't change the underlying need we men feel to look out for the people we care about. He's a good guy. I get where he's coming from, and I respect him for it."

Holly smiled. "Aren't you the perceptive one?"

"I make it my business, Holls."

She laughed. "Only Berto gets away with calling me that!"

He took her hand as they walked down the crowded street. "I'll have to see if I can earn the right to join him, then. Now, where do you want to go for lunch?"

They settled into a corner booth in La Hacienda, a Mexican place where Holly often lunched with Emma.

"*Hola*, Holly!" The owner brought them menus and poured water. "Usual for you?"

"Yes please, Miguel."

"What's the usual?" asked Pete.

"*Arroz con pollo*," replied Miguel.

Holly started to explain, "It's chicken...."

"With rice," finished Pete. "Could I get that, too?

"So," said Pete once they were alone. "You're okay with coming with me on Friday?"

She loved the way that smile hovered on his lips. "As long as you don't mind giving me a *ride* again...." She couldn't help it, the word play was so obvious, she had to.

"Mind?" There went that smile again. "I can't wait, sweetheart. But I have to ask, what happened to our one-off deal? Not that I'm complaining, you understand."

Holly had been asking herself the same question since she'd read his note earlier that morning. How could she backtrack so quickly when all her reasons for not getting entangled with him were still just as valid as they had been on Sunday?

"Well, we're going to be seeing quite a bit of each other these next few months. Since we are obviously so good at it, I don't see why we can't keep having sex."

Pete looked at her, brows drawn together, that pulse working in his jaw as he waited for her to say more. He didn't look impressed.

She laughed nervously. "Oh, come on. The way it looked over the weekend, if we continued sleeping together it was going to complicate things. The way it looks now, our trying to avoid sleeping with each other would be even more complicated."

Pete glowered a moment longer then rolled his eyes and smiled. "Do you really only want to use me for sex?"

Holly swallowed, hard before giving a little laugh and toss of her head. "Of course I do."

He was glowering again. "Why?"

"Pete, just be real about it. I told you before, we're from different worlds. There's no room for me in yours, is there?"

Pete hesitated. That was all she needed to confirm it. "Don't worry, sweetie. You don't need to come up with an explanation. I get it. I'm a realist. We're attracted to each other. We have great sex. As long as we're both clear about it, I think we can safely keep doing it for the next few months, until our paths are no longer likely to cross again."

She took a big swig of her water. That was how she could rationalize this to herself. She knew nothing more than sex would ever happen between them. But the sex was great and they wanted each other. There would be abundant opportunities over the next few months, so why not make the most of it? After the wedding there would be no reason for them to bump into each other again. That would be a natural end point. Knowing that from the beginning would make it easy to deal with at the end, right?

"Now, if you'll excuse me?"

Pete stood as she left the table and headed for the ladies' room.

~ ~ ~

Pete stared at the space where Holly had been sitting. What was it about her that got to him so badly? Any man—himself included, under normal circumstances—would be all over what she was offering: great sex, no strings and a predetermined end point. No commitments, no demands, nothing messy, just straight up honesty and lots of great sex. And it really was great. So why was he so uncomfortable with her proposition? Because he wanted more of her, or more from her? Maybe he did. But that was selfish of him. She'd been right; there was no room for her in his life. But not for her weird reasons about different world stuff. He'd have to get her to open up on what she really meant by that, because it didn't make sense to him. But still, there was no room for her in his life because it wasn't part of the plan. Not yet. He had a few more years yet, four to be precise, before he'd be prepared to take time away from Phoenix and invest it in a woman and a family.

He watched her return to the table. She was hot, no denying that. She was right. Why complicate matters with all the deep-and-meaningfuls? She was hot, he wanted her, and she was open and willing to sleep with him for the next few months. Really, what else did he need to know?

"So," he said once she was seated and Miguel had brought their food, "what time can we leave on Friday? Em wants us all there for dinner." He watched her fiddle with her ring as she thought about it. He realized it was a plain gold band on her wedding finger!

"I don't know," she said slowly. "If we leave at four we could be there by eight, right?"

"More like eight thirty or nine with the traffic on a Friday." His eyes were still fixed on that ring. He knew, at least he thought he did, that she wasn't married, so what was the story? Was she divorced?

"Could you leave at midday, say twelve, to give us the whole afternoon?" He smiled. "If you really want to *come* with me." He emphasized the word to make his meaning clear, and was gratified to see her eyes widen and the hint of a flush touch her cheeks.

She gave him her temptress smile, making him shift in his seat. "You know I want to. But I can't leave the store too early."

"Why not? Roberto said they could hold the fort."

She looked uncomfortable. "I just can't. You don't get it. It's my store. I have to be there. I'm not like you. I *have* to work."

Pete was a little taken aback by her rapid-fire response, but he was curious as to what her problem really was. "If that's a way to say you don't want to spend that much time with me, that's fine, sweetheart. Just say so. I'm a big boy, I can handle it." He gave her a hard stare, the look he used when he expected people to drop the excuses and tell him the real story. "Tell me?"

She shook her head. "No, Bigshot, that's not it at all, but I'm not sure you'll understand since you're not subject to the same obligations and responsibilities I am."

Pete frowned. "Enlighten me."

"I built that business from nothing. It's the sum total of my life's work. I *have* to work hard to keep it going, to keep it profitable, to provide an income for my staff. I can't just take off when I want to, not like you."

She surprised him. He was under the impression that her store was something of a success. He was a little ashamed that he'd even Googled it and asked around the few people he knew in the fashion world. It seemed the store, and Holly herself, had a great reputation.

"I'm sorry, are things not going well?"

She laughed. "Things are going great. It's a thriving little business and I turn a nice profit, but that's only because I work my butt off and don't flit around whenever the mood takes me."

Pete thought he was starting to understand. He knew so many self-made business people who shared the same fear. They believe that their success was completely tied to their own hard work, that if they didn't continue to work so very hard, it would all slip away. It saddened him because it kept them, and their businesses, small.

"You ever hear of working smarter instead of harder?" he asked.

"I like to think I am pretty smart, thank you very much!" she snapped.

He smiled and took hold of her hand. "I didn't say you weren't, sweetheart. I think you are very smart, you've built a thriving business. I'm just saying that in order to go to the next level, you need to get smarter about your own involvement. You need to run your business, not *be* your business."

Holly sighed, he was pleased when she squeezed his hand and met his eye.

"Thanks, Pete. I know you're right. I've heard it all before and I see the logic, but I'm not capable of letting go. I need to control my own security. I am successful, but not financially secure. I don't know how people like you take all the risks you must have to build something as huge as Phoenix.

Pete smiled and shook out his left hand so that a heavy silver bracelet slid down from under his sleeve. "Read it."

The heavy curb chain held a bar, engraved with one word: 'Work!'

She smiled at him and nodded.

"Now turn it over."

She twisted it to see the underside and read: 'Like you don't need the money.'

Holly laughed. "That's easy for you to say. You don't."

"It was no easier for me when I had this made than it is for you now. Jack and I were a year into Phoenix and we were feeling the same way you are. We wanted to keep it all in our control, and we needed the money. But it was only by learning to delegate and to take risks as if we really didn't need the money that Phoenix could become what it is."

"I admire that you made that choice, but I don't think I'm that brave, Pete. Like I told you, we're from different worlds, but that's partly because we're different people. I'll never take that leap because I'm too afraid to fall flat on my face, and too afraid of what would happen if I did." Her eyes clouded over. For a moment she looked very afraid, terrified. What was that about? The fear was quickly replaced by resignation. This wasn't the time to push it, but he wanted to know more. He wanted to help her.

"I don't think we're that different, Holly. Are you open to a little friendly advice?"

"Who wouldn't be from a self-made, multi-millionaire?" She smiled. "Go ahead, share your pearls of wisdom, Bigshot, but you know what they say about pearls before swine!"

Pete shook his head, lips pursed. "You're not going to get a rise out of me. All I'm going to say is, try baby steps. Getting out of your comfort zone is scary, so try just taking a little step, then another, instead of making that huge leap you were talking about."

"Makes sense. Any suggestions as to where I start?"

Pete grinned. "Compromise with me? Leave work at two on Friday?"

Holly laughed. "That was a roundabout way to get half of what you wanted."

He caught her eyes and held them with his own. "I'll get all of what I want, and so will you. If we can help you with your business hang-ups along the way, all the better. So, what do you say?"

"I say yes, I will."

Pete grinned, an idea taking to take shape in his mind. "Excellent! We're going to have a great weekend."

"I believe you could be right, but I need to get back to work if I'm going to cut out early on Friday."

"Okay, let me get this then I'll walk you back." Pete had been hoping for an extended lunch, but he wasn't going to push it.

Once he'd paid Miguel, they walked side by side through the lunchtime crowds. Pete noticed how many guys eyed Holly appreciatively as they passed. He put an arm around her shoulders possessively. She looked up at him, eyebrows raised. "Do you mind?" he asked.

She smiled and curled her own arm around his waist. "Don't mind at all."

All too soon they arrived back at her store.

"I'm guessing I pick you up here on Friday?"

"You betcha," she laughed. "It's going to be hard enough to leave that early without having to go home first too."

"I figured as much. So, until Friday then."

"Friday at three." She smiled.

Pete pulled her to him and dropped a kiss on the tip of her nose as he held her within the circle of his arms.

"At two, Holls. We have a deal remember? I take my deals very seriously."

She laughed up at him. "I was just testing."

He pecked her lips as he held her against him. "You don't want to test me, Holly, not unless you're prepared to find out how hard I can be." He proved his point, pulling her hips against him so his erection pressed into her. He didn't care that they were standing on the busy sidewalk outside her store. She didn't seem to care either as she reached her arms up around his neck, pressing the length of her body against him.

Her amber eyes met his. "Oh, I'll test you, Bigshot. Over and over again." She stroked her hand down his cheek then stepped back with a smile. "On Friday," she said, then disappeared inside the store.

Pete stood staring after her. She was going to drive him crazy! Was he, Pete Hemming, really standing out on the street staring after a woman he'd just been pretty much dry humping in public?

Staring through the storefront, he caught a movement, it was Roberto waving at him. Oh, God. He'd no doubt just seen that little performance. Pete raised a hand in reply and smiled as Roberto raised his eyebrows and nodded. Pete had a feeling he'd made a new friend there. He was glad; he liked the guy.

# Chapter Six

By one thirty on Friday, Holly was jumpy and irritable. She was nowhere near ready to leave and she didn't want to. She touched the cell phone in her pocket, ready to give in to the temptation to call Pete and tell him she couldn't go. She'd drive up tomorrow by herself. Except she hated to drive. Especially long distances. Especially by herself! She let out an exasperated sigh as she watched Erin and Anna, both busy with customers.

"Calm down, Holls." Roberto appeared at her shoulder. "You keep me around for a reason, darling. We both know it's because this place would fall apart without me."

Holly smiled in spite of herself.

"You, my dear, are simply decoration, not necessary to the survival or success of the place."

"Thanks!" she laughed.

"Seriously. Go touch up your makeup for that delicious man, then be on your way with a smile. You're going to offend me if you keep fretting like an anxious mother. You know I can run the place, no problem. If you carry on like this, I may start to think you don't trust me." He folded his arms across his chest and pouted. "You don't want to go there do you? You know you don't want to risk the wrath of Roberto!"

"I do not, and of course you're right."

"Always, darling, and don't you forget it."

"Okay, I give up. I'm going in the back to get my things together. Let me know when he arrives, will you?"

At two o'clock on the dot Roberto peeked his head around the office door. "Come on out, Cinders, your carriage awaits."

Holly smiled and picked up her bag. She was surprised to not see Pete and looked at Roberto. "Where is he?"

Roberto nodded through the storefront. "As I said, your carriage awaits."

She could see a silver limo waiting at the curb with a uniformed driver standing beside it. "What the..?"

"Chop, chop. You don't want to be late for the ball." Roberto patted her shoulder. "Go, relax. Let your hair down. Don't give this place another thought. I promise I will take very good care of it."

"Thanks Berto." She reached up and kissed his cheek. "You're the best."

"Yes dear. Now go. Give my love and congrats to Emma."

She walked out onto the street where the driver, a man in his late fifties by the looks of him, snapped to attention as she approached. He held open the rear door for her.

"Miss Hayes?"

"Yes."

"Mr. Hemming sends his apologies. He was delayed and asked me to collect you."

Holly stared at him. The only time she'd ever been in a limo was for a bachelorette party.

The driver smiled at her and held the door a little wider. "If you will?"

Holly continued to stare at him, not knowing what to make of this. The driver started to look uncomfortable. "I'm Albert," he said, seemingly at a loss for what to do or say next since Holly still wasn't getting in the car.

Holly's brain kicked in when she realized how rude she was being to this old gentleman. She held out her hand. "Nice to meet you, Albert. I'm Holly. Would you mind if I call shotgun?"

Albert grinned. "It'd be my pleasure, Miss Holly." He opened the passenger door for her and Holly buckled herself in.

"So, Albert," she said once he pulled out into the traffic. "Where are we headed?"

With a sideways glance he replied, "To meet Mr. Hemming."

Holly laughed. "Yeah, but where?"

"I'm afraid he asked me not to say."

Holly frowned. "And why was that?"

She could tell Albert was trying not to smile. "He said, if he knew you, you might change your mind about coming."

"I see."

"And, Miss Holly? If you don't mind my saying, I think he does know you. He told me not to be surprised if you wanted to sit up front."

"Well, I don't like to stand on ceremony, and I'm not like Pete, I'm not used to cars and drivers. I just see a nice man who is kindly giving me a ride, thank you."

Albert laughed, "You're more like Pete than you think. He sits up front with me whenever he can get away with it."

"Ha! I'd have imagined Mr. Bigshot sitting in the back, doing important stuff and giving orders!"

Albert guffawed at that. "Mr. Bigshot?! Don't let him hear you say that, he'd be horrified. He's as down to Earth as they come underneath it all, you know."

"I do know, Albert. It's just so easy to wind him up calling him that."

"You stick around, Miss Holly. I think you're going to be good for him."

"Ha! I'm just a passing fling, but thanks for the vote of confidence." Why did she have to blurt out such stupid things? Now the old man looked uncomfortable and she felt bad. "Sorry, it's just that I know it's not going to go anywhere serious between us, and I like him more than I should."

Albert nodded. "I say again. I think you're going to be good for him. And now, we're almost there."

Holly looked out of the window, "The airport?"

"Yes, ma'am." Albert slowed the car as they approached a chain link fence. He stopped and leaned out of the window to press some numbers into a keypad. The section of fence in front of them whirred and then rolled away to the side. Albert drove through the gap and stopped, letting the engine idle until the fence rolled back into place behind them. He drove on past a row of hangars until he came to the last one.

Pete stood outside, talking on his cell phone. He ended the call when he saw the limo approaching. Holly caught her breath at the sight of him. He was wearing jeans and a denim shirt which, although it looked old and perfectly faded, she knew had set him back at least five hundred dollars. She knew because she had been the one to persuade the designer to run a limited line in only two of the top men's stores in the city. Ugh! She really had to let go of the fashion fixation though. It wasn't the shirt, but the body it was stretched over that was making her heart race. The body, and the gorgeous smile on his face as he came over and opened her door before Albert could get out. He greeted her with a hug and a peck on her lips, then slung an arm around her shoulders and drew her to his side as he addressed Albert.

"Was I right or was I right?"

"You were right, smart ass!"

Holly looked between the two of them, surprised.

Pete laughed. "You're not the only one who calls me names and puts me in my place, you know."

"So I see. Good for you, Albert. Maybe you and I should join forces and really kick his butt."

Albert laughed. "I get the impression you can do that all by yourself, but if you ever need reinforcements, you give me a shout." He handed Holly his card and she slipped it into her purse. "For now though, I'm going to let you two get going." He covered his ears as the sound of jet engines firing up filled the air.

Pete checked his watch. "Yep, we're filed for two thirty. Thanks, old friend." Pete opened the trunk and took Holly's bag out then shook Albert's hand. "See you soon."

"Poker night Tuesday if you're down?" Albert turned to Holly. "It was a pleasure to meet you. I hope to see you again soon."

"You too, thank you." Holly gave him peck on the cheek. She liked the old guy a lot. He smiled and looked at Pete. "She's a keeper, son."

Pete smiled. "You're an old man, not an old woman. We don't need a matchmaker do we, Holly?"

As he smiled down at her, she felt that hollow pit of disappointment in her stomach again. Why, though? She already knew she wasn't a keeper in Pete's eyes. She was just the provider of some hot, easily available sex. She caught Albert's eye. *Oh, crap!* He could see how she truly felt.

She laughed. "Come on Albert, you don't think I'd let myself get tied down with this smart ass, do you?"

They all laughed at that, but as he got back in the limo, Albert shook his head and shot her a look that told her she wasn't fooling him. Not one bit.

Pete took her hand and led her around to the front of the hangar where the plane was revving up its engines. "Sorry about the change of plans. We finally got everything sorted to keep the Lear out here, and it'll save us four hours on the road. Are you okay with this?"

"I'm thrilled. You already know how much I hate road trips, and I've never been in a private jet before." She wasn't about to tell him how much this was scrambling her emotions. On the one hand, she was curious to see inside. She felt like a little girl excited to fly in a private plane. She was a little shocked at how much it turned her on that he owned it and was using it to take her away for the weekend. She certainly wasn't going to tell him that. On the other hand, it served as a reminder to her of how different they were. He was Peter the Great, Mr. Bigshot, with his limo, his jet, his mega millions. She was just plain Holly Hayes, proud owner of one small store, one small townhouse, and one old rust bucket of a station wagon. She pushed all that aside. For now they had the weekend ahead of them. She'd fly in his jet, they'd sleep together again. Why be greedy? She'd take what was offered and enjoy it.

"Let me show you inside." Pete grabbed her bag and let her climb the steps ahead of him.

Inside, Holly looked around. It was beautiful. The interior was done out in champagne colored leather. There were four club seats facing each other just behind the cockpit. A dark oak bar with a fridge and sink faced a bathroom. Beyond that, in the rear section, a sofa long enough to seat four ran along one side.

"What do you think?"

"It's amazing!" she exclaimed. "I don't know what I expected, but it wasn't anything this luxurious."

"Make yourself at home. I'll let Smoke know we're ready."

Holly admired his backside and muscular denim clad legs as he popped his head into the cockpit. He smiled as he turned around and caught her looking. "Soon," he mouthed, then raised his voice as the pilot appeared behind him. "Holly, this is Smoke, Phoenix Chief Pilot and an old friend."

"Nice to meet you." Smoke leaned past Pete to shake her hand.

*Oh my God! Another gorgeous man.* She'd put him easily on this side of forty, even though his perfectly mussed hair, was completely gray. She took in broad shoulders, narrow hips, and muscular arms all presented in a sexy pilot's uniform. *Yum!*

"You too," she replied.

Smoke went to pull up the steps and secure the door. After giving them a quick safety briefing, he made his way back to the cockpit and closed the door behind him. Pete took the seat opposite Holly and fastened himself in.

"I'll get us some champagne once we're airborne, but we have to strap down for now."

Holly nodded, still somewhat befuddled by this turn of events. Pete hooked his foot around her calf and smiled.

"You sure you're okay with this?"

"Yep, I'm just a bit surprised, that's all."

They thundered down the runway and up into the skies above the city. After a few minutes, Smoke's voice came over the intercom.

"You can unbuckle now folks. We'll be cruising at twenty two thousand feet, flight time forty-five minutes. I'll let you know when you need to strap back in."

Pete stood. "Champagne?" Holly nodded. "Come help me?" He leaned over her to unbuckle her seat belt. Feeling him so close, the butterflies took flight once more. She followed him to the galley. He unscrewed a weird looking cap from a bottle of champagne and she looked at him quizzically.

He laughed. "I hate popping corks in here. Just doesn't seem wise in a pressurized cabin, so I open it before take-off and screw it down with this."

Typical! He thought of everything and had it covered. He handed her a flute and then raised his own.

"What shall we drink to?"

Holly had a crazy urge to say, 'to us.' Instead she raised her glass and said, "Work!"

"Ha! Like you don't need the money, remember?" Pete went to the back of the plane and sat on the sofa. "This is much comfier." He grinned and patted the seat next to him.

Holly looked back at the cockpit door.

"Don't worry, he's flying the plane. He's not coming back here."

"Still, it's a bit weird though, isn't it?"

"Relax. Come sit with me."

Holly came and sat beside him, heart racing. Pete knocked back his champagne then tipped the bottom of her glass so that she would do the same. Why not? She downed it and felt the bubbles going straight to her head. Pete got rid of her glass

and drew her toward him. He locked his fingers in her hair and
his lips came down on hers. Holly moaned as he explored her
mouth, meeting his tongue with her own, feeling the heat
begin to mount between her legs. She wanted him so badly.
From the hunger of his kiss, she knew he wanted her just as
much. She felt his warm hands stroking her breasts through
her top. She moaned again as he increased the pressure,
squeezing and pinching her nipples. She pulled at his shirt,
grateful for the knowledge that what looked like buttons were
actually snaps and she could rip them open, which she did. She
stared at his bare chest, perfect pecs and rock hard abs.

"Holly, we have to." He rested his head against the back of the
sofa.

"Much as I hate to make your head any bigger...." She smiled
as she straddled him, kneeling on the sofa to face him, "I have
to admit, you are right once again."

He took hold of her hand and brought it to the front of his
pants so she could feel his erection. He was so hard.

"Don't worry, sweetheart. I don't think you could make my
head any bigger than it is right now. I need to be inside you."
He unfastened his jeans and pushed them down past his hips,
then slid his hand inside her panties. "You're soaking."

She could only nod as he stroked her, exploring her damps
folds with his deft fingers. He was in complete control of her
body again, taking her where he wanted her. She willingly went
with him, moving her hips in time with his fingers. She felt the
heat building. When she thought she couldn't take any more,
he withdrew his hand and quickly put on a condom. He pulled
her panties to the side and they both watched transfixed as he
guided himself toward her opening.

"Sorry guys," Smoke's voice over the intercom sliced through the moment, and Holly jumped to her feet. Pete closed his eyes in frustration. She could see that little muscle working in his jaw.

"ATC are telling me we're about to hit some turbulent air here, it might get quite rough for a while. You're going need to put those belts back on."

Pete looked up at her. "Want to finish this first?"

Holly shook her head. She didn't mind the turbulence, but hearing the pilot's voice like that had been a rude reminder that they weren't really alone after all. She let out a deep breath.

"Later." She straightened herself up while Pete got rid of the condom and pulled up his pants. She watched regretfully as he fastened his shirt. Once they were both presentable, she turned to head back to the seats up front. Pete caught her arm and crushed her to his chest, kissing her deeply.

He lifted his head and captured her gaze. "Not too much later, sweetheart. I need you."

Holly nodded, she felt the same way. She fastened herself back in while Pete poured them more champagne then came to sit opposite her.

"Jack and Emma aren't expecting us until later, we won't have to wait too long."

Holly tipped her glass to him. "I'll drink to that."

Thirty minutes later, as the wheels touched down on the runway, Smoke's voice came through again. "Hope that wasn't too rough for you. We'll be taxiing over to the FBO where Jack and Emma are meeting you."

Pete tapped a button on the arm of his chair, "What?! I asked for a taxi!"

"I know, but I talked to Jack this morning and once he knew you were coming he told me to cancel it. Wanted to pick you up himself."

Holly couldn't help but smile at the thunderous look on Pete's face. After a long silence, Smoke's voice came again.

"Sorry."

Pete rolled his eyes as Holly continued to smirk at him.

"No problem, Smoke. It's not your fault, you didn't know any better." He looked at Holly and said, "It's a conspiracy!"

She laughed. "We're only here because of Emma and Jack, remember? Anything else is a side issue."

Pete glowered at her. "A side issue?! Do you think I've been thinking about Jack and Emma all week? Or even thinking about the house I'm building? No! I've been thinking about you, sweetheart. All. Damned. Week. And now you've got me all hot and horny and we can't do anything about it!"

Holly's heart leaped. He'd been thinking about *her* all week? Okay, so it was no doubt only about the sex, but he was admitting she was getting to him. Just like he was getting to her.

"You're not the only one who is frustrated here, Bigshot. We'll just have to seize our moment when we can. I'm sure the others won't mind if we disappear for a while."

"But the others don't know."

"And...we're not going to tell them?"

"What would we say? You want me to ask our best friend and my partner to just excuse me while I go screw the Maid of Honor?"

"So I'm good enough to sleep with, but not good enough to tell your friends about? Is that what you're saying?" *Damn him, that's harsh!*

"No, Holly! That's not what I'm saying at all. I..."

Yet again, they were interrupted by Smoke as the engines powered down. "Okay folks, I'll be right out, the FBO guys will meet you and take you and your bags in."

"Holly, I'm saying...." Pete tried to continue, but stopped when Smoke appeared and came through the cabin. He opened the door and let down the steps to where a young man on a golf cart waited to ferry them to the building.

Holly hastily thanked Smoke and went down the steps. She took the front seat of the cart, next to the driver. Pete climbed on behind her. He put a hand on her shoulder.

"I didn't mean it like that Holly. I meant I didn't want the others to think, to know, that we're only sleeping together."

The driver's eyes widened, but to his credit he kept them fixed straight ahead.

"But I'm just using you for sex, remember?" Holly snapped.

The driver let out a small, strangled sound that they both ignored.

"Apparently!" Pete snapped back. "But I don't think that's your usual style, and I know it's not mine. I don't want the others getting the wrong idea. About either of us."

The cart came to a halt in front of the FBO building. Holly could see Emma and Jack inside, smiling and waving. The driver ran around to get their bags, but Pete took them from him. He looked at the wide-eyed youngster.

"You do not, repeat, *do not* mention or gossip about *anything* you just heard. Understood?"

The kid nodded his head, looking terrified now. Holly felt sorry for him. An angry Pete was a powerful force. She could see how anyone who didn't know him would be totally intimidated. But she did know him—at least she'd thought she did. She wasn't intimidated. Just good and mad! What was she, his dirty little secret? *No thanks!*

Pete slipped the kid a tip and visibly calmed himself.

"But, sir, it's a...."

"I know. Take it and beat it!" Pete turned toward the building, leaving the driver staring at the hundred dollar bill in his hand. Holly fell in step beside him.

Emma and Jack met them at the door with hugs and smiles.

"Yo, bro! You should've let me know you got everything squared away with Papa Charlie."

Holly and Emma looked at each other. "Papa Charlie?" asked Emma.

"The plane," explained Jack. "The last two letters of its tail number are P.C. Which in the phonetic alphabet is Papa Charlie."

"I only finalized everything this morning," said Pete.

Jack smiled. "It's a good job I talked to Smoke then, isn't it?"

"Yeah, great," said Pete, looking anything but pleased. "So, since you're here, what's the plan?"

Holly stood fuming to herself, watching the exchange but saying nothing. She hadn't given any thought to what the others would think. What did it matter? They were their friends. She felt insulted that Pete didn't want to tell them anything. Was he ashamed of her or something? She was angry with him, confused, and worst of all, she still wanted him. She needed to finish what they'd started on the plane.

"You're welcome, partner." Jack playfully punched Pete's arm. "A little thank you wouldn't hurt. What's eating you?"

Holly saw Pete's fist clench and unclench at his side. "Sorry. I'm a bit wound up." He looked straight at her and said, "My head is aching. I had some stuff build up that I haven't been

able to deal with yet." His blue gaze penetrated her. "You
know me though, I'll get on top of it soon."

"Well, do that on your own time," said Emma, oblivious to the
undercurrent between Holly and Pete. "The plan is, you and
Jack can go deal with whatever house stuff you need to. Holly
and I are going to talk girly wedding details, then we'll meet
you at the Boathouse later. Ben wanted us to eat there, but
then everyone's coming up to North Cove afterwards.

Pete nodded slowly. "Are we all staying at your place then?"

Emma nodded. "I'm hoping so."

"Sounds like a plan. Come on then." Pete picked up their bags
and the four of them walked out to Emma's car, which was
parked next to Jack's truck.

"Okay ladies. See you later." Jack pulled Emma to him and
pecked her lips.

"Oh, please!" said Pete, with a laugh that sounded forced.
"Stop pawing at her!"

"Nope." Jack smiled and dropped his head to kiss Emma
more fully. Her arms came up around his neck and they kissed
like a pair of teenagers about to be parted for the summer.

While they were so distracted, Pete murmured to Holly, "We'll
finish this later, sweetheart."

"We already did, Bigshot. If you're ashamed of me, there's
nothing else to say."

His eyes darkened and he leaned closer. "I am *not*...." he began,
then stopped himself. Catching hold of her wrist he called
over his shoulder, "We'll be back, guys. Holly left something in
the plane." He pulled her back toward the building.

*What the...?* Holly didn't want to go with him, but she could
hardly start struggling with him in the parking lot. His grip was
strong as he marched her back into the building. He led her

down a corridor then pulled her into a room filled with screens displaying weather maps and flight information. He closed the door behind them and leaned back against it, glaring at her.

"We are not going anywhere until we get this straightened out, sweetheart," his voice was low and controlled.

Holly paced the little room. "What the hell do you think you're doing, Pete?"

"I am trying to apologize for *your* misunderstanding and to figure out how we are going to handle this."

"Apology accepted," she snapped. "All handled, see? Now let's go." She reached past him for the door handle, wanting to leave while her anger was still stronger than her desire for him. He caught her wrist and pulled her to him, turning to trap her against the door and leaning the full weight of his body against her.

"Pete! I...."

"You what, sweetheart?" he asked with that damned half smile as he ground his hips against her. Every nerve ending in her body responded to him as his hardness pressed into her. He laced his fingers through hers and brought both hands up above her head where he held them against the door.

"I...." her words were lost as he gently bit her bottom lip. Thrusting his tongue into her mouth, he transferred both her hands into one of his own and stroked the other down her neck, trailing his fingers down the valley between her breasts. He teased her nipple, then squeezed it hard as he thrust his hips against her. She gasped and freed her hands from his so she could grasp his hard ass and pull him closer still as she rubbed herself against him. Her anger didn't stand a chance against her need for him.

He broke the kiss, his breath coming hard. "So?"

She smiled up at him. There was no way she was going to be able to resist this man, or anything he wanted from her. "Yes," she replied.

"Good." He dropped a kiss on the tip of her nose. "We'd better get back out there, but we'll continue this later."

She nodded.

"And, Holly. I was thinking of *your* reputation, not mine. I need you to understand that." His eyes bored into her; he still held her in the circle of his arms.

"How so?" She really didn't understand that part.

"I don't want them to think you're the kind of girl who is just in it for the sex."

She let out a harsh little laugh. "Even though you know I am?"

"I don't think you are though, sweetheart. Despite what you say. You obviously have your reasons about why that's all you want from me. I respect that. But no, I *know* you are not that kind of girl and I guess I just didn't want anyone else to think that you were." He stroked a strand of hair away from her face and ran a crooked finger down her cheek. "You're special, sweetheart."

Holly leaned her face against his hand for a moment, overcome by a rush of emotions and wants that were so much more than just physical. She closed her eyes and pulled herself together.

"Thanks, Pete." She kissed his fingertips and smiled. "Now we really better get back." She opened the door and stepped out into the corridor, needing to escape the intensity of the moment, the intensity of his eyes.

Outside, Jack was leaning against his truck, arms around Emma who stood between his legs. They didn't even notice Holly and Pete return, they were so engrossed in one another.

Pete ran a hand down Holly's back then squeezed her backside.

"See, we would have had time."

She smiled back at him, but said nothing.

"Yo, Benson. Put her down now. We've got work to do. Get your ass in that truck and let's go see what progress you've made with my house!"

Jack laughed. "Yes, sir! Peter, sir!" He saluted then gave Emma one more kiss.

Holly waved as they drove away. Pete blew her a kiss while Emma's eyes followed Jack.

# Chapter Seven

Pete drummed his fingers on the truck door while he waited for Jack to get off the phone. They'd spent the last couple of hours going over the plans for his new house. They'd walked the lot, Jack explaining again how the way he'd oriented the home site would give Pete the best views and more or less sunlight at different times of day and year. Pete was more excited than he chose to let on. He was eager to get the place built and finished. Growing up in Summer Lake, he'd always known that one day he'd build a house of his own here. He wanted his own kids to know the kind of carefree childhood he had. Building this place was completing another stage of his plan.

His thoughts drifted back to Holly. It was a pity she didn't fit into the plan. Apart from lusting after her pretty much since the moment he'd met her, he liked her immensely as a person, too. She was fun, funny, down to Earth and smart. She was great with people as he'd witnessed with Alonso and his family, with her staff, and with Albert. Even when they'd had lunch the other day, the people in the restaurant, from the owner to the busboy, had all known and obviously liked her. She had a smile and a kind word for everyone. At the same time, she didn't take any crap. She certainly wasn't afraid to call him out. Unlike so many women he'd known, who went out of their way to please him and win his approval, she spoke her mind and told it like it was.

In short, he admired her. She was the kind of woman he wanted in his life. Just not yet. He wished he could meet her four years from now. Who knew what might happen between them then? He stared out at the lake. That was crazy talk. He'd met her now. The only thing she was offering was sex, and how could he complain? He couldn't offer her anything more than sex either. Not for the next four years. He'd be stupid to think she'd still be available by the time he was ready. Some lucky guy was bound to come along and make her his own. He clenched his fist against the wave of anger that thought caused him.

"Do we need to get ready to go into town?" Jack's voice cut into his thoughts.

"I guess we do. Mind if I shower in the RV?"

Jack nodded. He was supposedly living in his brother's motor coach, which he'd parked on Pete's lot while he oversaw the construction of the house. In reality though, he'd effectively moved in with Emma. Her house stood on the same headland as Pete's lot. Pete smiled to think that soon they'd be neighbors up here, sharing the headland and the beach that lined the North Cove.

After they were both freshly showered and shaved, Jack said, "Let's go. We don't want to keep the ladies waiting."

Pete laughed. "It still seems strange to me to see the eligible Mr. Benson mooning around after my 'little sister!'"

"Laugh all you like, partner, but don't tell me you're not as eager to get down there as I am!"

"What do you mean?" Pete stalled for time, he still hadn't figured out how he wanted to handle this. What he could say or do about Holly?

Jack closed up the RV. Once they were in the truck he turned to Pete as he started it up. "Don't give me that shit. I mean Holly and you know it, bro. Whatever is going on between you two has high voltage sparks flying."

"It does?"

"Damned straight it does! And listen, I'm sorry if I messed up by coming to get you at the airport. You could have told me, you know."

Pete let out a frustrated sigh. "Yeah, I guess I could. See, I don't know myself what's going on with me and Holly. All I know is she's gotten under my skin."

Jack grinned as he turned the truck toward Summer Lake Resort. "I knew it. So what are you going to do about it?"

"It's complicated."

Jack laughed out loud at that. "Oh, man! You've got it bad, believe me, I know. I recognize the symptoms."

Pete glowered at him. "No you don't, bro. It's not like you and Emma. It's just complicated."

Jack laughed again, totally unconvinced. "Go on then, explain to me what kind of complicated."

Pete drummed his fingers, considering it. What could he say? What was the complication, really? They were sleeping together, that was all, nothing complicated about that, right?

 "Nah. It's not that big of a deal. Forget it."

Jack looked across at him, his eyes saying so much more than his words. "Whatever you say, man."

They parked in the square at the resort and made their way through the bar, looking for Holly and Emma. Pete's heart raced when he spotted her. She sat at a high top table with Emma and Missy. Quite a sight, three amazing looking women, but he could only see one. She was stunning, with her hair falling in soft curls around her shoulders. He wanted to tangle his hands in it, pull her head back, watch her lips part, ready for his kisses. She was wearing another one of those long slim dresses. It clung perfectly to the contours of her breasts. His imagination was already filling in the details of how it clung to her tight little ass, too. She was smiling, her eyes sparkling, gesticulating wildly as she spoke. She had Em and Missy in stitches as she rolled her eyes and fanned herself with a menu. He grinned, guessing she was telling a story about Roberto, whom she obviously adored.

He felt Jack dig him in the ribs, making him realize that he'd stopped dead when he'd seen her.

"Not that big of a deal, huh?"

Pete turned to his partner. "It can't be," he growled.

Jack stared at him. "You want to tell me what's going on, Bro?"

Pete blew out his cheeks and shook his head. "There's nothing going on, okay? Drop it." He started toward the girls' table with a grim look on his face. Jack matched his stride.

~ ~ ~

Holly turned as she sensed Pete's presence in the bar. That was impossible, she knew, but still she felt her body tense and tingle in anticipation. The butterflies swirled in her stomach and when she turned she locked eyes with him as he was making his way through the crowd to their table. Her heart thundered and her throat went dry as she took in his dark blue jeans and white cotton shirt, sleeves turned up to display muscular forearms. His broad shoulders stood above most of the crowd, and above them she could see his perfectly chiseled features were set and grim. *Oh, dear! Not a happy camper.* She glanced at Jack beside him, another drop dead gorgeous man, she had to admit. By comparison though, he exuded an air of fun and happiness, his eyes shining as he looked straight past her to Emma, who was sitting beside her.

When they reached the table, Missy greeted them first.

"Hey, guys! What's with the Mr. Happy and Mr. Grumpy act? Are you practicing to play good cop, bad cop?"

Holly and Emma laughed with her as Pete and Jack exchanged a look then laughed themselves.

"Hey, Miss!" said Jack "The only explanation I have is that I just laid eyes on my beautiful wife-to-be. You know that always puts a smile on my face." He leaned in to kiss Emma, then pulled up a stool beside her. "As for Mr. Grumpy there," he nodded at Pete, "he...well he's just a basket case!"

"Watch it, Benson," laughed Pete. "That 'grumpy face' as you call it, Miss, is actually grim determination and, as my partner will vouch, it means I'm about to get what I want."

"And what is you want now, Pete?" asked Missy.

Pete pulled up a stool between Missy and Holly and patted them both on the knee. Holly caught her breath as he slid his hand up her thigh a ways before removing it. "I already got it, Miss." He grinned at them both. "The best seat in the house, between the two most beautiful women."

"Hey, Hemming!" said Emma.

"Sorry, Mouse. I meant between two of the three most beautiful women, but you know I have to watch my mouth these days, 'cause Jack might get jealous."

Jack put an arm around Emma's shoulders. "Yeah, pay attention to your two women and leave mine alone."

Holly laughed, pleased to see her friend Emma finally happy and relaxed with a man who loved her so much. She envied Emma this group of friends she had here in this wonderful place. She was looking forward to spending more time with them in the lead up to the wedding. She'd gotten to know Missy last weekend and liked her very much. She knew the two of them would become good friends as they took care of many of the wedding details for Emma.

"So where are the others?" asked Pete. "I thought we were all under orders from Bridezilla here not to be late."

"Careful, Hemming," laughed Emma. "You call me Bridezilla one more time and I'm putting you in charge of flowers!"

"I'll be good, I'll be good!" Pete held up both hands with a look of mock horror. "Anything but flowers!" He pulled Holly and Missy's stools closer to his own and put an arm around each of them. "Though I don't mind if you want to put me in charge of bridesmaids."

Missy slapped his arm away. "Hands off, Hemming!" she laughed. "You only get to be in charge of one bridesmaid and, for both our sakes, I'm glad it's Holly and not me."

Pete tried to look hurt, but Holly could see the half smile lurking as he turned and wrapped both arms around her. "I pity poor Dan," he shot back at Missy. "He's going to have his hands full with you."

Holly couldn't believe it as he hugged her close and kissed the top of her head. "Did you hear that? I get to be in charge of you!"

Holly looked around at the others, who were all smiling in amusement.

"Not so fast, Mr. Grumpy! Are you sure you can handle being in charge of me?"

He grinned down at her. "I'm not at all sure, no, but I think it'd be fun to find out, don't you?"

Holly looked at Emma. "In the hierarchy of the wedding party, who ranks higher, the Maid of Honor or the Best Man?"

Emma frowned. "I think it'd have to be the Maid of Honor."

"No way!" chimed in Jack, "Best Man, hands down."

Missy laughed. "I spy the beginnings of a power struggle, and you know, Pete, normally my money would be on you, but I think you've finally met your match in our Holly here!"

Holly smiled at her. "Why thanks, girlfriend!" Missy high-fived her above Pete's head.

Jack laughed. "Sorry partner, but I'm with Miss on this one. I second the notion that you have met your match."

Emma nodded, smiling a knowing smile at them.

Holly could see what they were thinking. It was quite ironic really that they all thought they were witnessing the beginning of a relationship between her and Pete, while he didn't want to admit that that would never happen. That they were in fact just screwing each other!

"Here's the lucky guy who gets to be in charge of me," said Missy with a big smile on her face as Dan joined them, accompanied by Laura.

"Now, Miss, don't you go pushing my brother-in-law around," said Emma.

Another gorgeous looking man! This place was overrun with them. Dan looked a lot like Jack, but not quite as tall, and he had that kind of stubble that was almost a beard, but wasn't quite. Holly always thought it looked so very attractive but wasn't so sure about how it would feel. Her impression of Dan when she'd met him last weekend was that he was incredibly smart, incredibly sweet and considerate, and perhaps a little shy. So she, along with the rest of them apparently, was a little surprised by his reaction to Missy's words.

He smiled at her and asked , "Seriously? I get to be in charge of you?"

Missy nodded happily.

"In that case...." He held out his hand to her and she got down from her stool looking puzzled. "You're coming with me. Right. Now." With that he led her away from the table and the others sat staring after them.

"Wow!" Jack was the first to break the stunned silence. "Looks like this wedding party is going to be quite a party!"

Holly felt Pete's arm tighten around her shoulders as he said, "I'm banking on it, bro."

Laura took Missy's empty seat and said, "And it looks like I'm late to the party, as usual. Hey everyone."

"No party could start without my cousin," said Jack.

"Yes, thanks for coming," added Emma.

Holly looked up as Ben, who owned the resort and was the final member of the wedding party, pulled up a stool.

"Sorry guys, we've got a function upstairs tonight, and I wanted to make sure everything was set. I really want to get out of here after we've eaten. I need a break from the place. Is that still the plan, Em? For us all to head up to yours?"

"It certainly is. We could have had dinner up there, too, you know."

"I know, Mouse. But you just got engaged and I wanted this first little celebration to be my treat, not have you cooking for all of us."

"Well thank you. It is very sweet of you."

"Yeah, sweet, that's my problem." He laughed. "But come on," he passed menus around, "Let's eat and get out of here, can we?"

~ ~ ~

Holly had enjoyed dinner immensely. The food was wonderful and Emma's friends were great company. There had been much teasing as Emma had laid out her plans and areas of responsibility for each of them. What she'd enjoyed most was the way Pete had teased her and challenged her every chance he got. And the way he'd kept an arm around her shoulders for much of the night.

They were standing in the square, trying to figure out the logistics of getting everyone back up to Emma's place.

"I can take a bunch of us in the minivan," said Missy. "I know it's not a glamorous ride, but you're all welcome. We need to stop and pick Scot up on the way through."

"I'm in," said Dan. "I can't wait to see my little buddy." Holly knew that Dan had been working with Missy's son Scot for the last few months on some computer projects.

"Me too," Laura and Ben spoke at the same time.

"Thanks, Miss, but I'm going to chauffeur my lady home in her mouse-mobile," said Jack, referring to Emma's convertible, which really wasn't a good match for the country roads around the lake. He threw his own keys to Pete, whose hand shot out to catch them. "Would you bring the truck back up for me, bro?"

"Sure thing," said Pete. "As long as Holly will keep me company?" He raised an eyebrow at her.

Though Holly put on a big sigh, she was thrilled at the chance to be alone with him again. "I suppose so. Someone needs to keep an eye on you."

~ ~ ~

Pete started the truck and let it idle while Emma's Lexus and Missy's minivan pulled out of the square. He looked across at Holly, who was smoothing her dress down over her long slender legs. He badly needed to have those legs wrapped around him.

"You, sweetheart, are driving me nuts. Do you know this?"

"The feeling is mutual, Bigshot."

"I am so tempted right now to drive this truck down a dark country lane and make out like a couple of kids."

"Yes, but we can't, can we? Since you're too ashamed of me to tell anyone what we're up to."

"I am *not* ashamed of you! I thought you understood that."

"I do, Pete. You're just too easy to wind up."

He shook his head. "You're the only one that can do that, you know? I don't get wound up." It was true. Sure, Jack could get to him sometimes, but they'd known each other half their lives. He'd only known this woman a week.

She laughed. "It's only 'cause you're used to everyone and everything being just what you want them to be and I'm not, am I?"

"Dammit, Holly! You're exactly what I want. You know how much I want you."

"You're going to have to figure out how to make it happen then, aren't you? How and when. We both know it can't be now. We're going to have to get up to Emma's before they send out search parties."

She was right, of course. Much as he wanted to forget the others, drive her out to the cabin, and make love to her all night, he knew they couldn't. He did have to figure something out. He put the truck in gear, mostly to stop himself from unbuckling his seat belt to kiss her. If he kissed her now, there was no way they'd make it to Emma's tonight.

When they arrived at North Cove, everyone was sitting out on the front deck.

"Hey you two," called Emma. "Bring your bags up and I'll show you your rooms. You are staying, right, Pete?"

"Course, I am, if there's room. I didn't have a drink with dinner, and I could use a cold one right about now."

"I'll grab you both one," said Jack and headed into the kitchen while Emma pointed upstairs. "You're going to have to share with Ben this time."

Pete's stomach dropped, he was planning to sneak into Holly's room.

"That way the ladies can all have their own room." Emma had inherited this place from her great aunt, and it was huge. It had five bedrooms and had been used as a vacation rental for many years. There was certainly room for all of them, but he didn't like the way the sleeping arrangements were working out. Maybe Holly would be right next door to him?

"That's great, thanks, Mouse."

As he headed up the stairs, he heard Emma telling Holly, "I've given you the downstairs, since you'll be here a couple of nights. You've got your own bathroom and a sitting room overlooking the lake...come see."

Pete groaned. If he was going to get to her in the night, he'd have to avoid waking Ben *and* go creeping all around the house. This wasn't looking good! And he was still suffering from the pent up frustration of getting so close to having her this afternoon. He threw his bag on the bed, grateful the room held two queens and not the bunk beds he'd feared. He wouldn't even be able to take care of the frustration himself

with Ben lying just feet away from him. Holly was right; he had
to figure out how to make it happen. The when had to be
soon, he knew that much.

He joined the others on the deck. Jack handed him a cold beer,
and he took a long swig.

"Thanks, bro. I needed that."

Missy and Laura were chatting with Emma about bridesmaids
dresses, a subject that would not normally interest Pete at all,
but he imagined Holly in an off the shoulder number. Dusky
pink, exposing her slender neck and shoulders. Showcasing
those pert little breasts, matching the color of her nipples that
stood to attention for him whenever he looked at them. Jesus!
He had to pull it together!

"What color are you going for, Mouse?" he asked.

Jack gave him a weird look, but Emma was so involved with
her plans she didn't seem to think it odd that he asked.

"I'm thinking maybe a dusky rose," she replied.

Pete bit his lip and nodded as Holly stepped out onto the
deck, and he felt the rush in his veins. He may have to risk
sneaking around the house in the night after all. He turned to
Jack and Ben, determined to distract himself.

"So guys, what's the plan for the rest of the weekend?"

"Work, work, and more work for me," said Ben. "I know I
shouldn't complain, but I'm ready for the busy season to be
over."

Pete nodded. "At some point we need to get together with
Dan and figure out this fella's stag night."

Ben grinned. "Night? I say we make a weekend of it. I'm
thinking Vegas?"

Jack looked away. "I figured we'd just get the guys together for
a few beers?"

Pete slapped him on the back. "You leave it to us."

Jack nodded, not looking too convinced.

"What have we got lined up for tomorrow?" asked Pete. "Is there anything we can do on the house or is this one all about wedding plans?"

Jack shrugged. "Not much more we can do on your place until we get rolling, and I think Em's talking details with the ladies."

"You don't look too thrilled?" Ben raised an eyebrow.

Jack ran a hand through his hair. "No, I am. It's just that I'd planned to take her up to Napa this weekend. It kind of got lost in the shuffle. Marcos is over at the moment and I'd hoped to see him."

Pete smiled to himself as the beginnings of an idea formed in his mind. "Too bad," he said. "You haven't seen him since last year, have you?" He and Jack had known Marcos and his brother Antonio since their days in Austin. Marcos ran the family vineyard in Sicily, Antonio owned another in Napa.

"Nah," said Jack. "I haven't and I really wanted Em to meet him. She loves his wines, and Antonio's too."

Pete rubbed his chin. "Are you planning on using their wines for the wedding?"

Jack grinned. "Now there's an idea!"

"And there's no fixed plan after tonight then?"

Jack looked at him. "Have you got something in mind?"

Pete grinned, actually he did, but he wasn't ready to spring it yet. Instead he said, "I was thinking we could all do brunch at the resort in the morning, that's all. Looks like the ladies have got lots to talk about. I was thinking we might take a look at Four Mile Creek after brunch and leave them to it?"

"Brunch sounds great," said Ben. "It should be quiet enough for me to join you. I'd love to come out to Four Mile with you too, but you know that's not happening, not on a Saturday afternoon."

Pete had been hoping for that answer.

"I could do it," said Jack. "If Em's caught up in dresses and flowers with the girls. I know the last week has been crazy, but the three of us do need to get our heads together on the plans for the development soon."

The Phoenix Corporation was in the process of buying a sizeable piece of land on the Eastern shore of the lake from Ben's grandfather. The three of them were going into partnership to develop an upscale community of mixed residential and vacation properties.

"Let's see how it pans out, shall we? You may have your hands full tomorrow afternoon too, taking care of your lady's needs."

Pete was hoping that he'd be finding himself in that situation, if this plan worked out.

Jack nodded. "Let's play it by ear."

Missy was the first one to call it a night. "I'm pooped, guys," she said as she stood. "I'm going to check on Scot and Dan, and then turn in."

That was all it took for the rest of them to start saying their good nights, too, and head inside. Pete's eyes found Holly's.

"Goodnight, Pete. See you in the morning."

He frowned at her, he'd still be hoping to find a way to get to her in the night. She shook her head firmly. Her meaning clear. Boy, he could not catch a break!

Ben slapped his back. "Come on roomie, let's turn in."

# Chapter Eight

Holly leaned back in her chair and looked around the table. It was a beautiful morning out on the deck of the Boathouse restaurant by the lake. Missy and Laura were talking wedding cake. She, herself, was all about clothes and flowers and color schemes, she was happy to let them take care of the cake.

She envied Emma the life she had up here in Summer Lake. Jack was a wonderful man, not to mention gorgeous, and there was no mistaking the fact that he was completely in love with her. The gruesome foursome, as Emma liked to call her group of childhood friends, were great fun. Jack's brother, Dan, had joined them again this morning and they made quite a crowd. Holly noticed people look over at their table occasionally when one of the guys would laugh loudly or when Missy shouted at Pete when he teased. People stopped by their table to congratulate Emma and Jack or to have a word with Ben. Everyone in the place seemed to know Missy. The respect shown to each visitor to their table by Pete didn't surprise her at all. They were obviously the 'in-crowd' up here, and it felt strange to find herself a part of it. She wasn't used to being with a crowd of 'beautiful people' like this bunch. Beautiful outside and in. She liked it, though she kept reminding herself that she ought not get too used to it.

Pete's voice cut across the banter, "Enough talk of cake! What about the booze, Jack? Have you got that covered?"

"Not yet. Though I would like to get some of Antonio's wines in."

"That's your friend in Napa?" Emma looked at Jack. He nodded.

"You need to get some from Marcos too, so you don't cause a family feud."

"Who is Marcos?" asked Emma.

"Antonio's brother," replied Jack. "He runs the family vineyard in Sicily. You liked his Frappato, remember?"

Holly was surprised to see her friend's face fall.

"We were going to go up there this weekend. Marcos is the one who is in Napa at the moment, isn't he?" asked Emma.

"It's no problem," said Jack, "We'll see him again. I'd like to invite them both to the wedding."

"Why don't you go up there?" suggested Pete.

"We will," said Jack. "We'll just have to see when we can work it in."

"No time like the present. Marcos isn't over for long."

"It'd take too long to get up there though," said Jack.

"Not if you take Papa Charlie," said Pete. "You could leave this afternoon, take your fiancée for a romantic dinner, catch up with Marcos, and be back by lunchtime tomorrow."

Jack looked at Emma.

"But everyone's here," she said. "We couldn't just leave."

"Why not?" asked Pete. "No one's going to miss you, are we guys?"

Missy laughed. "Laura and I were trying to figure out how to get rid of you for a while anyway, Em. You're the best baker of all of us, but we want to do this cake for you, not have you supervising!"

"It makes no difference to me," said Ben. "I've got to get back to it once we're done here."

"And you know I'm going to be working with Scot, we won't notice who's here and who isn't," added Dan.

"And I'm off to Four Mile Creek," grinned Pete. "So that seals it. You guys aren't needed around here at all."

"But what about you?" Emma looked at Holly.

"Holly can come with us and help with cake," offered Missy.

"I was hoping you might come out to Four Mile with me," said Pete. "I'd like to get your ideas on the shopping center we're planning."

Holly knew that wasn't all he'd like to get, judging from the way he was looking at her. She looked from him back to Missy. "I...." she began.

Emma cut her off, "Sorry, Miss, but if I'm going to fly away and leave you all, it will be on the condition that Holly goes with Pete."

Holly jerked her head back to look at Emma. It was what she wanted, but she'd thought she'd have to stick with the girls.

Emma laughed. "Sorry, Holly, but we both know your talents do not lie in the kitchen. I don't want you anywhere near my cake! But I would love to think that you could guide these three into building a shopping plaza that'll be worth having up here."

Holly smiled. "I guess you do have a point, sweetie."

"Great," said Jack. "So, we can really go? I'd better call Smoke and have him get the plane ready."

Holly caught Pete's eye and he smiled at her. She guessed that he'd engineered this whole thing just so they could be together. She was thrilled.

~ ~ ~

Holly hugged Emma as they stood outside the restaurant. Missy had taken Laura and Dan back to her house. Ben had gone back up to the lodge to prepare for the Saturday afternoon rush. Pete and Jack were both making phone calls.

"You really don't mind me abandoning you?" asked Emma.

"Don't be crazy, sweetie. There's no way I'd let you miss out on jetting off to Napa with your gorgeous fiancé just to babysit me."

Emma smiled. "At least I made sure I'm leaving you in capable hands. And you have to tell me all about it when I get back."

Holly pursed her lips, but said nothing.

"Oh, come on!" Emma gave her a gentle nudge on her shoulder. "I told you that once I saw you together, I'd have facts and not just intuition to go on. The electricity between you and Pete is dangerous. I knew I was on to something getting you two together. Have you seen the way he looks at you? Be warned though, he *always* gets what he wants, and he wants you—badly. I knew you'd be great together, you're so well suited."

"It's just sex, Em." Holly couldn't afford to think about how well suited they were. Pete had admitted there was no room for her in his life. She had to be satisfied with a place in his bed.

"Ha! It's so much more than that, and we both know it!"

"Don't start, Em." Holly looked over at Pete. He stood talking into his phone. The sun reflected off the lake behind him, silhouetting his broad shoulders, making his hair shine gold.

As if he felt her eyes on him, he looked up and smiled. She knew she should stop this now, before she got too attached to him but, as always when he looked at her, she felt as if he held her captive with his eyes. She knew she would do anything he wanted, just to feel his lips again, his hands, his warmth, his hard body against hers. She may be on a path to self-destruction, but she intended to enjoy every minute of the ride. He ended his call and walked toward them.

She turned back to Emma, who was watching her with a knowing smile.

"Don't say a word, sweetie. Okay?"

"Certainly. I'll just get out of the way before the sparks start flying again." Emma smiled sweetly.

Jack was ending his call too. "Okay, Mouse. Smoke will be ready to go whenever we can get to the airport." He gave Pete a curious look. "He didn't seem too surprised by the request either."

Pete just smiled. "Have a great time guys. I think we'll take a cab out to my parents' place so I can get the old truck."

"You don't want to ride back up to Em's with us so you can take mine?" asked Jack.

"No, thanks. That's the opposite direction."

"Here you go," said Emma, handing Holly a key. "The fridge is stocked and there's plenty of booze. You're welcome to stay up there too, Pete."

Jack nodded. "I hope you are going to stay too, bro? I don't like the thought of Holly staying up there by herself."

Holly saw that half smile lurking as Pete said, "Don't worry, I'll take *very* good care of her. Now you guys stop fussing and get a move on. Say hi to Antonio and Marcos for me, and would you bring me back a case of the Cab Franc?"

"Done deal," said Jack.

Holly waved as they drove away. She was surprised when Pete took her hand.

"Alone at last," he grinned. "Let's go get a cab."


Pete gave the driver his parents address, then put an arm around her shoulders and pulled her closer to him on the back seat.

"That worked out nicely, didn't it, sweetheart?"

Holly smiled up at him. "Did you really orchestrate all of that just to get rid of them?"

Pete widened his eyes in shock. "Me? Would I do something like that?"

"Yes, you." She laughed. "Did you?"

"Damned right I did. I *had* to Holls. How else could I get you all to myself again? No way was I spending another night camping at Em's under a very uncomfortable tent pole!"

Holly rolled her eyes. "Wow! You mad romantic fool, you. And I thought it was my wonderful personality and scintillating conversation you were after."

Pete's brow lowered. "You're the one that keeps insisting that sex is all that's on offer."

"Lighten up, Bigshot. I was just teasing."

His smile returned, but his eyes remained dark. "I should have known. You *are* such a tease." As he spoke, he cupped the back of her neck and lowered his face to hers. He brushed his lips against hers and smiled. Holly drew in a sharp breath as his hand slipped under her skirt and warm fingers slid up her thigh. She looked at the rear view mirror, but the driver had his eyes fixed on the road ahead.

Pete ran his tongue along her bottom lip as he ran his fingers along the edge of her panties. She couldn't believe he was doing this in the back of a cab, but she didn't want him to stop. He slipped his tongue inside her mouth in a deep commanding kiss, as he slipped his hand inside her panties. She opened up, kissing him back greedily as the exquisite sensations spread out from the place he touched her. She could feel herself getting wet, the tension starting to build in her belly as his mouth on hers demanded surrender. Suddenly he lifted his head and withdrew his hand, eyes glinting. Damn! He had her pulsing with need for him.

He smiled down at her. "We're nearly there," he murmured.

"We were!" she retorted.

"Two can tease, sweetheart."

She drew in a deep breath. He was right there. She was frustrated, she didn't just want him now, she *needed* him. But as the lust receded a little, she was grateful that he at least was capable of some restraint. What kind of woman was she turning into? They were in the back of a cab, for God's sake— on the way to his parents' house!

The cab turned off the road and pulled through an arched gateway with the name 'Hemming' carved above it. They followed a driveway toward a huge house standing at the edge of the lake.

"Take a left here," said Pete and they turned away from the main house.

As they rounded a corner, Holly saw a cabin standing at the water's edge, next to its own beach, sheltered by huge pines. She gasped, it was such a beautiful setting.

"This is great, thanks," said Pete.

While he paid the driver, Holly got out and walked down to the water's edge. The pines smelled wonderful. The water lapped the pebbles on the beach. It was like a secret cove from a storybook.

The cab drove away, and Pete walked down to join her. Holly's throat went dry as she took in his broad shoulders, strong chest, and the muscular legs encased in dark blue jeans; he was incredible! She met his eyes and smiled. He came to her and wrapped her in his arms. Resting his forehead on hers, he looked deep into her eyes.

"So?" The gesture and the way he asked were so gentle, she would love to believe that the question was about much more than sex, but she couldn't start kidding herself now.

"What about your parents?" she asked. She didn't want to be 'that girl,' the one screwing their son in the guesthouse!

Pete looked confused for a moment. His smile gone. Had he really been asking about more than sex? His eyes narrowed as he recovered.

"Don't worry, they're not here. We could get naked and fuck right here on the beach if that's what you want. We won't be disturbed."

Holly was shocked by the harshness of his voice and his words. She looked at him, stunned.

"You're just here for the sex, right? Nothing else?"

Holly nodded, not knowing what else to say or what he wanted to hear. She'd never seen him this angry.

"Where do you want it then, sweetheart?" he spat out the last word.

She started to speak, but his mouth crushed hers as his hands came down and grasped her backside, clamping her to him as he ground his hips into her. She flattened her hands against his chest to push him away, but he tightened his arms around her and started walking her backwards. In a few steps, her back hit the trunk of a tree. One of his hands tangled in her hair and pulled her head back. His lips left hers to nip and suck at her exposed throat.

"Pete, I...." she breathed as he pulled down her skirt to lay in a pool at her feet. His hand dived inside her panties.

"Pete...." she tried again.

"What, sweetheart? We both know you don't want me to stop."

She moaned as he slid two fingers inside her, then withdrew them, spreading her wetness over her nub in tight little circles before he slid them back in, over and over.

She couldn't focus on anything but the feel of his fingers, the sensations building. She was supposed to want him to stop, but she couldn't. It felt so good. The next time his fingers entered her, he pressed his palm against her, the combined pressure taking her close to the edge.

"Pete," she breathed, "you're going to make me come."

He withdrew his hand, eyes still dark. "Not till you're naked. I need to see you."

She was panting, desperate for his talented fingers to return to their work.

"Take it off, Holly." He stepped back, eyes fixed on her breasts. "Let me see you."

She pulled her top over her head, unfastened her bra and removed her panties. A little thrill ran through her as the fresh air touched her skin, reminding her she was getting naked out here on the beach, in broad daylight. She reached out to Pete, wanting to see him too. He pushed her hands away. Leaning an arm across her chest he pinned her back against the tree.

"No need, you just want sex, right? Not me?"

His hand trailed down over her stomach and returned to its work. She moaned again as his other hand closed around her breast and he pinched her nipple, hard. He thrust his fingers deep and she arched her hips to him as he touched her G spot. His eyes, still hard, bored into hers. "Come for me, Holly."

She couldn't look away as he brought her to the edge. Even as her muscles spasmed over and over and she cried his name, she couldn't pull her eyes away from his. When she stopped gasping, he slowly withdrew his fingers and brought them to his lips, still holding her eyes as he licked her juices from his fingertips.

"Mmm, I need more of this."

She drooped against the tree, wondering if her legs would support her. Pete read her mind and picked her up, carrying her around to the back of the cabin where he sat her on the edge of a picnic table and took a seat on the bench between her legs.

He pulled her hips towards his face and an aftershock rippled through her. She hadn't fully recovered and he was about to.... Oh God! She leaned back on her hands as he held her open and trailed his tongue over her swollen flesh. Even his tongue was hot and hard as he flicked it inside her, making her collapse back onto her elbows. He grazed his teeth over her clit, just hard enough make her yelp at the delicious discomfort.

"Sit up!" She was stunned by the growled command that came from between her legs. So stunned that she obeyed instinctively, sitting upright. He reached up to touch her breasts. His mouth closed around her clit and he sucked as he twisted her nipples between his finger and thumb. The combined effects made her come again, a shuddering orgasm that left her panting.

Pete stood and she reached out hold him, but he stepped back away from her. Screw him then if he was going to be so moody! She lay back on the table, needing some support, her muscles were like Jell-O. She closed her eyes and let out a sigh, she was spent.

She opened them in a hurry when Pete took hold of her feet and pulled her around so she was lying lengthways on the table, her legs hanging off the end. He was unbuckling his jeans, eyes still unreadable, none of the fun in them that she'd grown so used to.

"Pete, I...."

She tried to sit up, but he put a hand to her shoulder. Without a word, he freed his cock from his pants. He was huge and *very* hard. She could see the veins standing out along the length of him. He took her hand and closed it around him. He felt like silk and steel, radiating heat, she could feel him throb.

"Is this what you want from me?" he asked, thrusting into her hand.

She nodded, biting her bottom lip in anticipation of the way he would feel inside her. He rolled on a condom then spread her legs wide. He stood between them, positioning himself at her opening. He coaxed her clit with his thumb once more. At her first moan, he thrust deep, stretching her even though she was already so wet. He embedded himself deep inside and held still, she could feel him pulsating as he filled her. He stood that way a long moment, breathing hard. She found his eyes, little beads of sweat had formed on his brow.

"Is this what you want from me?" he rasped. He pulled all the way out then thrust deep again.

"Yes, oh God, Pete. Yes!"

He held still, blue eyes boring deep into her. "Is this *all* you want?" He picked up his pace pounding into her then stopped. "Is this really *all* you want?" He moved slowly now, filling her, pulling out, tormenting her. "Don't lie to me."

Tears filled her eyes. Why was he doing this? It was nowhere near all that she wanted, but she knew it was all she could have.

He thrust his hips again, his hot, hard cock taking her to the edge, even as a tear threatened to fall.

He pulled her up so she sat facing him and pumped slowly in and out, still holding her captive with his eyes. "I *need* to know." He marked each word with a thrust. "Is. This. All. You. Want?"

"Nooo!" It came out as a scream that echoed around the pines and across the lake. She couldn't hide it, couldn't deny it. His eyes softened and his arms closed around her as he moved inside her. Her naked breasts chafed against his shirt as their bodies heaved together. She felt him tense and grow bigger before he exploded, triggering her own climax as they carried each other through wave after wave.

When she returned to Earth, he silently offered her his hand and led her inside the cabin where he went into the bathroom while she collapsed onto the bed. When he returned, he wrapped her in a blanket then wrapped his arms around her, holding her close as he rested his head on her shoulder.

"You are amazing, do you know this?"

Holly said nothing. She was physically and emotionally drained. She didn't know what to say, or even what to think. Why had he done that? Why tear down her defenses? Was it some kind of ego trip for him? She was glad she couldn't see his eyes, or he hers.

He peppered her neck and shoulder with little kisses. "Do you think we need to talk about it?"

She shrugged, wondering what he might have to say.

He said nothing for a long moment, then his hand found its way inside the blanket and stroked down her side till it rested at her waist. She didn't know if she could manage another round. But, instead of making its way southward, that hand surprised the hell out of her by tickling her. And did it ever tickle! She laughed uncontrollably as she tried to wriggle away from him, but he just kept tickling and laughing. She rolled over to face him and tried to tickle him back, but being fully clothed gave him a major advantage. They were laughing like a pair of kids when he caught her hands and drew her to him, the laughter fading into a deep, tender kiss.

When he finally lifted his head, his eyes were that violet color again, gentle, not a trace of hardness left in them.

"There's my proof," he smiled.

"What proof?"

"A woman would never get into a tickle war, or respond to a kiss the way you just did, if she was only looking to get laid."

Holly rolled her eyes. "Such a way with words!"

"Don't blame me, they were *your* ground rules."

"I suppose."

He kissed the top of her head and she closed her eyes. He could be so sweet. She'd be setting herself up for a whole world of hurt if she got too attached to him.

"I'd say it's fairly obvious we need to change those ground rules though. So, we need to talk about it. Agreed?"

"I suppose," she said again. Why the hell was he doing this? Wasn't the guy supposed to be the one who was happy with just sex? The one who didn't want to talk?

"Come on, Holly. What do you want out of this?"

She pursed her lips. "Nothing I can have, that's for sure!"

"What do you mean?"

"You said yourself, there's no room for someone like me in your life."

"What? I've said nothing of the sort. And what does 'someone like you' mean, anyway?"

Holly took a deep breath. "Okay, maybe you didn't say it out loud, but you didn't disagree with me when I said there was no room for me in your life. I know I'm not like you. I'm not rich or successful. I'm just plain old Holly Hayes. Someone like you is going to want a woman of similar status, a successful woman, who moves in all the right circles, who goes to your fancy fundraisers." She let out a bitter little laugh. "Someone who can cook! I am none of those things. I am definitely not girlfriend material. So, I thought it best to keep our arrangement purely physical."

Pete looked completely baffled. "Why?"

Holly blew out an exasperated sigh. Why was he able to blast through her defenses? And why, oh why, did she always have to blurt out the truth? She planted a kiss on his full, beautiful lips.

"Because you, Mr. Bigshot, would be far too easy for me to get attached to. I am nothing if not practical. I was trying to make it easy on myself."

Pete nodded slowly, but she wasn't sure he truly understood.

"Anyway, why couldn't you just take a woman offered on a plate and leave it at that? I would have thought any man would be all over an opportunity for commitment free sex."

He said nothing, just held her captive with his eyes once more. She could see his mind working overtime, the little pulse working in his jaw. She waited for the worst. He'd probably tell her they should just forget the whole thing.

~ ~ ~

Pete's mind was racing; racing to unscramble what she'd just said, the way he felt about her and how he could reconcile any of it with the unfortunate fact that, in one important respect, she was right....

"Okay, first things first. You've got me all wrong if you think status and material success are what matter to me. Think about it. My best friends include a broke single mom and the son of a dirt poor, abusive alcoholic."

Holly raised an eyebrow.

"I'm talking about Missy and Jack, two of the most important people in my life. So that argument doesn't stand. I don't even believe you think I'm that shallow, it's more about your own hang-ups."

Holly started to speak, but he silenced her with a kiss. He needed to tell her the rest before they got into discussing it.

"Now, I didn't argue with you about not having room in my life, because it's true, I don't. No, listen," he said, seeing her face tense up at that. "It's not that I don't have room for *you*, it's that I don't have room for anyone. Phoenix takes up my time and is my number one priority, and it will be for the next four years. That's the plan, and I live my life by the plan. It's what got me where I am. I date women, of course I do, but nothing serious, nothing long term, because it's not my time yet."

He waited. No idea how she would respond. He'd never spelled it out for a woman before, never felt the need. But he wanted, no...needed, for some reason, for Holly to understand. Her question caught him off guard. "So why ask for more than sex? Why not be honest, like I was and admit it's all you want?" Her voice wavered, "Why push it?"

It was a good question. "But you weren't being honest though, were you? You do want more, but you don't think it's wise." The truth dawned on him as he spoke. "And I want more too, but I don't think it's wise, either."

"So we're back at square one, aren't we? We can choose just sex or nothing."

Pete hated the way she said it, so matter of fact. He was usually the one to assess the facts of a situation and be realistic about the possibilities it presented, but he wouldn't accept that all he and Holly could share would be just sex or nothing at all.

"No." He said it so forcefully that she looked up at him, surprised.

"What other choice do we have?"

"I don't know, but I'm not prepared to accept that there isn't something."

She smiled sadly. "I know you're used to getting your own way, Bigshot, but sometimes you just have to face facts."

He smiled back. "Or get creative. Let's look at the facts, shall we? And see what we can create from them. Fact one, you don't want to get attached to me. Fact two, I don't have room for anyone in my life right now. Fact three, I don't want to walk away from this. Fact four, I don't want to be just that guy that you sleep with sometimes. Fact five, we're going to be spending some time with each other anyway, until the wedding. Does that cover it all?"

"I think so. But to me it still adds up to just sex, or nothing."

"I refer you to facts three and four, sweetheart." He had to find a way around this. "I will not just walk away from this, and I'm not prepared to keep sneaking around. Nor do I want the others thinking that either of us is just a sex hound."

She laughed at that. "You really think they'd judge us?"

Pete sighed. "No. If I'm honest, I don't. That's my own hang-up. Call me old fashioned, but I don't approve of people just using each other for sex. That's what I'm uncomfortable with. I don't respect people who do that, but I do respect you and I do respect myself." As he spoke, he was desperately trying to see how they could get creative. Finally the solution came to him and he grinned. "You don't want to get attached and I can't commit to anything long term. So how about we agree to something short term? How about we date for real? Just until the wedding," he added quickly. "You were happy to sleep with me until then, why not make the most of it? Let's see each other for real, knowing that it'll end after the wedding. What do you say?"

Her amber eyes stared back up at him while she considered it. He was aware of his fist clenching as he waited.

"Why not? It's not much different than we'd already said is it? There can't be any harm, right?"

"No harm at all." He pulled her closer to him. "We're going to have fun you and me." He pressed his forehead to hers and cupped her face between his hands. "So much fun."

# Chapter Nine

Holly smiled as they drove along the lakeshore out toward Four Mile Creek. The lake sparkled to their left and the mountains rose to the right. It was such a beautiful place, and she'd just agreed to spend the next few months coming here with Pete. As his girlfriend! Kind of. No! She couldn't let herself start thinking like that. He reached over and took her hand, smiling warmly.

"You okay, sweetheart?"

"Wonderful, it's so beautiful here. I imagine a new development will sell really well. What exactly is it you want my advice on?"

"The idea is to have a mixed residential and vacation community. There will be a lodge, but mostly it will be single-family homes. A mix of full time residents, second homes, and vacation rentals. I want a shopping center that will serve our demographic; high income, boaters, golfers, their wives. We need to somehow create a balance between serving everyday needs and creating a high end destination shopping experience."

Holly nodded, intrigued. "So you need everything from a grocery store, to a souvenir and postcard place, to a pro shop, to boating supplies, and fashion, right?"

"You got it."

"And what's the plan? Are you going to bring in independent retailers, or chains, a mixture of the two, or keep it all in house?"

"That's something I'd like your opinion on. Retail is not my forte. I definitely don't want chains. I thought we could do it in house, so we could set the tone and standard, but Ben thinks that would be too much of a headache. If we go with independents, Laura is interested in setting up another store here for her jewelry. One of the guys Jack worked with in Florida is keen to get back to California and is angling for the golf course and pro shop. But as for the rest, I really don't know. It's early days yet. I'd like to hear your ideas, get a fresh take." He glanced across at her. "Maybe give you some ideas about thinking bigger, too."

Holly was thrilled. Although she limited her own business to the one store, she loved to read about new shopping developments and did have her own ideas on what worked well with different demographics. She was eager to see the site, though she knew there was nothing there yet. More than that, she was flattered that Pete, with all the commercial sites he'd developed, valued her opinion.

He pulled the truck off the road and got out to unlock a gate that opened onto a dirt road. They followed it away from the lake as it wound up into the foothills, following a creek bed that held barely a trickle of water.

"All of this area will be part of the development," said Pete. "There's a strip on the other side of the road. That'll be divided into a few premium lots for lakefront homes with docks and then the restaurant and marina. There will also be a community boat ramp and park. It will pretty much mirror Summer Lake resort in that respect, but this will be a private community."

Holly nodded, imagining the hillside transformed. The road crested the hill and flattened out. Pete pulled over and got out.

"Come see. This is where the community center will be. There will be a clubhouse and the golf course, a community pool, and right about where we're standing will be the main plaza, as Jack insists on calling it. I swear he gets a little obsessive about this stuff. But, see...." he swept his arm out.

Holly turned to take in the view. The lake stretched away into the distance. She could make out the resort, away to her left on the opposite shore. The whole panorama was breathtaking.

"Wow! This would be shopping with a view."

Pete grinned. "I know you didn't need to come up here to get an idea of what kind of stores will work, but I wanted you see. Isn't it amazing?"

"It is, and seeing the place puts it in perspective. I could never have imagined this."

"So, what do you think? Will you help me with it?"

She smiled at his enthusiasm. "I'd love to, but I'd need more information on your demographics and goals."

"Great. How about I get the data to you on Monday, and you can tell me all about it over dinner on Wednesday?"

She laughed. "I think I'll need more than a couple of days to go over it. I do have a store of my own to run."

Pete shrugged. "So at dinner on Wednesday you can tell me how long you'll need."

He'd changed since she'd agreed to his idea that they should date for real until the wedding. He was more relaxed, openly affectionate, interested in her opinions, and making plans for what they would do together. He was doing everything a girl could want her man to do. It made her a little uneasy, though. He wasn't really her man. She couldn't afford to get too comfortable with it because in a few short months it would all be over.

"Okay, Bigshot. Dinner on Wednesday it is."

He wrapped her in his arms and dropped a kiss on the top of her head. "Good deal," he murmured into her hair.

They spent the next few hours exploring the site. It occupied a couple thousand acres on the Eastern shore of the lake. She listened as Pete explained some of the processes they needed to go through to get all the licenses and permits they would need. It all seemed so complicated, so high stakes with huge amounts of money involved. To Pete, though, it was just another deal, like so many he'd done before. He spoke with such confidence. She realized that she'd been wrong about him. He didn't expect things to fall into his lap or turn out as he wanted them to, he simply had no doubts or fears about being able to handle it when they didn't.

They made their way back down the hillside and out to the main road. Pete got out to lock the gate behind them, then climbed back into the truck.

"So, since tonight will be our first official date, what would you like to do? From here a right will take us back to Emma's or a left will take us back to my folks' place. They're in Denver this weekend. We could stay in the cabin. What do you think?"

Holly smiled, she liked the idea of both. She didn't really care either way, she'd be alone with Pete on their first real date. "You choose. As long as you don't expect me to cook."

Pete laughed. "I've been meaning to ask you about that."

"Emma wasn't joking. My talents do not lie in the kitchen." She felt the familiar heat spread through her as he held her gaze.

"Sweetheart, your talents lie in a different room, and I'd like to take you there again, soon."

She leaned across and placed a hand on his muscular thigh. "In that case, Bigshot, which one is closest?" As she spoke, she moved her hand up his leg until it rested on the growing bulge. Pete slammed the truck into gear and took a right, back up toward North Cove.

~ ~ ~

It didn't take long to get back to Emma's. Pete parked the truck and jumped down, eager to be inside. Holly scrabbled through her purse for the key and let them in. He closed the door behind them and led her through to the suite of rooms where she had slept the night before. He wanted her badly, but he wanted this to be different. This time it *was* different. It was more than just two people acting on lust, great as that had been. He snaked an arm around her waist and pulled her close. He traced her cheek with his fingers.

"Have I told you how beautiful you are?"

She smiled at him shyly, the temptress gone. "Thank you."

"You are, Holly. So. Damned. Beautiful."

He lowered his lips to hers, hovering an inch away while he looked into the amber of her eyes. Her hands came up to his shoulders as he lifted her top up and over her head, then freed her breasts from her bra. She unfastened his shirt and as she pushed it off his shoulders he stood back to look at her. *Beautiful!*

But there was only so much looking he wanted to do. He stepped forward and held her to him, loving the feel of her soft skin against his naked chest. She moaned as his hand closed around her breast. How he loved that sound. Her hands were on his belt and soon his jeans and boxers lay on the floor where her skirt and panties joined them. He dropped his head to kiss the sweet spot where her neck joined her shoulder. Again, that little moan as she pressed herself against him. The blood boiled in his veins at the feel of her breasts, his hard-on pressed into her belly. He let out a moan himself when she gently dragged her fingernails across his shoulders. He found her mouth in a hungry kiss, tongues mating, hands exploring.

He went to sit on the edge of the bed and brought her to face him, standing between his legs. He grasped her ass and kissed her stomach, wanting to taste every inch of her skin. He worked his way up, trailing kisses over her ribcage until he took her breast into his mouth. Her hands met in his hair as he sucked and teased the tight little buds with his tongue. He pulled her down onto the bed and crawled them up to the pillows. She lay on her back looking up at him, skin flushed, lips parted. He took one of the pillows and slid it under her hips, lifting her up to him. He held his weight to one side as he kissed her. He stroked her from her breasts, down to her wet heat, and back again. He was so hard now, it was almost painful, but the anticipation was such sweet torture he wanted to make it last. She was moving her hips in time with his touch. He could make her come this way whenever he wanted to. He loved knowing that he could take her there so easily. That her body was under his command.

"Pete," her voice was husky with need. "Please, Pete."

No way could he resist that. He reached for the condom he'd left ready.

"I don't need that if you don't."

It wasn't a risk he would normally take, but he didn't even hesitate. He trusted her completely. He positioned himself above her. Her arms came up around his back when he spread her legs wider with his knees.

"Open your eyes, sweetheart."

She opened them and locked them with his as he plunged inside her. Her wetness was so hot and tight around him, the sensations so much more intense with no condom. He wasn't going to last long. He moved inside her and she moved with him, their bodies molding into one, matching each other perfectly. He picked up the pace, thrusting deep and hard, no longer able to control his own need as he hurtled them both toward release. He was building, building, building until he let himself go. He saw stars as he exploded, coming hard, the fire burning through his veins, pumping into her as she clenched around him, crying his name. She dug her nails into his back and dragged them down the length of his spine, intensifying his orgasm from his scalp to his toes.

When they finally lay still, Holly turned her head, still breathing hard, and planted a sweet kiss on his cheek. He lifted himself onto his elbows, still inside her. He rained kisses down on her nose, her eyelids, her cheeks and her brow. He planted one last one on her lips then rolled to the side.

"Wow!" was all he could say.

She smiled. "Mmhmm. Wow!" she agreed.

They lay in silence for a long time, her head on his shoulder, his arm around her. Pete didn't know how to find words to do justice to what they'd just shared.

Holly didn't want to.

~ ~ ~

Pete smiled as she came into the kitchen. He was bare-chested, hair still damp from the shower. Surrounded by the contents of the fridge, with a pan in his hand, he looked like an advertisement for one of those naughty man-maid services. She let out a chuckle at the thought.

He raised an eyebrow. "What's so funny?"

"You. Barefoot in the kitchen doesn't quite go with the Bigshot image."

He laughed. "But see, that's where you're wrong. I'm an expert in the kitchen, and I'm about to make you a dinner you won't forget."

"You're making this a night I won't forget." She bit her lip as soon as the words were out. That was a dumb thing to say. She couldn't turn this into more than it was.

He smiled though. "That's my plan, sweetheart. This is our first date, remember? You're supposed to remember those."

"I don't know about you, but I never had a first date that started out that way." She raised her eyebrows and looked back toward the bedroom.

Pete grinned. "Me neither. See, I told you I'd make it memorable." He brought her a glass of wine. "Try this, it's the Cab from the vineyard where Jack and Em have gone."

Holly swirled and sniffed, then took a sip, "Oh, that's good. Very good."

"And it goes wonderfully with steak, which, if you approve, I'm going to grill for you."

"Sounds wonderful. What can I do?"

"Given your earlier confession and the fact that Em didn't want you anywhere near her wedding cake, I'd guess nothing that involves food prep."

Holly started to protest, "I'm not that bad..."

He silenced her with a smile and a kiss. "I'm not saying you are," he kissed her again. "I just don't want to risk finding out!"

"Oh, you!" She pushed at him, but he caught her hands and wrapped her in his arms. "There's something much more important I want you to do...talk to me while I make dinner? I've got the grill going out there."

That suited her perfectly. She really was a disaster in the kitchen. She would much rather drink wine and look at his perfect body than go and butcher vegetables. She followed him out onto the deck. He put a couple of sweet potatoes on the grill and closed the lid.

"They'll take a while, and everything else is under control for now, so let's sit, shall we?"

Holly took a seat on one of the huge wicker chairs and Pete came to sit beside her. She stared out at the lake for a long moment. She really did want to remember this. This beautiful evening, the wonderful setting of the lake and mountains. Most of all, the man sitting beside her who, she became aware, was watching her closely.

She turned to face him. Whenever she looked at him, she was stunned again by just how gorgeous he was. Maybe not the standard, pretty-boy handsome, his face was harsh in some respects, with those penetrating blue eyes. His nose and cheeks could have been carved from granite. But his beautiful full lips and that cheeky little dimple on his chin gave away a hint of all the fun and laughter that lay behind the imposing exterior.

"It's so beautiful here, Pete. I envy you guys."

He nodded. "We were lucky to grow up here. Luckier to have the chance to have a home here again. It's a good counterbalance to the city. What about you? Have you always lived in LA?"

Holly nodded. She didn't want to talk about it; her life seemed so ordinary and small by comparison. "Born and bred. My family has been there for generations. My sisters are raising the next generation already."

"Are your folks still around?"

"Yep," she didn't want to elaborate. She had nothing to hide, she just didn't want to highlight the differences in their backgrounds. Pete's parents, she knew from Emma, were both artists. They owned that huge place she'd seen this afternoon. They couldn't be more different from her own parents—the plumber and the housewife.

Pete either understood her reluctance, or wasn't that interested. He went back inside to check on dinner and she heaved a sigh of relief. She didn't want to taint this little fantasy with details of her mundane reality.

Pete reappeared in the doorway with a grin. "I've been meaning to ask. Do I need to be on the lookout for an irate husband coming after me?"

"What?" She narrowed her eyes at him. "What on Earth are you talking about?"

He laughed. "Just teasing. I've been curious about your ring. Since you obviously don't want to talk about your family, I thought I'd better check."

Holly automatically reached for the gold band on her wedding finger and twisted it. "Ah, I can see that." She smiled sheepishly. "But, no. I don't have a husband, or even an ex-husband stashed away anywhere."

"Glad to hear it." He waited, apparently expecting further explanation.

She blinked back a tear. "It was my grandmother's. She died last year."

"I'm sorry." He obviously was, his teasing tone gone. "You want to talk about it?"

She really didn't, but yet again, something about this man made her blurt out the truth. "I loved her to pieces, but she had some issues. She left me with this ring, and her huge gambling debts."

To his credit, Pete's face didn't register the shock he must have felt. Holly would bet that he had no experience with the sordid world of loan sharks and gambling addiction. Why in the hell had she told him? Even Emma didn't know the whole story.

He sat down beside her, took hold of her hand, and held her eyes. "Tell me." It was a gentle command, not a question.

She obeyed, surprised at herself as the words came tumbling out. "She always had a problem with gambling. I know it sounds crazy for a little old lady. She was always disappearing off to Reno or Vegas. She played poker with the guys in the neighborhood. She never knew when to quit. She got herself into some high stakes games. She'd pawned just about everything she owned and no one even knew. I went over to see her one day and her house was just...bare. I paid for her to get everything back and paid off her debts, but she made me promise I wouldn't tell the family. I thought she had it under control after that, but I was stupid...she just hid it better. Then she had a heart attack. It was the stress. She'd borrowed from loan sharks and they were after her. She'd borrowed so much by then that I couldn't pay it off."

He was still holding her hand and her gaze. She couldn't read his expression, but she pressed on.

"I talked to them. I took over the debt so they would leave her alone. They did. But she never recovered. She had another heart attack and died a few months later."

She couldn't tear her eyes away from his. Now the story was out she was starting to wonder why she'd felt the need to tell him. And starting to fear what his reaction might be.

"Like I said, she left me the ring and the debt." She shrugged. "Perhaps you'd prefer an irate husband," she said with a bitter little laugh. "I did tell you we're from different worlds."

She was shocked to see that his eyes were hard now. The little pulse working in his jaw.

"How much?"

"What?"

"How much do you still owe, Holly?"

"None of your business, Bigshot! Don't you know it's just as rude to ask a lady about her finances as it is to ask about her age?" She forced a laugh. She wanted to drop it, to move the conversation back to anything but this. She regretted telling him. What had she been thinking?

He still held her hand, but he wasn't laughing. In fact he looked...angry? Was he angry? Oh, no! He didn't think she was asking him for money did he?

"Tell me how much," he ground out the words.

"No! It's none of your business, I shouldn't have told you. Pete, I wasn't asking for help. I was just telling you, as a friend, because you asked. Please don't think that I.... That I would...."

His eyes softened. "I don't. I know you wouldn't. But you have to let me help. Those people are dangerous, Holly. We need to pay them off."

She stared at him. "Thank you. That's very sweet of you, but it's my mess. I can handle it."

"Tell me how much and let me pay it. You can pay me back if it's a pride thing. I understand that. I just can't stand to think what they might do to you. You have no idea how those people operate."

She couldn't bite back the bitter laugh at that one. "Believe me, Bigshot, I know all about how they operate. That's my world, remember? What surprises me is that you have any clue. Thanks for the offer, but I can handle it, okay?"

"No, not okay. You *have* to let me pay it. Why is it better for you to owe them than to owe me? In what world does that make sense? I just don't see it."

She was angry now. "In my world, Pete! That's where. In the world where I take care of my own problems. Where I'm capable of dealing with my own shit!" She took a deep breath to calm herself before she continued. "In the world where I like you, where we have just given ourselves a limited time to enjoy each other's company. Where I don't want things between us getting weird or screwed up because of money. Can you see that?"

He nodded slowly, about to say something else, "Yes, I can, but...."

"No, no buts. This afternoon you said you respect me. That means a lot to me, but not if it's empty words. Prove it. Show me that respect by dropping the subject, okay? I'm a big girl, I've got it covered."

He pursed his lips. she could see he didn't want to drop it.

"One condition," he said.

She shook her head. "You don't get it do you? It's not up for discussion!"

He glowered at her, face hard. She could see how he got the reputation for always getting what he wanted. Who could stand up to him looking like that?

"No, Holly. *You* don't get it. I do respect you. And although I don't want to, I will, out of respect, agree to drop it. *But,* not until you agree to my one condition. You have to promise me that if this gets ugly, if there is any problem at all, you *will* tell me and you *will* let me help."

She said nothing for a long moment. He obviously wasn't going to back down. He was offering her a safety net. She doubted she'd be able to persuade him to butt out completely. Another look at his face told her how true that was. He was still glowering, waiting for her to speak.

"Okay, but only because it won't come to that."

"Not good enough, sweetheart. You have to promise me that you will come to me for help if you need it."

She sighed, knowing she couldn't beat him. "Alright, I promise, but now can we drop it?"

She watched his face transform as he smiled. "Consider it dropped."

~ ~ ~

After dinner they walked down by the water's edge, hand in hand. Pete was not happy about what she'd told him. He was all too familiar with loan sharks and their tactics. You didn't build a company like Phoenix without running across some unsavory characters along the way. Whatever Holly thought he was, he wasn't the kind of guy who sat tucked away in his office the whole time. He and Jack had had some hairy experiences of their own in the early days. He hated the thought that Holly was at the mercy of those people. He'd let it drop and focused on having fun with her over dinner. He had to respect her wishes and stay out of it, but he couldn't stop turning it over in his mind.

"I can't believe this is Emma's very own private beach," said Holly.

He came back to the moment. "Hey, it's mine too. In fact," he looked back, "We are now actually on *my* beach. See that big rock? That marks the line between our two properties."

"Well, pardon me, Mr. Bigshot!" she laughed. "How could I forget that you own a beach, as well as a plane, and who knows what else!"

He stopped dead and turned to face her, towering above her, hands on hips in his most intimidating stance. "You'd better not forget it, sweetheart," he growled. He couldn't keep it up, though. He burst out laughing at the stunned look on her face. "Now who is the one that can't handle the teasing? I'm kidding, okay?"

She laughed. "Damn! You looked so serious there. I thought I'd offended you for real."

"What kind of materialistic creep do you think I am? Hey?" He poked her in the ribs as he asked, making her laugh and hold her hands up in an attempt to defend herself. "Hey?" he asked again as he started to tickle her mercilessly. She gave up trying to tickle him back and made a break for it, running off along the beach.

"There is no escape," he shouted as he chased after her, surprised at how fast she was.

"You'll never catch me," she called back over her shoulder.

He knew he would though. Holly wasn't aware that once she rounded the headland there would be no more beach as the shore rose steeply in a high bank. She'd have nowhere left to run. He was glad, too. He wasn't so sure he would catch her otherwise. She ran like a gazelle. She disappeared around the corner and he heard her footsteps stop. He smiled as he heard her curse.

"I've got you now," he growled as he rounded the corner. She was ready for him, laughing with her hands raised ready to block the tickle attack. She was no match for him though. He grabbed her and held her back against his chest with one arm while he tickled her relentlessly with his free hand. She felt so good, wriggling against him as she tried to escape, her efforts weakened by her laughter.

He paused a moment. "Do you surrender?"

"Never!"

So he tickled some more. "Surrender now?"

"Never!"

He kept on tickling until she was sagging in his arms from laughing so hard. He dropped a kiss on the soft skin of her shoulder. "Now, you surrender."

"I never surrender."

Something about the way she said it made him turn her around. He kissed her, tasting the sweet lips, dueling tongues, feeling her soft body against his own. He raised his head. "Not even to me?"

He saw confusion, desire, and defiance all fight for space in the amber eyes looking back at him. This was about so much more than tickling. Just when he thought she was going to answer him, she broke free and ran again, back around the headland and away down the beach.

*Damn!* He jogged slowly after her.

# Chapter Ten

Holly put down her fork and smiled at Pete. "That was amazing. Thank you."

"You are most welcome, sweetheart. I have a feeling making breakfast for you could become something of a habit."

She liked the sound of that. They'd spent the night making love and sleeping in each other's arms. She'd woken with her legs entangled with his, his arm slung across her waist. She could happily get used to mornings like this.

"Want to walk on the beach?" he asked.

"Yes, but let me clean up the kitchen first."

"I'll get it when we get back, there'll be plenty of time before the guys get home."

"It'll only take me a few and besides, you cooked, I'll clean. I may not be a chef, but I do pull my weight." She started clearing the table.

Pete came up behind her and put his arms around her middle. "Come on. We can do this later." He brushed his lips against the back of her neck, sending shivers through her.

She laughed. "You're not even dressed. I'll be done here by the time you're ready to go."

He reluctantly let her go, then swatted her backside. "Okay, you win, boss lady."

She had the kitchen cleaned up by the time he returned. He was wearing black cargo shorts and a blue T-shirt that matched his eyes perfectly. It also showed off his muscular chest and shoulders. Holly caught her breath at the sight. He was so damned hot!

Pete smiled knowingly. "Like what you see, hey?"

She nodded appreciatively.

"That makes two of us." He ran his eyes over her. "We could take this back to the bedroom instead?" He raised an eyebrow. "You wanna?"

She did, but part of her wanted to enjoy his company away from the bedroom too.

As if he understood, he held out a hand to her. "We'll get to that, but first I believe we had planned a walk on the beach."

As she took his hand and they headed out the door, Holly reminded herself that he was, above all else, a man with a plan. And that he stuck to it. She couldn't get carried away with all this. He'd been honest with her and she accepted it. The plan was that their little affair would end after Emma and Jack's wedding. She would make the most of it, but she couldn't let herself hope that it would be anything more. It didn't fit Pete's plan. End of story.

The morning was already warm as they walked down the path that led to the beach and on past the fire pit where Emma had a circle of chairs set out. Holly felt sad as she thought of Emma and Jack and all their friends spending evenings out here around the fire. Soon Pete would have his house built, too, and they'd have a lifetime of friendship ahead of them in this beautiful place. There was no room for her in that picture.

Well, maybe occasionally, as Emma's friend, but it was Pete she wanted to be here with. She bumped into him. She'd been so lost in her thoughts, she hadn't noticed that he'd stopped and turned to wait for her.

Laughing, he put his hands on her shoulders and kissed the tip of her nose. "Earth calling Holly! Is there anybody home?" He knocked on her forehead.

"Sorry, I was just thinking."

"Penny for them?"

She let out a short laugh, "They're not worth that much."

"In that case," he stepped closer, "allow me to chase them away?"

She raised an eyebrow, not understanding.

He brushed his lips over hers. "I believe I can distract you and help you clear your mind of worthless thoughts." He ran his tongue over her bottom lip, then nipped it gently.

Holly closed her eyes and slid her arms up around his neck. As she settled against his hard chest, she felt the heat his body radiated seep into her. His mouth came down on hers and soon she was lost in his kiss. All thoughts were chased from her mind. She was oblivious to everything but the feel of his lips on hers, his tongue mating with her own.

Eventually he lifted his head. "Did it work?"

It took her a moment to understand, then she smiled. "Almost."

He ran his fingers down her cheek. She cupped his hand and pressed his palm to her face. His eyes were violet again. "I may need a little more." She saw the corner of his lips curve up in the moment before they returned to hers.

The way he kissed her made her wish it would never end. His kisses were just like him, confident, commanding, yet so tender. His mouth held her captive as easily as his eyes. She let herself float away, only anchored by the warm circle of his arms.

She crashed back down to Earth with a jolt and sprang away from him when she heard....

"Yo! Hemming! Put her down!"

She looked up to see Jack and Emma standing at the top of the path, laughing. What the hell were they doing back so soon? She looked at Pete, wondering how he would react to being caught like this. He surprised her by standing behind her and wrapping his arms around her. She looked over her shoulder at him and he planted a kiss on her lips.

"Won't! And you can't make me!" he shouted back.

She laughed herself at that. For a Bigshot he was more like a big kid sometimes.

"Well then at least bring her up here and come say hi," Jack said with a laugh.

Pete kept his arms wrapped around her waist and her back pressed to his chest as he started walking them back up the path.

"Really?" she asked in a low voice. "This is how you want to play it?"

He grinned as he kept walking and tightened his grip. "Sure is, sweetheart. You're mine until the wedding and I want everyone to know it."

~ ~ ~

Holly smiled at Emma and shook her head.

"You *have* to tell me! What happened in the last twenty-four hours? Yesterday you were insisting that you and Pete were just sleeping together, and I come back to find a pair of lovebirds on my beach! Tell me!"

Holly hadn't even thought about what she and Pete might tell their friends. She, herself, had had no problem if they all knew the two of them were sleeping together, though Pete had been uncomfortable with that. He'd surprised her with his reaction when Emma and Jack had caught them kissing on the beach. Though it had been a very pleasant surprise. She still wasn't sure she should tell Emma about the time limit on their relationship. She wanted to ask Pete about that first, but he'd gone off with Jack to work on some detail that had the two of them switch back to work mode as soon as Jack had stopped teasing about the Best Man and the Maid of Honor making out on the beach.

"There's nothing to tell, Em. Calm down." They were sitting on Emma's front deck with the bridal magazines Holly had brought. "We're just having a little fun. Nothing to get excited over. Now can we get to work on finding you a dress?"

Emma glared at her. "I know what Pete looks like having fun. I know what you look like having fun. And what I just saw between you was a whole lot more than fun! So tell me!"

Holly shrugged. "Okay, so I'm not going to be able to fool you. How about I tell you when I can figure it out myself?"

Emma grinned. "That's more like it, and of course I won't push." She gave her very best innocent smile. "Though you don't need to spend too much time figuring it out. I can tell you right now, you are falling for each other. No doubt about it."

Holly rolled her eyes. "Whatever you say, little Miss Romantic. Now let's find you a dress." She couldn't consider that possibility, so she opened the first catalog and tapped on a dress. "Something like this?"

"That'd suit you much better than me."

Holly had to laugh. "Drop it, sweetie. We have to get serious about this dress. Have you two even set a date? It is a rather critical detail."

Emma shrugged. "We're working on it. It's not as critical as it would be for most people though. It's not like we have to book a venue, since it will be at Gramps' place. Ben is happy to cater it and lend us the band. All the other details are easy to take care of up here. We don't want hundreds of people. I've only got Gramps and you guys. Jack has a few more business associates. All of our friends are the kind of people who will be here if they can, no matter when it is. We're really waiting on Jack's mom, to see when we can get her up here."

"That's all great, sweetie. But the detail of your dress isn't going to get taken care of up here. You need to decide, we need to get it made, have fittings. Do you even have a tentative date in mind?" Everything she had said was true, but what Holly really wanted to know was how long she and Pete would have together. Although she was happy for Emma and couldn't wait to see her marry the man she was so deeply in love with, she was hoping for at least a couple of months before the big day. The happiest day of Emma's life was one Holly was starting to dread.

"We're thinking maybe a few months."

Holly smiled. A few months would be good.

Pete paced the den. She'd be here soon. He hadn't seen her since Sunday. Three whole days, but she'd hardly been out of his mind the whole time. Whenever he closed his eyes he saw her. Eyes shining down at him as she'd straddled him on the plane, when they'd almost.... Laughing as she ran from him on the beach.... Walking arm in arm with Emma, ahead of him and Jack, as they'd returned to the airport on Sunday.... Smiling up at him as she'd pressed her cheek into his hand on the beach. His mind was a jumble of pictures.

The one he kept returning to was of her eyes wide open, locked with his own, crying his name as he'd made love to her at Emma's house. Made love? His fist clenched at his side. Yep. That had been a whole lot more than just sex. He cared about her.

He had to be careful that he didn't start to care too much. He'd surprised himself with his suggestion they date for real until the wedding. It had been a lapse on his part, but he was glad she'd agreed. Since he'd allowed himself this weakness, he intended to make the most of it. He wasn't going to hide it from anyone. For this limited period, however long it lasted, she was his. But he already knew it would be hard to detach when it ended.

Fortunately, he knew how to compartmentalize. He always kept his eye on the big picture, didn't deviate from the plan, and the plan did not allow for a special someone in his life just yet. So, after the wedding, tough as it would be, he'd let her go and move on.

He didn't need to think about that tonight, though. Tonight was about enjoying what they had while they had it. She was coming for dinner, supposedly to talk about her ideas for the shopping plaza. He didn't care what they talked about, though, he just wanted to spend some more time with her.

The security system buzzed, alerting him that a car had entered the driveway. He checked the CCTV and saw her old station wagon. He frowned. He'd done a little more checking on her store yesterday. From what he'd found out, she'd built a solid business there and turned a very decent profit. Her old beater of a car and her tiny townhouse told him that she was probably turning most of it over to the loan sharks to pay off her grandmother's debts, and the huge interest those people took. He had to find a way to get her out of that mess. He watched on the screen as she got out of the car. Another long dress that clung in all the right places. It looked great on her. He smiled; it would look even better on his bedroom floor.

He opened the front door just as she was about to press the bell. "Welcome to my humble abode." He smiled, taking her hand and kissing it in a grand old-fashioned gesture.

"Hey Bigshot," she said softly, her eyes alight with pleasure. She looked around at the huge house and laughed. "Don't give me that 'humble abode' crap, there's nothing humble about this place! It took me ten minutes just to drive the length of the driveway!"

Pete laughed and shook his head. He loved how she was so up front and put him in his place. He hated when women tried to flatter or impress him, and that's what most of them did. Not Holly though.

"Well, if you're going to be like that, we'd better skip the grand tour. I was going to show you around in hopes of impressing you."

"You can show off to me, I don't mind that at all. I'm dying to see the place. Just don't give me the false modesty crap. It doesn't suit you."

He pulled her to him for a kiss. He caught his hands in her hair as she parted her lips, kissing him back. She tasted so sweet, what he'd intended to be a quick hello became a tangling of tongues and melding of bodies as they stood in the hallway.

She was the first to pull away, eyes shining as she smiled up at him. "Wow! Hello yourself!"

"Hi, sweetheart. I missed you."

She lowered her eyelids. "You too."

He caught her hand. If he didn't show her around now, the only place she'd see would be his bedroom. He led her through to the den. She looked around, eyes wide.

"It's gorgeous, Pete!"

The wall of the den was all glass to showcase the pool area with the beach and the ocean beyond.

"Can we go outside?"

He nodded and followed as she went out onto the pool deck and straight to the edge, where a low glass wall acted as a balcony without blocking the view. She leaned on it and looked out at the ocean. He leaned beside her, saying nothing. Before too long she straightened up and turned back to take in the pool. It was free form with a bar over in the corner. An outdoor dining area sat beyond that and there were loungers under a gazebo.

She looked up at him. "Holy shit, Bigshot, this is awesome!"

Pete burst out laughing. "I'm glad it meets your approval!"

"Approval? I'm dumbstruck! I knew you had a big place at the beach, but this? This place is something else!"

"Well, I like it."

"I'll bet you do, you lucky beggar."

"Luck has nothing to do with it." He laughed and shook out his left arm so that the heavy silver chain slid down against his hand.

She looked at it. "Of course. Point taken. Work, right?"

"Dead right, sweetheart. Now, do you want a drink?"

"I'd love one, please. Do you have any of your friend's Cab? That was wonderful."

"I do," he smiled. "I thought you liked it so I brought a couple of bottles up, just in case."

He left her leaning on the balcony again as he went to fetch a bottle and two glasses. On his way back, he stopped to admire her for a moment. What was is about her? Yes, she was hot, no question there, but he'd known a lot of hot women, beautiful women. None of them had ever had this effect on him. He'd been looking forward to talking to her as much as getting her into his bed. He wanted to learn more about her, her life, her work, her family. He wanted to persuade her to let him take care of her grandmother's debts. He stood there watching her, her long brown hair lifting in the breeze, her face inscrutable. It held traces of a smile, but a faraway look too, that made him feel sad somehow.

She turned and caught him staring. Putting her hands on her hips she raised her eyebrows. "Are you going to stand there all night, Bigshotbigshot? What's a girl got to do to get a drink in this place?"

"I was simply admiring the view," he replied. "I like it more than ever tonight. And your wine is on its way. Patience, it's coming."

He beckoned for her to join him at the bar. She slid up onto the stool next to him and took the glass he offered.

"Thanks for coming, Holly. I didn't want to wait until weekend to see you again."

She chinked her glass against his. "I didn't either. Though had I known you lived in a place like this, I probably would have chickened out."

That surprised him. "Why?"

"I don't belong in a place like this. It reminds me how different we are."

"I thought we covered this?" He felt frustration rising. "We're no different, you and I. Why do you keep saying that?"

"Take a look at my old car sitting on your half-mile driveway, come by my house and take in the view of the bus depot, then tell me we're no different."

She said it with that bitter laugh that was starting to annoy him. "Granted, I've made a lot of money, but other than that there's no difference. We both work hard doing something we love, using the best of our abilities so we can feel proud of our achievements, true or not true?"

"True, but my achievements are a lot smaller than yours. And though you dismiss it, the amount of money you make does make a big difference. It gives you a different lifestyle and a different outlook."

Why wouldn't she see it? "Holly you've got that backwards, it's the having a different outlook that allows me to make the money. And," screw it, he was going to say it, "I'll bet the amount of money you make right now would give you a different lifestyle if you weren't giving it all to loan sharks to pay extortionate interest on a debt that's not even yours."

She clearly didn't want to go there. "I'm a simple girl, Pete. Even if I had more money, I wouldn't change the way I live. There's nothing I need that I don't have." She smiled. "Well, except maybe a new car. A BMW, a blue one. That'd be nice." She flashed him a grin, but he wasn't going to let her sidestep it that easily.

"That's not the point though, is it? You don't need to be forking over that kind of money to criminals."

Her eyes narrowed. *Damn!* He shouldn't have kept after her, but it was eating away at him.

"I thought you agreed to drop that subject?"

"I know. I did. I'm sorry. But sweetheart, it's driving me crazy. Let me help? Please?"

She shook her head, but he wasn't ready to let it go.

"I'm not trying to be a big shot asshole. I just don't see why you can't borrow the money from me instead of from dangerous criminals. If you let me pay it off, you can still pay it back. I'll even charge you interest if you insist, but at bank rates instead of whatever ridiculous percentage they're gouging you for. Look at this from a purely business perspective, you know it makes sense."

He looked at her, waiting for the worst, but hoping for the best. Surely she could see the sense in what he was saying.

She shook her head again and let out a long sigh. "That's very sweet of you, Pete."

"I'm not being sweet, dammit, I'm trying to make you see sense, to keep you safe!"

She put a hand on his knee. "I am seeing sense. I appreciate your kindness, but we need to be realistic. In a couple of months we'll be done with our little interlude. You'll go back to your life, I'll go back to mine. Even if I weren't too proud and stubborn to accept help, it doesn't make any sense for me to accept help from you. So, once more, can we please drop the subject, or do I have to get mad and leave?" She smiled to soften the words.

He opened his mouth to argue some more, but she slid her hand further up his thigh. "We did plan to have dinner, and I really don't want to leave."

Pete blew out his cheeks, exasperated. He didn't want her to leave either. He accepted that he'd lost the battle, but was still determined to win the war on this one. He couldn't do as she asked and butt out completely, it wasn't right.

"I don't want you to leave either, sweetheart, but I still think you're being...." he jumped as her fingers dug in the ticklish spot just above his knee.

She raised her chin in challenge. "Being what?" she asked, her eyes sparkling with amusement now.

"A stubborn little...." Her fingers dug in again and he almost jumped out of his seat. They were both laughing now. "Are you looking for a tickle war, lady?"

She held up her hands, eyes wide. "Nooo, no tickle wars! I'll stop, I promise!"

Pete lunged to tickle her, but she was too fast and was down from her stool and gone. She ran to the far side of the pool and stood laughing, eyeing him to see what he would do. He followed her, adjusting his pants to accommodate his growing erection as he went. For some reason their childish games turned him on, in a big way.

She backed off as he approached. "No tickle wars, okay?"

He grinned and kept coming.

"No, Pete, you can't tickle me, you're too good at it!"

He laughed. "You shouldn't have provoked me then, should you?"

She was backing up to the loungers and had nowhere to escape.

He grinned. "I've got you now!"

"Nooo!"

"You could surrender?" Why did he want so badly for her to surrender to him?

"Never!" she shrieked as he made a grab for her. She managed to get both hands against his chest and gave an almighty shove. As Pete stepped back, he realized he was going into the pool. Just as he toppled, he managed to catch hold of her and take her with him. They made a huge splash as they disappeared under the water. As he surfaced, Holly's face emerged next to him, laughing and spluttering. Her hair was plastered to her head like a drowned rat. Even so, she'd never looked more beautiful than she did in that moment, so full of fun. He pulled her to him and kissed her, her arms came up around his neck as he crushed her to his chest. He stroked his hands down her legs and brought them up around his waist.

He'd thought this evening should follow a more traditional pattern, that they'd have dinner *before* taking it to the bedroom, but with her lips parted to allow his thrusting tongue inside and her legs wrapped around him, he knew that wasn't going to happen. He touched her breasts through the wet fabric of her dress and felt her quiver in his arms. He managed to unfasten his pants and get out of them without breaking the kiss. The feel of the water swirling around his cock heightened his desire. He wedged her against the side of the pool and pulled the skirt of her dress up to her waist. She clung tighter to his neck as he pushed her panties to one side and stroked her, tracing her folds then teasing her nub. When she moaned, he guided himself to her opening and thrust deep. Her legs tightened around his waist as he moved inside her. He cupped her ass cheeks in his hands and held her wide open to receive him. He was so close, she must have sensed it because she dug her nails into his back. He let himself explode deep inside her, taking her with him. They came together, gasping in the water as their bodies strained as one, carrying each other through the waves of a climax that left them both panting, clinging to one another.

He rested his head on her shoulder. "What are you doing to me, lady?"

"I thought it was you doing it to me? Either way, I like it."

"Me too."

When the strength returned to his legs, they waded to the shallow end of the pool where he took her hand as they walked up the steps.

"You ever won any wet T-shirt contests?" He loved the way her wet dress clung to her, showing off every contour of her body.

She laughed. "Not my style, sweetie."

He took a towel from the stock by the bar and began to dry her down.

"Hang on." She peeled the dress off and wriggled out of her underwear.

Pete took in the beautiful naked body before him.

She laughed. "You can tell that guy to go back to sleep for now."

Since he was wearing just his shirt, it was quite apparent that his cock was enjoying the view and getting ready for round two. He wrapped her in a fresh towel and hugged her to him. "Sorry about that, I think he likes you."

She smiled. "I'm flattered, and I like him too." Her stomach grumbled loudly. "But I'm starving and somebody promised me dinner."

He pulled off his shirt and tied a towel around his waist. "Then let's go find you something to wear and get you fed."

Holly munched on her pizza and took a sip of wine. "Mmm, this is sooo good."

"Isn't it? I probably eat too much pizza." He patted his stomach.

She laughed. "There's not a scrap of fat on you. You're solid muscle." And he was; she was enjoying the view. He was only wearing boxers so she was able to admire his solid frame. Strong shoulders and muscled chest above rock hard abs and that V that led down to…. She licked her lips at the memory. He caught her looking and smiled. She didn't mind, she knew she was having the same effect on him. He'd given her a plain white button-up shirt to wear, and of course as soon as she had it on, he'd undone the top three buttons. She was naked underneath it, his eyes had hardly left her.

They were sitting on the sofa in the den, their legs entangled in the middle as they each leaned back against an arm facing one another. She felt so comfortable with him and, despite what she'd said earlier about not belonging in a house like this, she felt so at home here in his space.

"So, do you want to hear my ideas for the plaza?" she asked once they were done with the pizza.

"I do, if you've had time to come up with anything."

"Not much, yet. I've set aside time tomorrow night to go through the data you sent, but I did want to share the main idea that struck me."

"What's that?"

"You said that you wanted to keep the retail in-house, but Ben thought it would be too much of a hassle. I came up with a hybrid where you could contract with independent retailers, but still have the in-house control you're looking for."

"Tell me more."

Holly launched into the details of what she had in mind, hoping it would make sense to him and that he wouldn't laugh at her. She detailed an option where the resort would keep control of staffing and store layout and independent retailers would manage the actual supply and stocking of merchandise. When she'd finished, she looked up at him, holding her breath, hoping he wasn't about to point out all the reasons it couldn't work that she wasn't smart enough to see. He looked at her for a long moment, the pulse working in his jaw. *Oh no. He must think I'm stupid!*

"That's brilliant, Holly, sheer genius."

She gasped. "You like it?"

"Like it? I only wish you'd come up with it years ago so we could have rolled it out as a solution to a couple of our projects that have struggled on the retail side." He grinned. "We may have to negotiate you some kind of fee if we run with it. Think about it." He took her foot and began to massage it between both hands. "I should warn you though, I negotiate hard."

"That's not fair, you're asking me to think about something, something important and then you're, mmm, making it...ooh...impossible to...." She couldn't think straight as he massaged his way up her calves. "That feels so good."

"It gets better and better," he said with a grin.

"I believe you, but you'll have to remind me later what I was supposed to think about." As he worked his way up her legs, stroking and massaging, Holly lost herself in the feel of his warm hands on her skin, not caring anymore what else he wanted her to focus on. It was gone.

# Chapter Eleven

Holly stared out of the window as they took off from the little airport at Summer Lake. She couldn't quite believe that for the fourth time in less than a week, she was flying around in a private jet. She looked across at Emma and Missy sitting opposite her.

"So, ladies, are you ready to shop?"

Missy grinned. "Ready, willing, and able!"

"Oh yes," said Emma. "Look out San Francisco, here we come!"

"Where are we meeting Laura?" asked Holly.

"The car is picking her up first and bringing her to the airport," said Emma.

"This is just so Pete," laughed Missy.

"I know," Emma smiled. "He and Jack went back and forth so much about a wedding gift they drove me nuts. They are so competitive. Jack didn't want Pete doing anything he could do himself. Since Pete is my brother in all but blood and my parents are gone, he wanted to foot all the costs that the parents of the bride normally would. Of course Gramps wouldn't hear of it. Jack was pissed and I wasn't being heard above all the testosterone!"

Holly and Missy laughed.

"Then Pete came up with this, he'd take care of all the dresses and of course he has to fly us to San Francisco and lay on a car and driver."

Holly smiled to herself. It really was a very 'Pete' thing to do. She loved that she was part of it, but knew that, for her, this life would soon be over. With Emma living up at the lake now she'd be seeing much less of her friend too, as well as saying goodbye to Pete.

Missy looked over at her. "Are you going tell us what's going on between you two?"

Holly shook her head. "We're just having fun. I doubt it will last after the wedding."

Missy wrinkled her nose. "I cry bullshit!"

Emma laughed. "Right there with you Miss. Have you seen them together?"

"I haven't seen them apart!" cried Missy. "They're inseparable. I thought you and Jack were bad with all the face-sucking goodbyes, but Pete is even worse. The big macho man with his 'See you later, sweetheart' and wrapping himself around her, the temperature goes up about a zillion degrees whenever they get within three feet of each other. The man is smitten I tell you, smitten!"

Holly couldn't help but smile, she wished he really was smitten. It was a nice fairy tale, for now, but that was all.

"And you," added Missy, "You're totally besotted with the man, so why won't you both admit it?"

Holly didn't want to hide it from her friends. "Listen guys, be gentle with me, please? Yes, you're right, I admit I am rather taken with him, but I'm trying very, very hard not to be."

"But *why*?" cried Emma. "You're so good together...what's the problem?"

"The problem, sweetie, is that Pete has a plan. Surely as two of his best friends you know this?"

Missy's face grew serious. "Of course he does, Pete always has a plan. Oh, sweet baby Jesus. The plan does not allow for a woman in his life until he's thirty-six, right?"

"Right," said Holly glumly. "So no matter how it *looks*, it's not going anywhere."

Emma looked as though she might cry.

"Come on, Em. Don't look like that. I'm okay with it."

"But Holly, you're so good together. You're perfect for each other, but Pete never, *ever*, deviates from the plan."

Any sneaking hope Holly had felt died with Emma's words. Emma was the idealist, the romantic, the one who never gave up believing that good things would happen for her friends if not herself. If Emma wasn't going to argue that there had to be a way around Pete's plan, then she had to accept that there really wasn't one. Hell, she'd already accepted it, hadn't she? Apparently not, because where she had been happy and excited, looking forward to a fun day with the girls, now she felt sad and deflated.

"I'm sorry, Holly." Even Missy, who could usually make a joke out of any situation, wasn't going for the laugh on this one.

"I'm okay with it. I know the score and I have since the beginning. We're just having fun. I thought that's what *we* were supposed to be doing today? So can we lose the glum faces and raid the champagne while we figure out which stores we're hitting first?"

She got up and poured them champagne, smiling at the screw top Pete had on the bottle. She looked back at the long sofa and tingled all over as she remembered how close they'd come back there. She took the drinks to the others and sat back down.

"So, we need Em's dress, our dresses, matching fabric for the guys' cummerbunds. And shoes, we can't forget shoes!"

Missy laughed. "Of course shoes, the answer to every girl's woes."

Emma joined in, but Holly could see her eyes were still sad. "Perhaps we should start with some shoe shopping? Nothing to do with the wedding, just to get our shopping juices flowing."

"Genius, Emma. Pure genius!"

They started planning which stores they wanted to visit and talk of Pete was soon left behind, if not forgotten. Holly forced herself to smile and make the most of the day. She doubted she'd ever know another one like it.

The plane touched down on the runway, and Missy released her death grip on the arms of her chair. "I can't think of one reason why a person would pay millions of dollars for the privilege of hurtling through the sky in their very own tin can. It's completely beyond me."

"You're just scared," laughed Emma.

Smoke's voice came over the intercom. "Welcome to San Francisco, ladies. I hope you enjoyed the ride. The guys at the FBO tell me your friend and your car are waiting for you."

When the intercom clicked off, Holly chuckled, "How about that for a reason, Miss?"

Emma giggled. "He is rather hot. Especially in that uniform."

Missy snorted, trying to hold back the laughter. "Yeah, his name suits him, Smoke – smokin'!" The three of them fell about laughing at that. "Emma, you'd better behave since we're about to go buy you a wedding dress. You have one very hot man of your own, Mrs. Benson, you're out of the running. Holly and I can fight for him."

"Ha!" cried Emma, "Why do I get the feeling that Holly can have him and the name Benson has something to do with that too?"

Missy's laughter stopped abruptly.

"Oh no, what?" asked Holly. "I thought you and Dan were getting quite friendly?"

"Yeah, we were. Friendly. But that's all it's going to be. He has a girlfriend."

"What?" Emma looked stunned. "Since when? Does Jack know? Why didn't we know?"

Missy held up a hand. "Since three years ago apparently. Yes, Jack does know, or knew and has forgotten, or doesn't realize they're still together. We didn't know because it's a strange situation and he doesn't talk about it."

"It must be a strange situation," said Holly. "Hasn't he been at Summer Lake with you guys every weekend for the last few months?"

"Yes, he has," said Missy.

Smoke emerged from the cockpit and came through the cabin to open the door and let down the steps. Laura was standing on the tarmac, grinning and waving. While Missy waved back at her and started down the steps, Holly registered Smoke's reaction to seeing Laura.

"Must be something in the water," she muttered to herself.

"What was that?" asked Emma pausing at the top of the steps.

"I'll tell you later, get a move on."

Once Emma started down the steps, Holly turned to Smoke. "Thanks for the ride. Pete said we should let you know an hour before we head back to the airport, is that enough time for you?"

"That's great, thanks. It gives me time to file our return flight plan and be ready to go."

Holly waved down at the others who were waiting. She raised an eyebrow at Smoke. "Could I introduce you to Laura before we leave?"

Smoke grinned and followed her down the steps.

"Laura, this is Smoke. Phoenix Chief Pilot and an old friend of Jack and Pete's. Smoke, this is Laura Benson, Jack's cousin."

The two of them shook hands and locked eyes.

"There's not enough room for all of us on this thing," said Holly, climbing onto the golf cart. I'm going to commandeer it to get to the ladies room and send it back."

"Me too," said Missy. She jumped on the back followed by a giggling Emma.

"Go, go, go!" Holly told the man driving it, when Laura turned away from Smoke to join them. "Sorry sweetie, no room!" Missy waved happily from the back of the cart as they drove away. "We'll send it back for you."

Laura eventually caught up with them at the front of the building where they stood smirking by the limo Pete had arranged for the day.

"Oh my God, you guys! How could you?"

"How could we what?" asked Emma sweetly.

"Sorry, sweetie," laughed Holly. "Had to get to the bathroom."

"How about a thank you?" grinned Missy.

Holly knew she'd done the right thing when Laura clasped her hands together and grinned. "Thank you, thank you, thank you! Where did you find him and can I keep him?"

"Come on," said Holly, smiling at the driver who stood waiting. "In the car everyone, we can do this on the way. There are shoes and dresses out there with our names on them."

In the back of the limo, Missy poured champagne while Laura babbled.

"Did you guys see him? I think I may still be drooling!"

"I know I am," said Holly, "But he only had eyes for you. He lit up the moment he clapped eyes on you!"

"But you were sooo mean running off like that. And I am so grateful!"

"So did you get his number?" asked Missy.

"We exchanged cards." Laura tried to say it with a straight face. "It was a little awkward, you know? But he said he would be at the wedding, so I'll see him then if nothing else. Will you hurry up and set a date, Em, and make it soon?"

Holly's heart sank. She'd much prefer it if Emma and Jack went for a long engagement.

~ ~ ~

Holly sat back in her seat and pushed her plate away. "That was wonderful," she declared.

Emma and Missy agreed.

"I'm glad you enjoyed it," said Laura. "This is one of my favorite places for lunch."

She'd brought them to a place down on Fisherman's Wharf after a morning spent in a shoe-frenzy for all of them, followed by a fruitless wedding dress hunt.

Holly hadn't wanted to make appointments at the major bridal stores. She knew Emma's taste and temperament too well. She figured she would end up making something herself created from the details Emma liked along with her own design skills.

"What's the plan for the afternoon?" asked Missy.

"I want to walk Em through one more store. If we don't find 'the one' then I suggest we start focusing on bridesmaids dresses to give Em's brain a rest."

"I don't mind if we go straight to bridesmaids dresses," said Emma. "I think my brain is fried already."

"Just one more, sweetie. You can do it." Holly patted her hand. "I promise I won't make you do any more today, but this place may be the one. I have a hunch."

"Okay then," Emma nodded obediently.

"You're so laid back about it, Em. I think I'd be driving you all nuts dragging you into store after store if we were shopping for my dress," said Laura.

"Yes, but that's because you have dress sense and know what you want," said Emma. "I, on the other hand, am clueless, but very fortunate to have Holly. She is a fashion guru. She knows what works on me better than I do *and* can make it all happen. I just do as I'm told."

Holly laughed. "I think I got the easy job. She is quite docile when it comes to clothes. It may be harder for you two with the cake, since she knows what she's doing there and is used to being in charge in the kitchen. Beware, the Bridezilla may strike yet!"

"Why do you think we're keeping it top secret and under wraps?" laughed Missy.

Emma frowned. "Yeah, I'm still not so convinced that's a good idea..."

"Em, Honey, it's decided. You get to make your top layer, but the rest is one thing too many for you to deal with, so let me and Laura handle it. Better still, forget about it—do us all a favor!"

"Okay, okay!"

~ ~ ~

Holly's hunch proved right. She let Missy and Laura pick out a bunch of dresses with Emma and go to try them. She went to talk to the in-store designer, who she had met at several fashion shows in LA. She was a tall, willowy girl in her mid-twenties who seemed to design for figures like Emma's; shorter in stature with fuller curves. Holly described what she had in mind.

Tara smiled, transforming her angular features. "Hang on, I may have something." She disappeared into the back and returned in just a few minutes with two gowns. She held up the first one, it was silk with an embroidered bodice and full skirt. If Em were to go for a traditional style, this would be the one. Holly believed she would want something a little different though.

When Tara held up the second one Holly grinned. "Jackpot!"

It was satin, a simple Greek style, which would drape wonderfully. It had Emma's name written all over it, it would accentuate her curves beautifully.

"This is perfect! What sizes do you have it in? I'd like her to try it."

"There's only this one, but I'm guessing it will fit her. She's my ideal model."

"I know. That's why I thought we'd find 'the one' here. I'll go see and let you know how it goes."

The dress fit Emma perfectly. They filled the dressing room with squeals of delight.

"Em, you look gorgeous. I think I might cry!" Missy eyes were indeed shining with tears.

"It's like it was designed just for you," said Laura. She turned to Holly. "Was it? Did you have this all set up?"

Holly laughed, she was thrilled. "No, but I told you I had a hunch. I know how Tara designs and thought something of hers might work for Em."

"And I told you Holly is a genius." Emma smiled. "I knew she'd find me my dream dress, but this is so much more. Whenever I dream of my wedding day I keep changing the dress in the picture. I couldn't even imagine the right dress, and Holly found me the perfect one in reality." She twirled in front of the mirror. "See, it even feels like me!"

Holly grinned, hearing that confirmed it all. "Sweetie, if you can feel that comfortable while looking that sensational, then my work here is done. I am happy." Even as she grinned, she wished she was as happy as she sounded. She wondered if she would ever shop for her own wedding dress. Pete was the first guy she had cared about in a long, long time and it was a road to nowhere. She already knew it would take her an even longer time to get over this…this…whatever it was they were doing.

"Finding something that will suit all three of us might be quite a challenge you know."

They'd taken care of Emma's dress and were beginning the quest for bridesmaids dresses. Holly looked at Laura; she was tall and tan with long black silky hair and pale blue eyes. Missy was much smaller, about the same height as Emma. She, too, had dark hair, not as long as Laura's, but her complexion was much fairer with steel gray eyes and porcelain skin. Holly, herself, brought chocolate brown hair to the equation, amber eyes and, at five seven, fit right between the others height-wise.

She looked at Emma. "Sweetie, have you decided what color scheme you want?"

Emma grinned, she was still too excited about her own dress. "Not really. I like pink, but I'm open to opinions?"

Laura shuddered. "I don't do well in pink, but I'm not going to kick up a fuss if that's what you want."

Missy pulled a face but said nothing.

"Like I said," smiled Emma. "I really am open to opinions." She looked at Holly. "What do you suggest, oh great fashion goddess?"

"Well, as far as color goes, we've got to consider the setting and our own coloring. Then for style, we've got three different shapes to work with. So, let's get to it."

She worked her way around the rails, pointing out a selection of styles and colors to the lady that was helping them. "Can we get these in each size to start with? We'll set up in the dressing room and take it from there."

Two hours later, Holly stood between Laura and Missy for Emma's inspection. "And the verdict is?" she asked.

"Absolutely gorgeous!" cried Emma. "If I didn't love my own dress so much, I'd want one of those too!"

After trying on so many different dresses, only to find each time that the style or color worked beautifully for two of them, but not for the third, Holly had started to think they may have to take a different approach. She'd wandered back out through the store and found it; a rich purple colored satin number, body hugging with asymmetrical pleats, gathering it all to one side at the waist. It was a little sexier than your typical bridesmaids dress, but it worked well on every one of them.

"I'm going to have to call you Team Slinky." Emma laughed, obviously thrilled with the look.

Laura and Missy kept admiring themselves in the mirrors.

Holly laughed. "That's us. Team Slinky it is, girls!"

Missy gave a twirl then put her hands on her hips and wiggled her backside. "I can live up to the name. How about you Laura?'

Laura put on a supermodel pout and walked the length of the dressing room and back with a step that would have graced any catwalk. She came to a halt in front them, one hand on her hip and purred in a sultry voice, "Team Slinky, at your service." They all fell about laughing.

"Watch out *chicas*!" laughed Holly, "We've unleashed the models within, God help those poor men. We may need to buy extra fabric and give them drool catchers."

That brought a fresh wave of laughter.

Emma finally caught her breath. "Okay, since I'm trying to get past all my silly fears, I'm going to share one."

The others sobered up quickly, as Holly wondered where her friend was heading with this.

"Don't worry, I'm over it, I think. It's just that seeing Laura slink around like that made me think of all the tall, dark, sultry beauties that I thought were Jack's type." She looked at Laura. "That's part of why I freaked out so badly when I first saw you on the beach with him. I had no idea who you were, I just saw another tall, dark, svelte beauty and it hit all my insecurities. He swears that's not his type, but there have certainly been a few of them around."

Laura smiled at her reassuringly, "I hope you really are over it, Em? They never were his type, you know."

"Don't worry," smiled Emma, "You're his cousin, you have to defend him, but it's okay. I am secure in the knowledge that he only has eyes for me these days."

"About time, too!" teased Missy. "You made the poor guy work his ass off to earn your trust. Any other guy would have walked."

Emma hung her head. "I know, but I couldn't help it." She brightened up. "But the fact that he did take all my stupid crap and never gave up is a big part of why I now feel so secure and confident."

"I'm so glad, and so happy for you both," said Laura. "And you know, Miss, the tall, dark, leggy thing wasn't just Em's imagination. They used to come after him all the time. He never sought them out, but something about him attracted those types in particular. There was one that used to drive me nuts, Mia was her name. She and her partner Jade do a lot of the retail developments for Phoenix, so you may meet them at some point."

Holly caught Laura's eye and tilted her head towards Emma, who was looking a lot less confident and secure than she'd been proclaiming just a moment ago.

Laura got the message. "Yeah, she drove me nuts 'cause Jack was sooo obviously not interested in her, but she would never give up. Even when Pete and Jade would go out, Mia would try to make it a foursome, but Jack would never go along with it."

Holly watched her friend closely, she didn't know if she felt worse for Emma or herself. She didn't want to hear about the woman Pete worked with *and* went out with.

Emma met her eyes. "Yes, but that's the point isn't it? All of that is in the past." Bless her. Em was trying to reassure *her* now. "Pete and Jade haven't seen each other in months."

"Yeah, but only 'cause they've not had any new retail sites on the go," Laura continued, "I just hope they don't bring those two up to Summer Lake for Four Mile."

Holly tensed at that.

Laura looked between Holly and Emma. "Okay, can we change the subject now? Before I put my foot in it any more than I already have?"

"Great idea!" agreed Missy. "And besides, we can't be standing around here talking, Team Slinky needs shoes."

# Chapter Twelve

Pete sat with Jack on the deck of the restaurant. They'd spent the morning with Ben going through the details of the land purchase from Ben's grandfather. It was looking like they'd be able to close on it next week. The three of them had similar ideas for what they wanted to do out at Four Mile. The one aspect where they diverged was on the shopping plaza. Pete smiled as he remembered Holly's visit to his house. He liked her idea and was looking forward to persuading Ben that was the option they should run with.

"What you smirking at, bro?" Jack was watching him.

He grinned. "How all of this is going. Remember at the beginning of the summer we said it would be one to remember? Who'da thunk it'd pan out like this? You're living up here, building me a house so that I can do the same someday. You're getting married! Who would've believed that? And the Four Mile deal is coming together nicely. What's not to smile about?"

Jack grinned. "It is pretty awesome, huh? Four Mile is looking like it's going to be a big deal for us. How would you feel if I were to incorporate a mini HQ into the plans?"

Pete sat back in his chair and folded his arms. "I'm not following you, partner. Mini HQ for what?"

"Phoenix. Like a satellite office. I know we haven't discussed it yet, but I don't think Em wants to move back to LA full time, and I don't want to be a weekly commuting husband. I mean, obviously operations are based in the city, but I was never a full time fixture there until last year. I think I'd like to be based here."

Pete's brows knit together.

Jack looked defensive now. "I'm not suggesting a major shift of personnel or anything. It could be just me, Nate, Lexi, and a small staff, if you want."

Pete drummed his fingers on the arm of his chair.

"You don't like it?"

"Shall I tell you what I don't like about it?'

"Go ahead, 'cause I thought you'd love it."

Pete struggled to keep a straight face. He loved to wind his partner up and it was easy to do when Jack was as attached to an idea as he obviously was to this one. "I have two problems with it." Pete could tell by the way Jack ran his hand through his hair that he was getting agitated, steeling himself to counter whatever these objections might be. "Shall I tell you what my first problem is?"

"For fuck's sake, yes! Quit stalling and spell it out, bro, 'cause I'm not backing down on this one so we need to get into it."

Pete shrugged. "Okay, so my first problem is.... That I didn't think of it!"

Jack rolled his eyes. "Asshole! You had me going there."

Pete laughed. "Sorry, you're just too easy to wind up these days. Must be wedding stress."

Jack ran his hand through his hair again and smiled. "Maybe. I want it to be perfect for her, give her the big day she used to dream of." His face clouded over.

"What?"

"It's just any time I think of the jerk she used to be married to, I see red. She never got to have the wedding that she wanted." His face brightened again as he smiled. "But then I suppose I should be grateful, it's only because he was such an asshole that I get to be the one in her dream wedding."

"I would never have believed that you would turn out to be such a big old pussy cat," said Pete, laughing as he stretched out a foot to toe his friend in the knee.

Jack grinned. "It's being around that little Mouse that does it, and if I'm perfectly honest...."

"Which you tend to be."

"...I want to get married as soon as we can set it up."

Pete raised an eyebrow. That was not what he'd been hoping to hear.

"Call me a coward," said Jack, "But part of me is worried that she'll find something to get freaked out over and get scared again. I know it's inevitable at some point. She's not going to overcome her past all at once, just because I proposed. But I want us to be married by the time it happens. She won't run out on me if I'm already her husband, but I'm not convinced she wouldn't back out if something freaks her before we tie the knot. You know what she's like."

Pete nodded; he knew Emma all too well. He was the one who had nicknamed her Mouse when they were kids. He knew she was head over heels in love with Jack, but he also knew how easily she spooked and ran in order to avoid getting hurt.

"So, when are you thinking?" he asked, not sure he wanted to hear the answer.

"I don't know yet, but soon. I wanted to see how long she needed to sort out dresses and all that stuff. Thanks for sending them off in Papa Charlie today, that probably shaved a few weeks off."

Pete nodded. He could have kicked himself. He wanted to contribute to the wedding, but for the sake of a few more weeks with Holly he would have happily let the ladies take their time in getting together to shop.

"Anyway, what was the second problem?"

"Huh?" He had no idea what Jack was talking about.

"You said you had two problems with my idea of having an office here."

Pete grinned. "Yeah, that. The second problem was that you didn't mention me. I'm going to have a house up here, why don't I get to work here, too?"

"I didn't mention it because I never even considered that it would be possible to drag you out of the city."

"Well start considering it," laughed Pete. "I'm not ready to shift up here completely yet, but having an office here will at least begin the transition."

"Excellent! This is the beginning of a whole new era, bro!" Jack held his fist out and Pete bumped his own against it.

"It's looking that way."

Jack started doodling on a napkin and Pete knew he was already laying out office space. "When you draw it up, make sure my office is bigger than yours." He grinned.

Jack laughed. "Sure thing, I'll even make space for a bed in yours, which I won't need. I'll be able to go home to my lovely wife every night while you stay faithful to Phoenix."

Pete nodded—that was the plan.

Ben came out to join them. "You two want to stick around for some lunch? All the checkouts are taken care of. Now it's the calm before the afternoon storm of new check-ins."

"Sounds great," said Jack. "Let me call Dan and see if he wants to bring Scot over." He walked away to call his brother, who was spending another weekend working with Missy's son on whatever computer magic they were up to. Pete was pleased the two of them had hit it off so well.

"So what's your big idea for the shopping plaza?" asked Ben as he took a seat. "I don't see how we can have independents in all the spaces and still have overall control of it."

"That's 'cause it's a new and different way of doing things," said Pete. He explained Holly's idea of engaging boutique style retailers to rent space in the plaza. They would each supply their own merchandise, but all the staff would be employed by Four Mile itself.

Ben mulled it over as he sipped his lemonade. "So, *we* get to keep control of staffing without any of the stocking issues, and the independents get to supply the merchandise and personality for each store without the same time or financial commitments, is that what you're saying?"

"Pretty much," said Pete. "What do you think?"

"It's definitely different. I can see some details that would have to be nailed in the contracts but," he smiled, "in principle I think it's genius."

Pete grinned. He'd have to tell Holly that. She needed to know it wasn't just flattery on his part. She really had come up with a brilliant idea.

Ben was still talking, Pete dragged his attention back to his old friend.

"I can't believe this is the brainchild of those consultants you work with. They must have really got their act together. Sorry, Bud, but you know I was less than impressed with what they'd done for you in Florida," he gave Pete a lecherous grin, "but I can see why you keep them around."

Pete shook his head. "Nah, I finally got Jade off my back. And after you gave me your assessment of the Miami project, I realized they're really not that good."

"Who's not that good?" Jack returned to the table.

"Mia and Jade, we were talking about the plaza."

Jack's face drained of color. "Oh, God, no!"

"What, what's wrong?" Ben looked alarmed, but Pete started to laugh.

Jack looked at him with huge eyes. "No! It's not funny man! That Mia can*not* come up here. Promise me Pete! Emma would freak!"

Pete kept on laughing at Jack's panic.

Ben looked between the two of them. "Someone want to explain this to me?"

"Mia has been trying to get her claws into Jack here for the last few years. The consultants down in Miami? The tall dark one? With the legs? She doesn't like to take no for an answer."

"Pete, seriously." Jack looked horrified. "You have to promise me we won't use them for Four Mile. That woman is a menace and you know what Em's like. That really would freak her out!"

Ben was laughing with Pete now. "I remember those legs. Perhaps I could work on distracting her for you," he said.

"You're more than welcome to," Jack shot back. "Just not up here. I don't want that woman within a hundred miles of Summer Lake!"

"Calm down, bro," laughed Pete. "As I was explaining to Ben before you came dangerously close to heart attack territory, the plan for the plaza has nothing to do with Mia and Jade. It was actually Holly's idea."

"Holly?" Ben looked surprised.

"Perfect!" exclaimed Jack. "Having Holly up here could not be more perfect! Em will be thrilled, the Mia disaster will be avoided and," he raised an eyebrow at Pete, "I don't suppose you'd have a problem with it either?"

Pete sat back in his chair again, refolding his arms across his chest. He hadn't even considered having Holly come up here to oversee the project. For all the reasons Jack had just given, it did seem perfect. He really did want to give her some kind of consulting fee, but that had been about her debts. If she took the project, he could legitimately pay her. On the other hand, it would be a long-term project. It would mean he'd get to keep seeing her, except they'd already set their time limit. She'd given him no indication that she wanted to change their arrangement. And even if he wanted to, he couldn't. As Jack had said, he had to stay faithful to Phoenix. But, hell, if she was going to be up here working, what would that mean? He didn't know what it would mean, and he wasn't going to be able to work it out with Jack and Ben grinning at him like that. He looked at them. "I don't know that she'd agree to it, but it's not something we need to finalize today, is it?"

"I guess not," said Ben.

"Whoa, hang on a minute, bro. There's one thing we have to finalize right here and now," said Jack. "Whether Holly agrees or not, we do not have Mia and Jade on this one, agreed?"

Pete smiled and nodded. "Agreed." He had dated Jade on and off for the last few years. It had been a convenient arrangement whenever they were working together. Since he'd met Holly though, he'd turned Jade down three times. He no longer had any interest in her whatsoever. Even if Holly didn't take the project, he didn't want Jade around anymore than Jack wanted Mia.

~ ~ ~

"Nearly home, ladies," Smoke's voice filled the cabin. "Time to buckle in if you will."

Missy wrinkled her nose. "Even his voice is smoky. I may have to fight Laura for him."

Holly was surprised. "I thought you liked Dan."

"I do, but he has a girlfriend, remember?"

Emma frowned. "He can't be that into her considering all the time he spends up here. He certainly seems to like you, Miss."

Missy shrugged. "He comes to spend time with Scotty, not me. You know my luck with men, Em. I only ever want the ones I can't have. Anyway," she pointed out of the window as the plane touched down, "there are your two men, ready for a night out by the looks of them. I'm going to cry off tonight, though. All that shopping has worn me out."

When the plane came to a halt, Smoke came through the cabin and let the steps down. They thanked him as they left. Then Pete and Jack were greeting them.

"What do we want to do this evening, ladies?" asked Jack.

"I was just making my excuses," said Missy. "I'm heading home to put my feet up."

Holly looked to Emma, not wanting to admit that she herself was tired and achy.

Em looked back at her. "I'm pretty whacked myself. What would you like to do?"

Pete came to her side and said, "How about I nab Holly to do some Best Man/Maid of Honor organizing type stuff and let you go home with Jack?"

Emma smiled. "You wouldn't mind, Holly? I'm not exactly used to all that shopping and my feet are killing me."

"Of course not," Holly was thrilled to get an unexpected evening alone with Pete.

"Settled," said Jack. "Miss, we can drop you off in town if you like?'

"Thanks."

~ ~ ~

After the others had left, Pete took Holly's hand as they walked to his truck.

She smiled up at him. "What have you got in mind, Bigshot?"

She was surprised when he wrapped her in a bear hug and dropped a kiss on the top of her head. For a moment, she relaxed against him, breathing in the scent of him and enjoying his comforting warmth. She really was quite tired, but she was up for whatever 'organizing' he had in mind.

"Well," he smiled and held her at arm's length, "Seeing Missy and Em were both so exhausted, I thought you might be feeling the same way. So I figure we could, if you like, grab a takeout and a bottle of wine and go sit in the hot tub at the cabin. It's going to be a full moon tonight and if we time it right we'll get to watch the moon rise. Unless you'd rather go into town for dinner?"

Holly stared at him speechless. Then she pinched him.

"Hey!" he laughed. "What was that for?"

"Just making sure you are real. Sometimes I think you really are too good to be true. I was thinking on the plane how much I would love to spend the evening in a long hot bath and here you are offering me a hot tub, with dinner, wine, a full moon, and you thrown in!"

The corner of his lips lifted before they brushed briefly against her own. "Come on then, what kind of takeout do you want?"

~ ~ ~

Holly couldn't believe how big the moon looked as it rose above the mountains and reflected off the lake. They'd eaten Chinese food, and she'd entertained Pete with tales of their day shopping. He'd wanted to know about their dresses, hers in particular. She'd even told him about Team Slinky.

Now they were sitting in the hot tub as the moon rose and the stars came out. Holly leaned back and let the jets pummel her tired back. Pete took her foot and began to massage it, which felt so good. For a moment she closed her eyes and enjoyed the sensations. Then she pulled herself up, placed both her hands on his cheeks and kissed him, before sitting back down to put her foot back in his lap.

"Thanks Pete."

"Hey, I'll rub your feet anytime." He ran a hand up her calf and began working that too.

"That feels so good."

He stroked a hand up her thigh and smiled when her eyes flew open. "Close them again, sweetheart. I'm going to work all your aching muscles. Once I've got you good and relaxed, then we can get to something that will make you feel even better."

She closed her eyes, her body tingling with anticipation. When he'd finished with her calves, he drew her to him and sat her between his legs. She leaned back against his chest as he worked her neck and shoulders.

"Damn," she murmured. "You really are magic."

He dropped a kiss on the back of her neck, sending shivers all through her. "I've told you before, flattery will get you everywhere with me." As he spoke, one hand strayed down to her stomach and he pulled her closer against him. He held her there, his thumb slowly tracing circles just below her navel.

She leaned back, hoping his hand would circle its way southward, but her head snapped up as she heard a car approach the cabin. A door slammed shut and the car drove away. She looked at Pete. They were both naked out here! Pete moved to stand.

"Yo, bro. You here?" It was Jack's voice.

Pete sat down with a thud. "What the...?"

Jack stumbled round the corner and looked at them, eyes wide. "Oops, sorry guys." he said, but his grin faltered as he sat down heavily on the picnic bench. "Didn't mean to intrude."

Holly scooted lower in the hot tub, not wanting to expose her naked breasts. Jack was apparently a little the worse for wear.

"What's wrong, Jack?" Pete's voice was gentle; he could have been a father talking to a fractious toddler.

Jack put his elbows on his knees and, on the second attempt, managed to rest his chin on his hands. "You got to help me, bro." He swung big sad eyes toward Holly. "*You*! You have to help me!!"

She looked at Pete, not sure what to say or do.

Pete shook his head at her. "It's okay."

"No, Pete! It's not okay! And it won't be okay if you don't help me. She's freaking! She's freaking the fuck out about Mia. She's gone. Said she had to go see her Gramps, but I know she's bolted for the mouse hole! *You*," he swung his head back to Holly, "You have to do it, *please?*"

"Do what?" Holly didn't get what he wanted from her.

"The plaza! It's the only way. If you do it, Mia won't come here. Em freaked out just at the thought of it. If that woman comes here, I'll lose Em, I know it. Pete you gotta help me, bro!"

"Don't worry partner, we'll figure it out."

Holly was again surprised by his gentle tone. Pete stood and grabbed his towel, motioning for Holly to stay put. She hadn't been intending to stand up, naked as she was.

Pete smiled over his shoulder as he led a staggering Jack inside the cabin. "I'll be back."

She sat in the bubbles watching the moon. From what Laura had said today, it was fairly easy to piece together what had happened. What she couldn't understand was what she was supposed to do about it.

Pete came back with two glasses of wine and handed one to her. He dropped his towel and climbed back in. Even in the circumstances, she couldn't help but admire his powerful body. For once though, he didn't seem to notice her appreciative glance as he sighed and sat down.

"Sorry about that. He's sleeping like a baby now."

She smiled. "What happened?"

Pete blew out his cheeks in an exasperated sigh, "Well, you gathered that Emma's done one of her little freak outs?"

Holly nodded, she had talked Emma down herself enough times recently.

"Okay so, first you need to know about Mia...."

"I do," she interrupted. "Laura told us about her today."

"Ah."

"And Jade," she couldn't help but add.

Pete met her eyes for a second then looked away. Hmm, that didn't bode well.

"What did she say?"

"She told us that Mia had a thing for Jack, but that Jack wasn't interested. She also mentioned that you used Mia and Jade as consultants on your retail developments and that they may be coming up here." She decided against adding anything about Pete's relationship with Jade. Whatever it might be. She didn't think she wanted to go there and it really wasn't any of her business.

"Then you're up to speed. What you don't know is that tonight, as soon as they dropped Missy off, Emma started asking about the plaza and who would be working on it. When Jack said he didn't know yet, she freaked on him. She thinks he's got Mia waiting in the wings to come up here. You know how Rob didn't let being married to her stop him from sleeping with other women? Well Em's got it into her crazy little head that Jack's planning on doing the same."

"Oh, for God's sake. Where is she? Do you think I should go talk to her?"

"No, she's at her Gramps'. He'll talk her down. She made Jack drop her there on the way home. Said she was fine, just needed to calm down. When Jack called to see if she was ready to come home, she said she's staying the night. So, Jack had a whiskey or three and worked himself into a state trying to figure out how to fix it. He doesn't normally drink much. I think the stress is getting to him."

"Poor guy. She's my best friend and even I could shake her sometimes." Holly smiled. "Still, I don't get what he expects me to do about it?"

"I'd mentioned your ideas for the plaza today. He's decided that you should come up here and run the project, which would solve his problem and make Em very happy."

"I see." Holly's mind spun. She was concerned about Emma, felt sorry for Jack, and was confused about the suggestion of her running the project. What would that even mean? She was acutely aware that Pete hadn't mentioned how he himself felt about the possibility.

He tangled his fingers in her hair and smiled. "Some crazy friends we've got, hey sweetheart?"

"Totally batshit!" she agreed.

That had him laughing. "I haven't heard that expression in years."

"Yeah, I don't even know what it's supposed to mean. It just seemed the appropriate phrase."

"So what do you think?"

"About what?"

"Would you be willing to manage the plaza project?"

"I don't know, Pete. I don't even know what that means, what it would involve. I don't see how I could do it with the store and everything. *If* I could do it, even. I mean, I've never done anything like that."

"We'd have to work out the details, but I don't doubt you could do it. It would pay you *very* well, but it would mean spending a lot of time up here for quite a while."

His face wasn't giving her any clues as to what he thought. He certainly didn't seem thrilled about it. She was no good at guessing and she was feeling very uncomfortable. She had to ask.

"That would mean I'd still be around after the wedding?"

"Yes, for a long time after."

"But I thought we agreed that the wedding would be the end for us?"

Pete's brows came down. "I didn't say you'd have to be around me."

"Of course," she replied a little too quickly, desperate to hide the fact that she'd been hoping that this might mean they could extend their agreement further.

"Just think about it, hey? It would help Jack out and you know Emma would love having you around. Not to mention how good it could be for your career."

~ ~ ~

Pete could feel his fist pressing into his thigh under the water. What had he expected? He'd hoped she might love the idea. Of course she'd only reminded him of what they'd agreed to. It had to end. So why drag it on? She was right. He drank his wine and stared out at the moonlight dancing on the lake.

~ ~ ~

A bleary-eyed Jack came out onto the porch where Holly and Pete were drinking coffee.

"What time is it?"

"Yeah, good morning to you, too," grinned Pete. "It's only seven. Want some coffee?"

"Thanks. I'll grab a cup while I call a cab. I'm going back up to North Cove to sort this out. Holly, will you do it?"

She opened her mouth to speak, but Pete beat her to it. "We'll work something out."

Holly closed her mouth again. It seemed he really didn't want her to. Fair enough. She smiled at Jack. "Tell Em to call me?"

"Will do. I'll be in touch later. Thanks guys and, umm, sorry about last night."

Pete laughed. "Don't sweat it, partner. That's what your Best Man's for."

Jack smiled, running his hand through his hair as he went back inside.

~ ~ ~

"What do you think they're going to say?" asked Missy.

"I have no friggin' idea," replied Ben.

"I think I might," said Pete.

"You don't think they're going to call it off?" Ben looked concerned.

"No, not that," said Pete. Jack had called him and asked him to round everyone up for lunch at the Boathouse. He and Em were coming down and had something they wanted to tell them all. Pete had a sneaking suspicion that they were going to name the day, and that it was going to be soon. Since Holly had made it clear last night that they were done after the wedding, he was hoping it wouldn't be too soon. He looked across at her. He wasn't ready to say goodbye. They hadn't had nearly long enough together. Even last night had been a loss with Jack showing up like that, then snoring away on the sofa all night. He'd just have to make the most of whatever time they did have left.

He watched Jack and Emma walk across the parking lot, arms around each other, smiling. They definitely weren't calling it off. Apparently Em had calmed down and all was well between them. He steeled himself for what was to come, convinced he was about to hear how much longer he'd have with Holly.

"That's in two weeks!" exclaimed Missy.

"Yup." Jack grinned. "The weekend after next." We talked to my mom this morning and she can get here, so it's all systems go."

"Geez, it's gonna be tight," said Ben. He had offered to cater it and lend them the band.

Emma smiled at him. "Yes, but you can do it, can't you?"

"You know I can, and I will."

"How about you, big guy?" Jack was looking at him, but Pete was stunned. Two weeks? That was all? He was stunned by his own reaction as much as anything else. He felt like he'd been sucker punched and all the air had left him.

"Yeah," was all he could manage.

"And I know I've got Team Slinky to help me get everything done," said Emma.

Missy laughed. "Hell yeah, we're up to it, aren't we, Holly?"

Pete watched Holly smile and nod. Did she really look as stunned as he felt or was that just wishful thinking?

~ ~ ~

Once Smoke told them they could take their seat belts off, Pete unbuckled and came to sit beside Holly. She didn't meet his eyes.

"So, two weeks to make it the most of it, sweetheart. What do you think of that?"

She smiled, but her eyes didn't shine. "I think we'd better enjoy it while we can, don't you, Bigshot?"

He pulled her from her seat and into his lap so he could hold her close. Her arms came up around his shoulders and she smiled up at him, lifting her lips to his. Her kiss tasted so sweet, her lips soft as he brushed them with his own. They parted, willingly kissing him back as he clung to her.

She was breathing hard when he lifted his head, her eyes soft as she gazed up at him. It was going to be so hard to let this woman walk away. But he wouldn't think about that now. Didn't have to. She raised her lips to him for more.

"Stay with me tonight, sweetheart?"

She gave a little nod before her hands met behind his head, pulling him back down into that kiss.

# Chapter Thirteen

Holly sat in the grand reception area outside Pete's office. This felt strange. She'd agreed to come and see him here because he wanted to show her some of Jack's workups for the plaza. She knew he ran this big company, but knowing it was very different from sitting here in this huge steel and glass building that he and Jack had built, hundreds of people running around on seven floors doing their bidding. It felt weird, unreal.

She smiled at the secretary sitting behind the huge oak desk. Judy, she'd said her name was.

"Sorry to keep you waiting. He really should be out in a minute. It's my fault. He told me to keep the schedule clear, but I finally got a call he's been waiting on, so I put it through. I didn't think it would take this long."

"No problem," Holly replied. "I don't mind waiting." She'd been here less than five minutes.

"Sorry," Judy said again, looking flustered.

Holly hoped Pete wasn't a mean boss. She couldn't imagine that, but his secretary did look put out and was doing a lot of apologizing. She went over to Judy's desk and sat on the corner of it.

"It's okay, sweetie. I really don't mind." She wanted to reassure the woman. "If he gives you a hard time, he'll have me to answer to."

Judy's eyes widened as the door behind Holly opened and Pete appeared in time to hear the tail of end of what she'd been saying.

His voice boomed, "Who'll be answering to you? And Judy, I said no calls!"

Holly shot to her feet and spun around. "You'll be answering to me, Bigshot, if you dare give Judy a hard time!"

Pete laughed and wrapped her in a hug. "Didn't I tell you she's awesome, Jude?" And thanks so much for putting Bowers through."

Holly looked from him to Judy, and back again.

"Hey, sweetheart." He pecked her lips.

"I knew you needed him," said Judy, "but I hated to make Holly wait. And yes," she smiled at Holly, "she is absolutely wonderful. Anyone who will call you Bigshot and be prepared to put you in your place is alright in my book."

"Oh, she's not just prepared to Jude, she well and truly kicks my butt!"

"It's about time someone did," laughed Judy. "Please stick around, Holly. We need someone to keep him in line."

Holly smiled. She would like nothing more than to be that someone, but that was just a fantasy and she knew it. "Sorry Judy, but I think I'll tire of him in a week or two. He is a bit full of himself, isn't he?"

Pete let her go and looked at Judy. "See what I mean? Kicks my butt!"

Judy laughed. "I'll leave you two to spar it out. You've not forgotten I'm at the doctor with Tom this afternoon, Pete?"

"I have not. And you won't forget to call me tonight to let me know how it goes?"

Judy's eyes softened. "I won't. It was nice to meet you Holly."

"You too."

Judy collected her purse from under her desk and walked for the elevator.

Holly followed Pete into his office. "Welcome to the workhouse."

She let out a low whistle. "Some workhouse. It's more like a posh hotel!"

Pete laughed. "I'm saying nothing because apparently you already think I'm full of myself!"

Holly grinned. "You're not exactly lacking in confidence, are you?"

"I could be soon, if you keep being mean to me."

Holly laughed at that. "What could I ever say that would put a dent in *your* ego, Bigshot?"

He sat in his chair and leaned on his elbows on the desk. He looked up at her, long lashes lowered over those devastating blue eyes. Her heart quickened. She was good at keeping the banter going, but he might win if he carried on like that.

"Holly," he sounded serious now.

She perched on the edge of his desk. "What, Pete?" Between his tone and the way he was looking at her, this couldn't be good.

"You said you would tire of me in a week or two."

Her throat went dry. "That's when our time's up." Her heart was hammering. Why was she so convinced he was about to end it now?

"What if it wasn't?"

"Wasn't what?"

"What if you take the plaza project?"

"I don't understand."

"We thought we'd have a few months, not just a couple of weeks," he took her hand in his, eyes intense violet. "Holly, I don't want to say goodbye yet."

The air rushed out of her lungs. This was so not what she'd expected. She didn't know if she was good enough to do the plaza. She didn't want to mess it up, to let him down!

"I don't know, Pete. I don't know that I could do the plaza, even if I wanted to."

"And you don't even want to?" His voice was emotionless.

"It's just...I don't...." How could she tell him everything she was thinking?

"It's okay," he smiled now. "The two don't go hand in hand. You can take it if you want to and not have to see me at all. I wouldn't normally be so involved in the retail side. You could work with Ben on it. But, Holly, I think you should do it, do it for yourself, do it for Emma and Jack, do it for the money. It makes all kinds of sense."

He was right it did, but it wasn't the thought of the plaza that had her heart hammering in her chest. She thought about it for a moment and then had to ask, "How would it work though, if we carried on? What would be the cut-off point then, Pete? How long is long enough? I want more than two weeks, but if we keep this up what would we do?"

Pete sighed. "I know, sweetheart. I'm sorry, I was being stupid. Let's just make the most of it. Stick to the plan."

The disappointment was like a lead weight in her stomach. She'd asked those questions in the hope they could find the answers to them. But his mention of 'the plan' stopped her from explaining that to him. There really was no point in hoping for more. His plan meant she couldn't be part of his life, so why drag it out? The more time they spent together, the harder it would be to say goodbye. And the longer it would take to get over it. It was better this way. In two weeks she'd go back to her own life while he got on with his plan.

"Yeah," she plastered a smile on her face. "Stick with the plan. And the plan for today is?"

He smiled and stood to face her, placing his hands on either side of her hips on the desk. "To spend some quality time with you while I still can." He kissed the tip of her nose, then brushed her lips with his. "So, I need you to agree to look at Jack's workups when I send them over to you."

"But, I thought...."

His lips came down on hers, soft and warm, "You thought what, sweetheart?" His hand closed around her thigh and she felt the familiar heat start to build. "I thought you were going to..."

His mouth came down again and her lips parted, responding to his demanding kiss. He lifted his head. "Yeah, I thought I was going to too, but now I know we only have ten days left. So.... You are going to agree to look over the mockups and to seriously consider taking the project, aren't you?"

His warm fingers were inching their way up her thigh. She couldn't think straight as his other hand cupped the back of her neck. "Pete, I...."

"Aren't you?" He smiled as his fingers reached the lace of her panties and he touched her through them. "Please say yes?"

"Mmm," she took hold of his tie and pulled him closer for another kiss.

He stepped between her legs, replacing the pressure of his fingers with the pressure of the bulging heat in his pants as he rocked his hips against her. He was unbuttoning her blouse.

"Pete! What if someone...."

"They won't." He had her bra unclasped now, pushing the cups to the sides as he kissed the dusky tips.

She tried one more time with the little will power she had left. "But if someone...."

He closed both hands around her breasts, grazing her nipples with his thumbs. "They won't."

She moaned and let her head fall to the side at the surge of heat that rushed through her as he thrust his hips.

"When Judy's not around, the door won't open from that side until I push the button. It makes sure I won't be disturbed while I'm doing important stuff. And *you* are important stuff."

She was moving her hips in time with his thrusts as he continued to touch her breasts. She was under his spell. She knew it and didn't care. He was going to make her come like this, half undressed, perched on the edge of his desk. Suddenly, he stood back and let his hands fall at his sides.

Her eyes flew open and he gave her a wicked grin. "But I'll stop if you want me to."

"Nooo!" Her body felt bereft of his heat and his tantalizing touch. "Don't!"

"Don't what?" He teased the very tips of her nipples with his fingertips, sending electric currents zinging along the nerve ends that led straight into her panties.

"Don't stop," she panted.

He got rid of his shirt while she freed his straining cock from his pants. He stepped closer again, her wet panties a flimsy barrier between them as he pressed his hardness into her heat.

Her breasts brushed against his naked chest when he scooted her backwards. He leaned forward, forcing her to lie back on the desk, until he was on top of her.

"You're sure you don't want me to stop?" he teased as he stroked her through her panties. She moaned through his kiss. "And what about these? Can I get rid of these?"

Her panties were nothing more than a damp scrap of lace now. She gasped as he took them in his hands. She heard them rip, then felt his hot shaft pushing at her.

"Sorry, sweetheart. I couldn't wait." He rocked his hips and nudged inside her. He interlaced his fingers with hers and held her hands on the desk above her head. "You ready?"

She nodded. She needed to feel him deep. His pulsing head just inside her was driving her crazy. She wanted more, needed all of him. He brought one hand down and circled her nub as he made the tiniest of movements with his hips.

"Oh, God, Pete!" His expert touch had her right back at the edge, but she wanted him, all of him. "Please, Pete. Please!" She started to come and he plunged deep, filling her. Her body arched up to meet him. He was so hard and hot, his heat set her on fire as she moved with him. He didn't give her time to recover, keeping up the wild rhythm of his hips, the waves of her orgasm receding, then surging again. She brought up her legs, wrapping them around his back, deepening their connection.

"Holly!" he rasped her name against her neck as he found his own shuddering release. She clung to him as they soared together.

"It suits you." They'd cleaned up in the bathrooms off of Pete's adjacent meeting room. Holly was sitting in his chair as he returned to his office.

"What does?"

"The desk, the chair, sitting there like that." He smiled and the breath caught in her chest. He looked crisp and sharp, not a wrinkle in the shirt that stretched over his broad shoulders, not a hair out of place. No one would guess that ten minutes ago they'd been writhing half-naked on his desk together.

He pinned her with his gaze and grasped the arms of the chair, caging her in as he lowered his face to hers. "Tell me you'll think about Four Mile, Holly. I know you don't want me, but I think it's time for you to spread your wings. Take the project, who knows where it could lead you."

Holly stared back into the depths of his eyes. He thought she didn't want him? Was he crazy? How could she not want him?

"Tell me you will?"

She continued to stare, dumbstruck by what he'd just said.

His lips quirked up and he started to nod. He tucked his thumb under her chin and nodded her head in time with his own. "There, not so hard is it?"

Finally she smiled. "Okay, I'll think about it." He was right. It did make all kinds of sense for her to do it. It would broaden her horizons, open who knew what doors for her. She just had to separate it in her mind from Pete himself. How could he think she didn't want him? She pursed her lips. If she agreed to the project, she'd still seem him sometimes, at least. She'd no doubt hang out with Emma and Jack, and surely he'd be around?

She'd have to think about it. Would she be able to think about anything else?

"Good. One more request."

She laughed. "Are you always this demanding?"

"Always," he grinned. He pulled her to her feet and into his arms. "Have dinner with me tonight? Let's get out of here and go back to my place?"

Holly pretended to think about it for moment. She was surprised when he locked his gaze with hers.

"Please?"

He looked so serious. She reached up and kissed his lips. "I was only kidding, there's nothing I would like more."

She was even more surprised when his face flooded with relief. He put an arm around her shoulders and led her to the door.

~ ~ ~

Pete kept his arm around her as they walked to the elevators. He was aware of heads popping out of offices to stare after them when they passed. He didn't care. He'd never let the troops see him with a woman before, but at this point he really didn't give a shit. He'd only have her for ten more days. Even if she agreed to work on Four Mile, it wouldn't be the same. She'd be around for the job, not for him. She wouldn't be his like she was right now.

"Hey, Pete," Nate popped out of his office near the elevators and his jaw dropped as he looked at the two of them.

Pete grinned, enjoying Nate's reaction. "S'up, Nate?"

"Sorry, I, uh...."

"Holly, this is Nate. He works with Jack and is finally setting up an office here, now that we're done in Houston. Nate, meet Holly." Pete didn't let go of her shoulders while they shook hands.

Nate recovered his composure. "Nice to meet you, Holly."

"Were you after me for something?" asked Pete.

"Yes. Jack told me they're getting married in two weeks. I wanted to know if we're still doing a stag night for him?"

"Hmm." Pete frowned. "That kind of fell by the wayside in the rush to get everything ready. I'll talk to Ben and Dan and get back to you."

"Sure," Nate nodded.

Pete turned to Holly, "Have you arranged anything for Em?"

"Originally we'd planned to get her down here for a night out, but that was before we knew we only had two weeks."

"We'll work something out, Nate. I'll let you know."

"Great. Well, nice to meet you, Holly."

"You too."

As they emerged from the building, Pete asked, "Want to leave your car here and come with me?" Holly agreed as he'd hoped she would. He opened the passenger door for her to climb into his truck and patted her backside on the way up.

"Hey!" She laughed. "Careful with the merchandise! There are no panties under there, remember." She sat and smiled at him.

"No panties, huh?"

She laughed, "That's right, Bigshot. I just had every girl's fantasy come true."

Pete's eyes widened and he felt interest beginning to stir in his pants again, "Every girl's fantasy?"

"Well, one of mine at least."

"Do tell?"

"Well, I just had this gorgeous, powerful CEO get me into his office under false pretenses, then rip my panties off, and take me on his desk."

Pete grinned. "It does sound kinda kinky when you put it like that."

"How else could I put it?" She laughed. "That's what just happened."

"And you said this guy was gorgeous?" He liked hearing that.

"Drop dead gorgeous. I'd say he was panty dropping, except he tore them off, and that's even hotter."

Pete was getting hard again. She drove him crazy. Even with silly banter in a parking lot. "Does this guy feature in any more of your fantasies? "

"All of them!" He knew she was only teasing, but she pulled off looking dead serious.

"In that case, I suggest we get back to my place and discuss this further."

She put a hand to his chest and pushed him back. "I've been waiting for you to do just that!" she said before closing the door in his face.

~ ~ ~

Holly leaned on the balcony and looked out at the ocean. She didn't think she'd ever felt this happy. Or this sad. Pete was wonderful. They had so much fun—and such great sex. He made her feel so comfortable, and so beautiful. He'd made her a great dinner, which they'd eaten sitting out here overlooking the ocean. They'd also worked on another of her CEO fantasies. On a lounger. By the pool.

Pete was everything she'd ever hoped to find in a man, and a whole lot more than she'd ever dreamed. Emma had been right, they were perfect together. He'd even been helping her past her hang-ups about money and status. He'd shown her there really was no difference between them. He believed in her and was teaching her to do the same. But, because of dumb, sucky timing, they weren't going to have a relationship. They weren't going to keep seeing each other to see what developed. No. They were going to have ten more days. Then they would say goodbye. Finished. Over. She sighed. He was inside returning a call. He had ignored it at dinner, but it was some work thing he had to deal with.

He came back out and leaned on the balcony next to her, staring out at the last of the sunset. "Sorry about that."

"No problem, you're the CEO. It goes with the territory."

She saw his lips quirk at that, the ready smile never far away.

"And you like sleeping with the CEO?"

"I do."

"Then I have another request."

"What's that?"

"Stay with me?"

That surprised her. "Okay," she'd already thought she was. "I didn't think you were going to send me home tonight with no car and no panties."

He didn't laugh. "I don't just mean tonight, Holly. Stay with me until the wedding?"

Wow! Now that one she had not been expecting.

"You don't want to?"

"Oh, Pete, I do…."

"But?"

How could she tell him she was afraid to get even more attached to him? Well she knew how, she'd just say it, like she always did and to hell with the consequences!

"But I'm afraid to."

"Afraid?" He turned to face her and the blue gaze held her captive. "What are you afraid of, sweetheart?"

"I'm afraid it will make it even harder to say goodbye."

His shoulders sagged a little. "Don't worry, I'm a big boy, I'll survive."

Holly frowned at that. "I have no doubt you will, Bigshot. I, on the other hand, actually have a heart, and I don't want to get it broken!" she snapped.

Now it was Pete's turn to look confused. "I thought you were letting me down gently. You mean...you care?"

She rolled her eyes and shook her head. "Is it not totally obvious?"

"No it isn't! You're the one who keeps insisting we can't go past the wedding."

"Yes, but only because you insist there's no future in it. The more time we spend together, the more time I want. Pete, it's going to kill me to say goodbye to you next weekend. What would it be like in another three months or six months?" Tears stung behind her eyes, but no way was she going to let them out.

"But I thought...."

"What Pete? What did you think?"

"I thought that you.... That I.... Damn! I don't what the hell I was thinking." He wrapped his big arms around her, and she could feel his heart thundering is his chest. He stroked her hair. "I'm so sorry, sweetheart. I had no idea it would be this hard. On either of us."

# Chapter Fourteen

As Pete came bounding down the stairs, Holly stopped, glass halfway to her mouth. Emma swiped the glass from her hand. "You are actually drooling, Holly!"

"Mmm," she couldn't make her mouth form intelligible words. Pete looked devastating! He was wearing a steel gray suit with a black T-shirt underneath. His hair was perfectly mussed and his blue eyes were blazing as he strode towards her. She swiped her glass back from Emma as her friend was having the same reaction to Jack as he came down the stairs next.

She took a big swig of her wine before Pete took the glass from her. He stepped in close, lips quirking, clearly enjoying the effect he was having on her.

"So?"

She took in a deep breath to steady herself. It didn't work as she breathed in the scent of him; his spicy cologne and the distinct maleness that was simply Pete. "Oh, hell, yeah!"

He grinned at that. "Which question are you answering?"

She smiled. "Is the CEO gorgeous?"

His shoulders shook as he chuckled. "I know that much. My question was, shall we sneak off and leave these guys to it?"

She smiled. "My answer remains the same. In fact, looking like that, that's my answer to any question you care to ask."

His lips met hers briefly, making her want to drag him back up to his bedroom, not caring that the whole gang was here.

He smiled down at her. "And if I want you all to myself?"

"It's going to be hard to escape them all this weekend. We'll just have to snatch our moments."

He pulled her close. "I want to snatch you now."

"Hemming, put her down!" Jack was laughing at them. "Are you organizing tonight, or not? 'Cause, you know I'm okay with not. I'd rather take my fiancée to dinner." He smiled down at Emma. "We could go to Mario's?"

Emma's face lit up.

"Oh, no you don't," said Missy. She called out to where Dan, Ben, and Nate were talking by the pool, "Hey, guys! The Best Man may be failing in his duties. You're going to have to get these two going."

Pete pecked Holly's lips. "No failure here!" He grabbed Jack by the collar and pulled him away from Emma, who giggled and planted a quick kiss on Jack's lips.

"Come on guys, we have to show my partner one last good time." He looked back at Emma. "Just a figure of speech, Mouse. No offense."

"None taken."

"Go on," said Missy. "Get out of here, go do your boy thing. We've got to get Em ready. Whatever you've got lined up for the groom pales in comparison to the hotness that is Team Slinky. And we're hitting the town!"

Jack wriggled in Pete's grasp. "I vote Team Slinky! We should at least have another here until the girls are dressed. I want to see!"

Holly smiled when Pete's eyes found hers, he was considering that possibility too. In his moment of hesitation, Jack broke free and headed back to Emma.

"Oh no you don't." Dan's arm shot out and grabbed his brother.

"Looks like you were right, Missy. The Best Man is distracted." Dan smiled at Holly. "But we'll drag them both out of here if we have to so you ladies can get ready."

Nate joined Dan in restraining Jack while Smoke and Ben approached Pete. "Come on, big guy. Time to say goodbye to the pretty ladies."

Pete grinned. "Have fun, girls, we'll see you tomorrow."

Holly blew him a kiss before Ben slammed the door closed behind them.

"Okay," said Missy. "Now we must all clear our minds of the six hot men that we just allowed to leave this place."

"I'm not sure I can," said Emma.

"Then have more wine." Holly refilled Emma's glass.

"I'm with Em," smiled Laura. "How am I supposed to clear my head of all that smokin' hotness?"

"By drinking more wine!" Holly refilled her glass too. "This town is overflowing with hot men. Once we get to the club there will be hundreds of them. You can dance with as many as you like. But, for tonight, the ones that just left are off limits and we must *not* give any of them another thought, understood?" She raised her glass. "Team Slinky!"

Three glasses met hers. "Team Slinky!" they laughed.

She wished she was as into Emma's bachelorette party as she was trying to make out. It was Friday night. The others had all come in to the city to give Emma and Jack the traditional singles' send off, but Holly wished she could be spending the evening alone with Pete. A Friday night on the town with him, looking like he did tonight? What she wouldn't give! Yet it would never happen. Next Friday would be the rehearsal dinner, Saturday the wedding. Then it would all be over. She gave herself a little shake and refilled her own glass.

When they were finally ready, Emma squealed, "We need photos of Team Slinky!"

They all wore little black dresses. Holly had managed to find the short black equivalent of their bridesmaids' dresses. She knew the style worked so well on each of them and would suit Emma too. The full-length, rich purple made for beautiful bridesmaids. The thigh-high, black version they were wearing now would make for a very interesting night out, she had no doubt. They'd had great fun drinking wine and doing each other's hair and makeup, now they really looked the part.

Phones came out of purses and they took dozens of photos out by the pool. Holly set her phone to video and balanced it on the bar before running back to join the others, posing and pouting.

When they finally managed to get out of the door, the driver was standing beside the limo waiting.

"Albert!" Holly ran over and hugged him. "How are you? Pete didn't say it would be you. I thought you'd be driving him and the guys."

The old man grinned. "Evening, Miss Holly. He asked me to take very good care of you ladies. Miss Emma, congratulations to you."

"Thanks Albert." Emma hugged him too.

Holly introduced Missy and Laura, who followed suit and each gave him a hug rather than shaking his hand.

Albert was beaming. "Well, I sure got the best job tonight. If I may say so, you ladies look stunning!"

"Thanks Albert, we're Team Slinky!" said Missy.

"I would have to agree with that," laughed Albert.

"Oh, please would you take a photo of the four of us together?"

"Of course."

Laura handed him her phone and Albert took several pictures. "Would you mind if I took one for my scrapbook?" he asked. "I've got all the celebrities I've driven, but Team Slinky beats the lot of 'em." He pulled an old camera from the glove box and they all posed against the limo as he clicked away.

When they were done, Holly remembered that she'd left her own phone balanced on the bar. She ran up the steps and used the key that Pete had given her to open the heavy front door and went back inside to get it. When she returned, the others were already sipping champagne in the back of the limo. She locked the front door and stood a moment, wishing this really was her life. That she really lived here with Pete and that she wasn't just a temporary stand-in who'd be gone in a week.

She heard a click and then, "Smile!" Albert was pointing his camera at her. "Say Pete!" She laughed at his play on words. She'd miss Albert too, he was a good man. She ran down the steps and gave him another hug before she climbed in the back to have a glass of champagne thrust into her hand by Laura.

~ ~ ~

Pete stood next to Jack, sipping his beer. They'd come to one of their old haunts and the two of them had automatically gravitated to their favorite spot—a little balcony where they could watch the dance floor and still actually hear each other speak. The place was heaving. The dance floor writhed with sweaty bodies.

"You enjoying this?"

Jack nodded. "It's good to get the guys together." He tilted his bottle to where Nate and Ben were dancing with two blonde chicks. One was shimmying her large and barely covered bosom up and down Ben's chest, while her friend was dancing with her back to Nate, shaking her booty against his groin.

"They sure look like they're having fun!"

Pete laughed, "Those two would find half-naked women in a monastery. We've got no worries there." He looked past Jack. "Uh-oh, incoming at your nine o'clock." He'd spotted a tall, leggy brunette making a beeline for Jack, her little redhead friend at her side.

The brunette put a hand on Jack's shoulder. "Dance with me?"

Pete smiled when Jack made a big show of lifting his bottle for a swig of beer with his left hand, showing off the heavy gold band he called his 'engagement ring.'

"I'm waiting for my wife."

The brunette turned away. Pete shook his head at the redhead who lingered, looking hopefully at him.

Jack rolled his eyes as Pete's smile became a laugh once they'd gone. "Well! It's true. I'm waiting for her to become my wife."

"Man, you've got it bad!"

Jack grinned. "Real bad. I've never been happier. Though I'd be happier still if you'd let me take her to Mario's tonight instead of coming here."

"Man up!" laughed Pete. "It's one night with the guys. You've got the rest of your life to take her to Mario's. Come on, let's get another."

As they headed to the bar, Pete knew how Jack felt. He'd much rather be spending this evening alone with Holly.

They found Smoke and Dan at the much quieter back bar, far away from the dance floor. The two of them were deep in conversation about the new satellite navigation system Smoke was having installed in Papa Charlie.

"Here's my brother!" Jack slapped Dan on the back.

"Hey, you having a good time?"

Jack nodded.

Pete turned his head at the sound of his name being called.

"Hey Hemming!" Oh, fuck! This was not good. He tried to position himself so he'd block Jack's view of the newcomer, who was pretty drunk by the looks of him.

"Hemming, how you doing, man? Have a drink with me!"

"Hey. We were just leaving," Pete lied.

"Great, where we going?" The guy's eyes were glassy as he staggered into Pete and grasped his hand.

Pete caught him and heaved his huge frame onto a stool. "You've had enough."

The man's eyes narrowed. "Never got why you don't like me, Hemming," his raised voice drew the others' attention. Pete turned away from him. A heavy hand came down on his shoulder, and he took a deep breath. If Jack weren't here he'd tell the guy exactly why he despised him, but this was Jack's night. Pete needed to get him out of here before he realized who this asshole was.

Pete turned back to face the man. He could see how women would find him attractive, but right now he was drunk, his handsome features softened by too much alcohol.

"I said, you've had enough. Take it home."

The guy banged on the bar. "Service!"

The bartender came over. "I'm sorry, Mr. Rivera, but I'm going to have to ask you to leave."

*Oh, shit!* Pete sensed Jack tense behind him.

"I'm going nowhere! Bring me another shot, and for my friends here. Pete and," he leaned around Pete and raised his eyebrows.

Jack's face was murderous. Pete tried to pull him to his feet. "Come on, we're out of here."

Jack didn't move. Dan and Smoke were making 'what the fuck?' faces at Pete. He didn't have time to explain.

"Ah," the man grinned. "You're the guy!"

Pete again tried to get Jack to his feet, but Jack threw his hand off. "I am?" His voice was low and menacing.

"Yeah, the guy she's got her claws into now. Sweet little Emma."

Jack was on his feet now, Pete had never seen him so angry.

"Jack, leave it man, he's isn't worth it!"

Jack's eyes didn't leave the man's face, but he gave a slight nod.

"Don't. You. Dare. Say another fucking word to me!" With that he turned on his heel to follow Pete. Dan and Smoke closed in behind.

"Hey, man! Just a piece of advice from someone who's been there?"

Pete spun around, knowing he needed to stop Jack.

"She's great in bed if you like plain vanilla, but you'll get bored. I did."

Pete couldn't get a hold of Jack. He moved like a big cat, covering the distance back to the bar and had the man by the throat against the wall before any of them could react. He was shaking the guy, ready to kill him.

"Jack!" It was Dan that spoke. "Jack, let him go. He's not worth it. Jack, please don't?"

At the word, 'please,' Jack dropped the guy and turned to Dan. "Sorry Danny, let's go."

Pete understood the exchange between the brothers, sons of a vicious drunk who used to beat them.

He couldn't believe that Rivera was stupid enough to open his mouth again. "Enjoy my leftovers!"

Jack spun around. His fist connected with Rivera's face, knocking him out cold. Jack glowered around at them. "Tell me I was wrong?"

Pete shook his head, none of them could. Emma's ex was the biggest asshole he'd ever met.

The bartender came hurrying over. "I'll sort this out, you guys had better get out of here."

"I'll stay and deal with it," Jack's shoulders sagged. "He'll probably want to press charges."

"He has no grounds," said the barman.

"I think he does," replied Jack.

Rob was coming to now. The barman had him sitting up against the wall, slapping his face none too gently to bring him around. "Mr. Rivera, you are not going to press charges, are you?"

Rob's eyes narrowed.

"Mr. Rivera, that wasn't a question."

Pete exchanged a look with Jack, what was that about?

"Nothing happened here, did it, Mr. Rivera?"

Rob glowered at the barman, then turned a hateful look at Jack, then Pete. "No."

The barman looked up at them. "He won't be pressing charges, I assure you. Though you guys may want to be leaving now?"

Pete took Jack's arm and steered him away before he could argue. "Dan, would you and Smoke let the others know we're leaving? If they want to stay we can send the car back for them."

Pete guided Jack toward the club's entrance. He needed to get his partner out of here. Once they emerged into the cool night air, Jack started to look more like himself again and less like a man with murder on his mind. They found the limo and sat up on the trunk while they waited. Pete said nothing. He knew Jack would talk when, and if, he wanted to. They sat a long while in silence.

"I thought he'd be smaller," Jack said eventually.

Pete raised an eyebrow.

"Everything I'd ever heard about the guy made me think of a little weasel-shit."

Pete had to laugh. "What the hell is a weasel-shit?" He was relieved when Jack grinned.

"You know, the weedy little guy with a mean streak. A coward, not big enough or strong enough to face you, but you know you've got to watch your back 'cause he's sneaky."

Pete nodded. "No, Rivera's a lot of things, but he's no weasel-shit."

Jack sighed and cradled his fist, "What am I going to tell Em?"

Pete looked at his friend's hand, "Shit! Do you need to get that looked at?"

"Nah, it's fine, but Em's not going to like it."

"She'll understand."

Jack nodded. "Yeah, she will. She'll probably be surprised I didn't kill him. I know I am."

Pete smiled. "I thought you were going to when you had him against the wall."

Jack looked at him. "I might have if Danny hadn't been there. I've never been into violence. You know that. Not coming from where we do. But damn, Pete, I could've killed him. You have no idea. Maybe someday, when you meet a woman, you'll understand. With Em, making her happy is what makes me happy. The thought of her with someone else makes me see red. Thinking of that someone hurting her. It's just…. It's crazy making is what it is. I always thought if I met him I'd kill him. Thank God Dan was here."

Pete considered that. The thought of someone hurting Holly? Wasn't that what was driving him crazy? The thought of the loan sharks and what they might do to her? Making her happy made him happy. The thought of someone making her unhappy was weighing heavily on him. That someone was him. She was unhappy that their time together would end next week. He hated that. He was unhappy about it too, but that was just the way it was. There was nothing he could do.

"Hey, bro, where'd you go?" Jack was looking at him.

"Sorry, nowhere. But, where are we going to go, that's the question? You want to call it a night? We could pick up a case and go back to your place. I wish we'd let the girls stay at Em's. We could've gone back to my house to play pool."

Jack gave him a funny look.

"Uh-oh, what are you scheming, Benson?"

"I want to see Em."

Pete thought about it. "It's meant to be guys' night out."

"Yeah, and look how that turned out. I want to see her. Tell her what I did."

Pete had to admit he like the idea himself, but still. "It's her bachelorette party. She's supposed to be out with the girls."

"Yeah, I know." Jack grinned. "Team Slinky! I'd love to see what that looks like, and I know I'm not the only one."

Pete grinned back. "Yeah, but crashing her party?"

"She didn't want to go any more than I did, and you know it." His face fell. "Did Holly tell you where they were going?"

Pete shook his head, then grinned. "No, but I can call Albert!"

"Let's do it!"

Jack looked much happier now, so who was Pete to stand in his way? He dug his phone out of his pocket to call Albert while Jack texted Dan to see if the rest of them wanted to come.

~ ~ ~

Holly snatched Emma's phone out of her hands, laughing. She handed her a drink instead.

"Sweetie, come dance again. Leave the poor man alone. You've done well so far, and you'll see him in the morning!"

Emma grinned sheepishly. "I just wanted to...."

"Well you can't! Now back to the dance floor."

Emma downed the rest of her drink. "Yes, Ma'am!"

They elbowed their way back to Laura and Missy, who were fending off two guys dancing around them.

"Team Slinky seems to be a hit!" Laura laughed as three more men crowded around them.

"Sure is," said Missy, elbowing one of them as he grabbed her hips from behind and started moving with her.

Emma trod on a foot as another tried to get up against her. She looked at Holly. "Can't I go and sit down again? This isn't appropriate for an old, almost married lady!" She laughed.

Holly shook her head, "No chance, sweetie." She neatly dodged hands that were trying to grab her ass as one of the guys breathed down her neck. She twirled away and ended up with Emma in her arms. "We came to have fun and that we shall do!" She shimmied her shoulders. "Remember this?"

Emma laughed. "Course I do!" She shimmied back. The two of them held on to each other and danced together so no one could get near. Laura and Missy did the same.

"Damn!" Holly realized this was having the opposite effect to what they'd hoped. Instead of being shut out and moving on to hunt elsewhere, the guys were now dancing in a circle around them. Some of them openly drooling at their girl on girl double act. She scanned the club, looking for an escape. She wanted to dance, but not like this. Her eyes lit up as she spotted a very familiar face.

"What is it?" asked Emma.

"I spy the cavalry!" grinned Holly, waving madly. "Lots of very hot, very safe men to dance with." When she finally caught his attention, he grinned and spoke to his friends. They made their way across the crowded dance floor.

She flung her arms around his neck. "Roberto!"

"Holly, Holls, darling! And little Miss Emster." He kissed Emma's cheek. "Congratulations, Little one." He cast an eye over Missy and Laura. "Well, lookit this, it's Team Slinky!"

Roberto shouted introductions. Holly knew his partner John very well and recognized some of the others. She wondered how it worked that gay men always seemed to be so good looking. Most of Berto's friends could easily be models. Then again, knowing him, they probably were! They danced so well too. The girls danced happily with them as the grabby guys from earlier drifted away. This was much better.

She squealed as the next song came on and turned to Roberto. "Salsa! Dance with me!" she shouted and he grinned. They moved together perfectly. She and Em had taken a salsa class with Berto and John last year and they had all loved it. John danced with Emma. The four of them turned heads. As the song changed, Berto spun Holly away and John caught her.

"Trading partners!" shouted Berto as he moved in on Emma. Missy and Laura were swept up by two of his friends. Berto beckoned to another, he shouted in his ear and sent him over to the D.J. Holly watched the exchange and knew what was coming. When the song came to an end she clung to John. "Lambada with me, sweetie!"

John laughed and pulled her close, pressing his thigh between her legs as they moved. He smiled down at her. "You know, someday, lovely, you really need to find a straight guy to do this with."

She laughed as he spun her away then pulled her back, molding her body to him, as they moved with the music. "Not happening, sweetie. We're too good together!"

She looked over at Berto and Emma who looked like they were having sex standing up, as did every couple dancing around them who knew the lambada, and most seemed to. Holly let her head drop back, hair swinging. John held onto her with his over-muscled arms and expertly moved her body with his own. How she loved to dance!

Pete scanned the club. It wasn't a place he was too familiar with. He wasn't a big clubber and this one played a lot of Latin music. He danced well, but didn't like dance floors like this one. This, to him, seemed to be more about public foreplay than dancing.

Jack stood by his side. "They've got to be here somewhere."

Dan and Smoke were scanning the crowd too. Dan's face lit up. "I see Missy!" Pete wasn't surprised that she was the one he'd been looking for.

"Where?" asked Jack.

All their eyes followed as he pointed to a group in the middle of the dance floor. Missy and Laura were dancing together, mingling with a group of guys.

"What the...?" Jack had spotted Emma. "I didn't even know she could salsa! And look at that guy!"

Pete found her and grinned. "You've got no worries there, bro. That's Roberto, he works for Holly. Great guy, but he's not going to be stealing your woman, I can guarantee it."

"Yeah? So can I," Jack growled as he set out for the dance floor.

Pete hurried after him. "Bro, his boyfriend wouldn't let him!"

Jack stopped and grinned. "In that case, I like him!"

They cut their way through the crowds, Pete was still trying to catch a glimpse of Holly. He found her as the song was ending. She was dancing with some big, tall, muscle-bound dude. Pete felt his fist clench at his side. It looked like she was having a good time too! He couldn't believe his eyes as the song changed and she clung to the guy. The lambada? Shit! They were all over each other! She was rubbing up against him, they were moving like they were.... Damn! You didn't dance like that with someone you didn't know. They must know each other pretty well judging by the way their hips were moving together.

Pete needed to stop the guy. He couldn't hold her like that, move with her like that! Jack's words echoed in his mind, *'Making her happy makes me happy.'* It was true it did, and he didn't like it, hated it in fact, when some other guy was the one making her happy, like this one was right now. He needed to get to her. He elbowed his way through the heaving mass of couples. Never mind public foreplay, this was more like an upright orgy of grinding bodies!

He was almost to her when someone stepped in his way and a strong hand gripped his arm. Roberto!

"Pete, darling! How lovely to see you."

Pete felt himself dragged forward, taken by surprise by the vice-like grip. He glanced over to see Jack and Emma tangled up in each other, just before Roberto brought him to a halt and tapped Holly on the shoulder. Her eyes opened wide when she saw Pete. There was no mistaking the delight on her face.

"Very nice display, children, but now this man wants his honey back." He slid an arm around John's waist, "And I want mine!" He blew a kiss at Pete as they glided away.

Pete felt pretty dumb. He should have known. But he hadn't been able to think. He'd just reacted, instinctively. Was that what jealousy felt like? He didn't know and right now he didn't care. She was smiling, holding her arms out to him. All he could think about was holding her again, having her dance with him, moving like she meant it. He wrapped her in his arms and kissed her. She molded her body to him as they moved together. Now, it would be a good night.

# Chapter Fifteen

"For two people who are just having fun, you and Pete seem awfully intense."

Holly glanced over at Missy, who never took her eyes off the road, before she turned to stare back out the window at the lake. "I suppose it's intense because we know we've only got a week left."

"Seems crazy to me," said Missy. "You two are like the perfect couple. But for Pete and his stupid plan."

Holly nodded. "Tell me about it. But it is what it is. That's how he lives his life. He wouldn't be the man he is if he didn't follow his plan."

"I know," sighed Missy. "He's been that way since we were kids, and you can't say he's not done well on it. But still, it makes me sad."

"What do you think it does to me?" asked Holly. "Part of me wants to bawl my eyes out and beg him to forget his stupid plan. But that's not my style, and I know it wouldn't help anyway. It'd be asking him to change who he is. I don't want to him to change. It'd be doomed from the start."

Missy nodded. "You're right, hon."

"And here I was hoping you would tell me that I'm wrong. That there's some way around this that I'm not seeing."

"Sorry, but if there is, I'm not seeing it either."

Holly smiled sadly. "So how about we change the subject?"

"Sure. Want to tell me what we're going to do with all this fabric?"

They were on their way to Emma's Gramps' house. Holly needed to work out how they were going to decorate the place for the wedding.

"Wish I could, sweetie. But that's what you're going to help me figure out when we get there."

Missy laughed. "Now *that* I can relate to. No plan, just make it up as we go along."

"Yeah," said Holly. "That's the way I roll."

Gramps was waiting for them on his front porch.

"Hey, Gramps!" Missy greeted him with a hug. Holly did the same.

"You two don't look any the worse for wear. I hear you kids had quite a night of it?"

Holly grinned. "Yeah, it wasn't quite the night we had planned."

Gramps caught her eye. "Take it from an ole fella, the best times in life are never the ones you plan."

Holly swallowed and smiled back at him. He always seemed to know everything. "I'd have to agree with you there, Gramps."

He patted her arm. "That's 'cause it's the truth. You'll see. Did the boys get their suits?"

"They did," laughed Missy. "But it was touch and go this morning."

Everyone had ended up staying at Pete's last night, after what had become a joint night out. Even Ben and Nate had rolled in there at some ungodly hour. Holly and the girls had been ready to go and do their last bits of shopping by nine, but the guys hadn't been too enthusiastic about getting ready to go tux shopping before Smoke flew them all back to Summer Lake.

"I picked your suit up this week too, Gramps," said Holly. "It's in Missy's van."

Gramps' eyes twinkled. "You're a good 'un Holly. No way did I want to be going down to the city and around them stores."

Holly laughed. "And why should you when you have your very own fashion consultant and personal shopper?"

Gramps laughed. "Well thanks. You got me gussied up and now you need to see what you can do with this old place too, right? You don't need me, do you?"

"What would you do if we said yes, Gramps?" Missy teased.

"Ha! I would tell you, Miss Melissa, that I have fishies waiting on me. You'll know where to find me if you really need me.

~ ~ ~

Pete hung his new tux in the closet with Jack's, then ran back down the stairs. Jack was out on the front deck, drawing on one of his huge pads.

"What you working on, bro?"

Jack grinned. "Plans for what I'm going to do to this place. Em's agreed to let me renovate. I'd wondered about building us something out at Four Mile, but she's so attached to this old place."

"She's got too much history here," said Pete. "And besides, you wouldn't have me as your neighbor if you moved over there."

"I know. Sorry your place has taken a back seat with all the wedding stuff."

"Hell, seeing you two get married is more than worth the delay. And now that you mention it, what other wedding stuff do we need to be doing? Seems like everyone is off organizing something or other and we're sitting around here like a pair of old women."

Jack grinned. "Yeah, Em's got everyone running round like a well-organized army. I thought you were the planner, but I'm half expecting her to start giving out clipboards."

"She's a woman on a mission. Seems crazy to think that you two will be married in a week."

"Yeah, and then lying on a beach for two weeks after that," smiled Jack. He was taking Emma to St. Lucia for their honeymoon. He looked at Pete. "Two more weeks delay on your place, but I'm sure you'll find something to keep you busy while we're gone. Or more to the point, someone. I'm guessing the Maid of Honor will be keeping you entertained."

Pete closed his eyes and took a deep breath. "Nah."

Jack laughed. "What do you mean, 'nah'? You two are almost as bad as me and Em!"

"Yeah, she's fun."

Jack frowned. "But?"

"But we won't be seeing each other after next weekend."

"Why the hell not? What about the plaza?"

"I'm still trying to get her to take on the plaza. But, don't worry, even if she won't, I'll find someone other than Mia and Jade for it."

"And if she does?"

"She'll work with Ben, not me."

"What the hell, Pete? I thought you really liked her?"

"I do. That's the problem."

"The problem?"

Pete unclenched his fist and looked at Jack. "It's not part of the plan, is it?"

Jack shook his head. "Fuck the plan, Pete! Do you think I was planning on getting married?"

Pete shook his head. "No, but this is different."

"How?"

"Oh, come on! You know me better than anyone. You've known the plan since we first even dreamed about starting Phoenix. I have to get everything else in place before I can make room for a woman in my life."

"Pete, that's crazy! It was a great plan to keep you from getting distracted by women, but when the right woman shows up in your life, you need to make a new plan. I have."

"Yeah, but that's not how I work, is it?"

"So you're just going to end it with Holly?" Jack was looking at him as if he really was crazy.

"Yup." He didn't want to. Knew it would be hard, but he had no choice, did he?

"Fair enough, then. If she's not as important as the plan, then she's just not that important. I guess I'd gotten the wrong idea about you two."

"Jesus, Jack! She *is* that important! She's.... It's just...." Pete cut himself off, surprised by his outburst.

Jack's eyebrows were raised. "It's just what?"

"Just nothing. You're right. She's not *that* important." Even as he said it, he knew it wasn't true. Jack's face told him *he* knew it too. But how could he let her be more important than everything he'd spent his whole life working for?

"When you come to your senses, talk to me," said Jack. "For now, we need to get back into town, talk to the band and run a few more errands. We need to move if we're going to be done in time to meet everyone for dinner."

~ ~ ~

Holly swung her feet as she sat at the airport waiting for Pete. Laura was talking to Smoke in the little flight planning room. She'd come to sit out here to leave them alone—and to get out of that room. All she could see in there was Pete's face, blue eyes blazing as he'd 'persuaded' her, up against the door, to accept his apology. The way he'd run his fingers down her cheek, told her she was special. She sighed and kicked the chair in front of her. Just not special enough!

It'd been a busy couple of days with everyone scrambling to pull the wedding together. When Pete had said he was going over to see his folks, she'd stupidly assumed she was going with him. Instead, he'd said something about not being too long. Emma had quickly asked her for help and said she and Jack would drop her back at the airport. What had she expected? Why would he take her to meet his parents? But still, after Friday night, after the way he'd been with her, she'd felt so close to him. Felt like they were a real couple. His not wanting to take her to his parent's place had felt like a slap in the face. A cold hard reminder that she wasn't, nor was she going to be, a part of his life.

"Hey, sweetheart!" She looked up. He had no right to be so damned handsome. And he certainly had no right to look like he cared so much! He came toward her, eyes soft with concern. "Are you okay?"

She nodded. She had to snap out of this. He'd done nothing wrong. She'd known the deal from the start. She forced a smile she didn't mean and spoke the words she did, as she stood and he wrapped her in his bear hug. "Much better now." Now that she was back in his arms.

He kissed the top of her head and stroked her hair. "I'm going to ask again. And this time I'm not taking no for an answer," he said.

"Ask what?"

"Say you'll stay with me until the wedding?"

She was no longer in danger of getting more attached to him than she already was, that would be impossible. She met his eyes. "I'll stay with you."

His smile spread, but his eyes remained solemn. "Thank you."

Laura and Smoke came down the corridor. "Are you ready to go?"

"Yeah, let's get out of here," said Pete.

"I hope no one minds," said Holly, "But I've asked Smoke to drop me first."

She knew Smoke was happy to drop her and Pete off before he took Laura back to San Francisco. From the smiles all around she knew the others liked the idea too.

~ ~ ~

"Sorry the view isn't as good as yours," Holly called down the stairs to Pete. They'd come to her house so she could collect everything she'd need to spend the week with him.

"It's a great little place," he shouted back up. "You need a hand up there?"

"No thanks." She'd deliberately asked him to wait in the kitchen. She hated bringing him here at all. It wasn't that she was ashamed of the place. To the contrary, she loved her little townhouse, though she knew it was small and ordinary compared to Pete's massive place at the beach. It was more than that though, she didn't want to fill the place with memories of him. So she'd confined him in the one room she could easily avoid.

"I won't be long." She crammed clothes and toiletries into her bag and closed it. She'd hardly been here in the last few weeks. She looked around, knowing that she'd more than make up for her absence, moping around for the next few.

She joined him in the kitchen. "Ready to go?"

He frowned. "What's the rush? We could hang here?"

That was the last thing she wanted. "No, let's get going."

~ ~ ~

Pete looked at Holly curled up on the sofa in the den. He'd gone to get them another glass of wine and come back to find her with her eyes closed, knees curled up to her chest. Beautiful. She was so capable, she'd taken care of so many details over the weekend. So strong, she stood on her own two feet, as she kept reminding him. So independent, he'd noticed she didn't readily accept help from anyone, not just him. Yet curled up like that, she looked so vulnerable, he wanted to take care of her. He didn't want to step in and be the 'Bigshot' she so often accused him of being. No, he just wanted to be there for her. With her. Stand beside her as she fought her own battles. Be her soft place to land when she needed one. He shook his head. Not happening. He needed to stop thinking like that.

She opened her eyes and smiled at him. "There you are. I've told you, the service is terrible in this place."

He laughed. "Here's your wine, impatient one. I was just admiring the view."

He sat back on the sofa and pulled her head into his lap. "Go back to sleep if you want."

"I wasn't sleeping. Just resting my eyes."

He smiled. "Then rest them some more." He felt her relax.

"Mmm, maybe just a minute." She closed her eyes again.

He stroked her hair and stared out at the ocean, trying not to think about what he'd do this time next week when she was gone.

As he watched the last pinks and golds of the sunset fade, Pete realized she was fast asleep. He shifted, hoping not to disturb her as he got to his feet.

She opened one eye. "Sorry, Bigshot. I'll bet you're not used to 'em falling asleep on you, are you?"

He had to laugh. "I'm not! See, I told you you're bad for my self-esteem." He picked her up. "I think it's time to call it a night, sweetheart."

Her arms came up around his neck as he carried her upstairs and she kissed his chin. "It's early."

"Yeah, but it's been a busy weekend and we've both got work in the morning."

She ran her fingers down his throat. "I could keep you awake for a while."

"You could?" He felt his interest stirring. "And why would you want to do that?" He held her eyes as he nudged his bedroom door open with his hip.

"Because I want you."

He lay her down in the middle of the bed. "You do?"

She bit her bottom lip and, taking hold of the hem of his T-shirt, pulled it up over his head and off. He loved the way she looked at him. She wasn't shy about the fact that she found him so attractive. She ran her hands down his chest.

"I do."

"Then I guess you'd better take the dress off."

She smiled and crawled to the edge of the bed, where she got off and stood up. "Why do you have such a big bed?"

Sometimes she said the damnedest things at the strangest moments! "Because I'm such a big guy?"

He felt the strain in his boxers as she eyed him. "You can say that again. Show me."

He unfastened his jeans and kicked them off, boxers too, so that he lay naked on the bed as she stood fully dressed beside it. "Take the dress off, Holly."

She met his eyes. "What if I don't want to?"

He loved the way she teased. "The dress is coming off," he kept his voice low and commanding.

She took a step away from the bed, eyes shining. "You can't make me."

"Oh, but I can, sweetheart and I will." The thought of doing so was making him harder. He got up from the bed and she backed away with a come-get-me smile. He lunged but she dodged, taking another step backwards, but not, he noticed, too far out of reach. This time he caught her wrist and pulled her to him. She wriggled, but didn't make too much of an effort to get away.

"Last chance. Take the dress off."

She shook her head. Her skin was flushed, nipples erect, completely aroused as she waited to see what he would do. He wrapped an arm around her waist and slid a hand inside her panties. His fingers explored her damp folds and he bent his head to nibble her neck, drawing a moan from her.

"Surrender?" he murmured.

"Never!" She tried to pull away, but he spun her around to face the dresser.

He met her eyes in the full-length mirror that stood between two chests of drawers. "Are you going to take it off?"

She shook her head, her breath coming quickly as he continued to work the bundle of nerves between her legs. He leaned forward, pushing her down until her arms shot out to support herself on the drawers. He moved fast, lifting the back of her dress so her naked ass cheeks were exposed as she bent before him. Grateful she was wearing a thong, he hooked a finger in it and pulled it to the side. The sight of her like that, flushed face and breasts in the mirror, tight little ass bent in front of him, had him aching to be inside her. He held her hips steady and nudged at her heat. He lost it when he felt how wet she was and plunged deep. She gasped as he thrust inside her over and over, picking up his pace as he watched the pleasure on her face. He found her nub and worked her with his thumb as he drove into her. The heat began to build in his veins. He dropped his mouth to her neck, kissing and nibbling, sending her over the edge. Hearing her scream his name took him with her. Her tight wetness closed around him and he exploded, filling them both with his heat.

~ ~ ~

He lay on the bed staring up at the ceiling. How the hell was he supposed to let her go? She made him laugh. She made him think. She made him question everything. She made him horny. So damned horny. She made him come like no woman ever had. She made him happy.

She emerged from the bathroom. She was still wearing the damned dress. She made him hard again! He felt his erection grow. How was that even possible so quickly?

She met his eyes with a smile. A soft, shy smile, no teasing in her eyes now.

"Sweetheart?"

"Mmm?"

"Take off the dress." He held her gaze and felt the change in her. She said nothing, but he knew this time she'd do it for him.

She reached down and lifted the hem, pulling the whole thing up and over her head. She stood naked before him. His cock was fully erect again, eager for her to come join him on the bed. He sat up against the pillows.

"Come here."

She climbed up onto the bed and he pulled her on top of him. He held her hips and moved against her as she sat astride him. Then he raised his arms above his head and held the headboard, giving himself up to her. "I'm all yours."

Her fingers closed around his shaft, sending a tremor though his body as she guided him inside her. Oh, so slowly, she lowered herself onto him, driving him crazy as she sat up tall, stroking his chest and gently rocking her hips against him, holding him tight inside. The view from down here was one he knew he would never forget. Her pert breasts were swollen, her perfect body moving with his, using him to take her pleasure. She was biting down on her bottom lip and he could feel by the way she was closing around him that she was about to lose it. She started to move faster on him; he knew he could take her over the edge any moment he chose.

But *she* took him.

"I'm all yours, Pete." Her words filled his mind and his body. They were the heat that surged through his veins. He let go, claiming her as his own, filling her with his hot need. He pulled her down to him, holding her tight to his chest as he thrust up. She closed and clenched around him as her words reverberated through his veins and his soul with every thrust. *'I'm all yours, Pete.'* Whatever plans he might have, his body knew the truth and was claiming it. This woman was his, just as he was hers.

~ ~ ~

Holly came downstairs to the smell of coffee and bacon. She felt a little edgy this morning. It was strange to be starting a weekday together. It was more than that though, she couldn't believe she'd said that last night: *'I'm all yours, Pete.'* Really?! Yes really. It was the truth and, as per her stupid usual, she'd spoken her truth. He'd been so sweet too. He'd held her close afterward, told her how special she was, how beautiful. Stroked her hair. Gazed into her eyes. Poor Pete. He was truly such a decent man. He was trying to make her feel better. They both knew she wasn't really his. If only she could keep her big mouth shut.

Oh God! Pete dressed for work was a sight to behold. Pale blue shirt, light gray pants, suit jacket draped over the sofa. She could go for a few more CEO fantasies right about now.

"Hey, sweetheart. Want some coffee?"

"Yes, please." If only this was her real life.

"Come sit outside with me? I told you making breakfast for you could become a habit."

She followed him outside, wishing it was a habit that wouldn't have to be broken in a week.

Pete dug into his eggs, grinning at her. "So, I figure I could drop you off at the store on my way in. Will you have time to meet me for lunch?"

She shook her head. "We've got a big delivery today. I'll be lucky if I get time to even eat lunch."

Pete frowned. "You have to eat!"

"Sweetie, I don't always get chance."

He was still frowning. "What time will you be done tonight?"

"Probably not until seven or so."

"Okay, I'll come for you at seven. If you're not done, I'll help you until you are."

She almost choked on her coffee. "You don't need to do that!"

"I want to do that, sweetheart. Then I thought we could go out for dinner, if you'd like to?"

"I'd like to, but…."

"No, buts. It's decided. I'll be there at seven."

"Pete?"

"Yes?"

How could she tell him everything she wanted to say? "Thank you."

# Chapter Sixteen

As he sat in the restaurant waiting for Holly, Pete fiddled with his phone. He couldn't believe it was Wednesday already. On Monday he'd had Judy call the store and ask for Roberto. He'd found out from him what Holly and each of her staff liked for lunch. He'd driven around himself to three different places to get their favorites, then delivered it in person. It'd taken a great deal of willpower to not stick around, but he'd simply given Holly a quick kiss and left. He'd gone for her at seven, but she'd refused to let him help, sending the others home and locking up instead. He'd taken her to his favorite restaurant, then taken her home and made love to her.

Yesterday he'd done the same. Roberto was a very willing accomplice. He'd delivered lunch to the store again, this time with flowers for each of them, including Roberto. He grinned to himself, remembering how touched Roberto had been. Last night they'd swum in the pool, eaten a simple supper, and then walked hand in hand on the beach, chasing each other through the surf. Then they'd gone home and made love all night. He couldn't think of it as anything else. He made love to her. She made love to him.

When she'd spoken those words on Sunday night, they'd changed everything. *'I'm all yours, Pete.'* They were the truest words ever spoken. They'd melted the defenses around his heart and he knew it was going to get broken. He knew because he was the one about to do the breaking. True as those words were, yes they changed everything, but at the same time they changed nothing.

Maybe in a few years they'd still be true. He hoped that by some miracle they would be, that she'd still be his by the time he was ready. He didn't believe in miracles, though. On Sunday they would say goodbye. He had to.

He was still hoping that she'd agree to implement her ideas for the plaza. That she'd take the consulting job, and the big fat fee that went with it. He didn't hold out much hope, though. He wanted to maintain at least some connection, he wanted a safety net. Holly, on the other hand, was more courageous. He was quite convinced that he may never see her again. That she'd make sure of it, give herself the time and space to heal, put it all behind her. He understood that.

He looked up as he sensed her enter the restaurant. He was aware of the heads that turned as she passed. She was stunning, her long brown hair flowing around her shoulders, long lean body moving gracefully as she made her way toward him. She wasn't aware of them though—to be fair she never was—but in this moment her attention was all focused on him, smiling, amber eyes shining as he rose to greet her. She didn't stop until she was wrapped in his arms, planting a tender little kiss on his lips.

"Hey, sweetheart."

"Hey, Bigshot."

~ ~ ~

Holly rested her head back against Pete's shoulder. They'd had a fabulous dinner, a wonderful evening. Now they were sitting out looking up at the stars on one of the pool loungers, his arms around her waist, her back to his chest. She breathed a big sigh and felt his arms tighten.

"Penny for them?"

She smiled. "Just breathing in the moment."

He kissed her neck. "It's a good moment to breathe in."

She pushed away the sad thoughts that threatened to flood her mind; couldn't let herself think about how few moments they had left.

"Have you thought any more about the plaza?"

Had she ever. She'd been in constant battle with herself. "I have."

"And?"

"And I still don't know, Pete. There's so much to consider."

"It'd be a good move for you."

He was right, as always. In many respects it would be. She'd love the chance to work on it. The money wouldn't hurt either. It could be the beginning of a whole new career.

"What's stopping you?"

That was the problem. *He* was! How could she work with him, even just work for him and not *be* with him?"

"You know what's stopping me."

He was quiet a long time then. "I told you, I can take myself out of it. You can work with Ben and Jack."

"Maybe so, but I'd still be hoping to bump into you all the time."

Again, a long silence. "I'd be hoping to bump into you, too. Might even have to engineer the occasional 'chance' meeting."

Her heart leapt, then sank again just as quickly. "Yes, but that's all it would be, isn't it?"

He pulled her closer, but said nothing for a long time. "It's not all I want, but it's all I can offer."

She nodded sadly. "And that's why I'll probably end up saying no." She felt the tears prick behind her eyes, glad he couldn't see her face.

"I won't see you at all, will I?" he asked.

She shook her head, unable to speak.

"What if I promise not to engineer anything? I don't want to screw up what could be a great opportunity for you. Could you do it then?"

She shrugged, still not wanting to risk trying to speak around the lump in her throat. She would love to take the project, but she knew if she did, it would be in large part just a way to keep a connection with him. She desperately wanted to leave a door open, some chink of hope. She knew deep down, though, that what she really needed to do for her own sanity was to cut all ties.

"Please do it?" His voice was low and husky.

She didn't answer.

"Think about it, sweetheart."

Pete sat at his desk, drumming his fingers. He'd taken care of everything he needed to do before leaving for the wedding. In a couple of hours he was supposed to pick Holly up from the store and head out to the airport. Smoke was going to have a busy night; he'd be taking them and Nate up to the Lake, collecting Dan and Laura on the way. Emma wanted them all to get there as early as possible. Tomorrow would be a crazy day getting Gramps' place set up before the rehearsal dinner tomorrow night.

He'd been toying with an idea for the last hour. He didn't want to go tonight. He pressed the number one on his phone: Jack's speed dial.

"Yo, bro!"

"S'up, Partner?"

"Doing great. It's all coming together. What time you going to be here?"

"I'm not."

"Huh?"

"I was going to feed you some crap about not being able to get away tonight."

"Ooookay?"

Pete drummed his fingers on his desk, trying to figure out what to say.

"Fuck the plan, Pete!"

Pete stared at the phone in surprise.

"Bro, I do know you better than anyone. You don't want to come up here tonight because you want one more night alone with Holly. True or false?"

Pete let out a short sigh. "True."

"So do it! Come up in the morning. But man, you're a fool. If she's got you this bad, you need to say fuck the plan and start working on a new one. One that includes her."

"It's not that simple."

"It could be."

"Jack!"

"What?"

"It's how I live my life."

"Well, change it! Adapt, overcome, survive."

"You don't get it, bro."

"Too damned right, I don't, Pete. Maybe we're just different. I've never known much love in my life. When I found it with Em, nothing, and I mean *nothing*, was going to get in my way."

Pete sighed. Jack had gone through more than most men would stand for to win Emma's trust.

"Maybe it's different for you. You had a different childhood, always felt loved, so you're not hanging onto this the way I have. But Pete, if you let love walk away, you'll always regret it. Life doesn't always give you second chances, you know."

"Who said anything about love?"

Jack laughed. "You and Holly, every time you look at each other!"

Pete pondered that a moment.

"Listen. I've got to go. Get your ass up here when you can, okay?"

"Okay."

"And, Pete?"

"Yeah?"

"You know I'm right."

~ ~ ~

Holly shut down her computer and stared at the black screen. The next time she fired it up it'd all be over. When she came back to the store on Tuesday, she'd no longer be with Pete. There'd be no more lunch deliveries. No more flowers. No nights at his place, by his pool, in his den, in his bed, in his arms. No more quirky smile, no more demanding blue gaze. No more Pete. She blinked, refusing to let the tears come. She'd save them for Monday. Over the last few weeks she'd relaxed into allowing Roberto and the girls run the place. They didn't need her. She was more willing to accept that now.

She'd be gone for a long weekend. To Roberto's surprise she'd told him she was taking Monday off, too. She would allow herself that one day to stay home. On Monday she would let the tears come. For one day she'd indulge in all the sadness she felt, grieve for everything that would never be. On Tuesday she'd be back in here. She'd make a start on her life post-Pete.

She was still considering taking the Four Mile project. Trying to convince herself that it was about her career. Not about him. If anything, he had given her a gift. His 'Work like you don't need the money' motto had given her a fresh perspective. She was ready to think bigger, to stop clinging so tightly to the small and easily controlled business that she'd built. She could see now that once she stopped focusing on the desperate need for money, she could expand her horizons and, as he so rightly said, make more of it in the process.

She was starting to think that maybe she could take the project. If it meant she'd see him sometimes.... Well, she'd rather have that than nothing at all. Wouldn't she? She shook her head, still undecided. How could she ever move on, forget him, as she knew she must, if she was still living for the chance of seeing him again? She didn't have to decide right now. For now she was going to get back out into the store. Later she'd go with him. Enjoy the wedding. Make the most of the little time they had left.

As she came out of the office, she was surprised to see Laura, whom she'd thought was still in San Francisco, looking at the purses by the window. Laura had her back turned, but her friend, a tall woman with short blonde hair and bright red lipstick spotted Holly and nudged her. Holly grinned and started toward them. The woman turned and Holly realized it wasn't Laura at all. From behind, the long dark hair and tall slender figure had looked the same, but face to face, this woman had much sharper features and, like her friend, was wearing bright red lipstick and a little too much make up.

The red lipstick curved up in a condescending smile. "You must be Holly?"

Holly smiled and nodded extending her hand.

"So nice to finally meet you." Cool fingers wrapped around her own in a limp handshake. "I'm Mia Sylvester and this is Jade Evans."

The blonde woman smiled and offered the same lifeless handshake. So, these were the consultants. The tall brunette who stalked Jack, and Jade, the one Pete dated. Holly swallowed at the thought. They were both beautiful, no denying it.

"Welcome to Hayes," she wasn't about to lie that it was nice to meet them.

"I love your store." Jade's smile didn't convey the same warmth as her words.

Holly looked at the woman who had no doubt shared Pete's bed. Her blood ran cold at the thought. "Thank you."

"I hear you're going to be helping the boys with their little project at Summer Lake?" Mia raised a perfectly arched eyebrow.

*Wow! The boys? Little project?* And how had she heard anyway? "Nothing's been finalized yet." She really didn't want to talk about it with these two.

Jade put a hand on her arm. "If you like, you could partner with us. If it's all a bit daunting for you? I know you've never done anything like this before."

Holly couldn't think of anything she'd like less.

"We work with the boys all the time," said Mia airily. "We could clue you in on what they like, show you the ropes."

"That's very kind of you." Kind wasn't the first word that came to mind. Holly's heart raced. She hated thinking that these two might know what Pete liked better than she did. In any sense. "As I said though, nothing has been finalized yet."

"Of course," said Mia. There went that condescending smile again. "Take my card and let us know." Holly automatically took the business card.

Jade smiled, a smile that made Holly want to throw a glass of water in her face. "You can always get in touch with me through Pete. I work closely with him."

*Wow again!* Message received, loud and clear. Holly smiled, not trusting herself to reply to that.

Roberto appeared at her side. "So sorry to interrupt. Could I borrow you for a moment?" He turned to Mia and Jade, "Do forgive me ladies." He took Holly by the arm and steered her to the back of the store, leaving the two women staring after them.

"Thanks, sweetie."

"I know an ambush when I see one, Holls! Who the hell are they?"

Holly realized she was shaking as she watched them leave. "Ugh! They were a reminder that I need to forget the Four Mile Creek job!"

Roberto frowned. "What have they got to do with it? It'd be a great opportunity for you."

Holly shook her head. "No, Berto. It would be more than I could handle. Those two just served as a perfect reminder of that." What had she been thinking? She wasn't going to be with Pete after this weekend, but he wasn't going to become a monk. He'd never claimed he didn't date. He just didn't get involved in anything serious. She knew now she couldn't take the job. Couldn't risk seeing, or even hearing about how 'closely' he and Jade were 'working.' No. She needed to cut all ties. Just seeing that woman, thinking about her with Pete, had been like a dagger to the heart. She needed to follow Pete's example and stick to her original plan; enjoy it while it lasted then firmly close the door on it. Forever.

~ ~ ~

As she made her last minute checks, she sensed *him* enter the store. It was as if her body was so in tune with him that she picked up on whatever vibration it was he put out. She still couldn't see him, but she knew without a doubt that he was here. Then she spotted him, talking with Roberto. She smiled at the unlikely friendship the two of them had struck up. They were deep in what looked like a serious conversation. Roberto gesticulating as he made a point, Pete's brows drawn together, frowning as he listened. Again she was struck by how imposing he was. The stark contrast between the laughing, tickling Pete and the man who stood in her store. Rigid stance, suit she could see was Italian, hand tailored. She'd guess from the cut she knew who'd made it—and how much it cost! The crisp white shirt and bright blue tie set off his eyes perfectly. They were blazing. What on Earth were those two talking about?

As she reached them, Pete gave Berto a meaningful look then turned to her with a smile, his handsome features transformed. Holly's heart swelled with love. *Wait! What? Love?* This was a really bad time to start thinking along those lines! She let herself sag against him for a moment as he wrapped her in his bear hug.

"Hey Bigshot" She smiled up at him, wishing it was all so different.

"Hey, sweetheart." The eyes that smiled down at her held such tenderness.

This was so unfair. She wanted to scream and shout and demand a recount. At the same time, she was a realist. "I'll just get my bag from the back."

~ ~ ~

"Are we going straight to the airport?" she asked once they were in his truck.

"No. I need to go home."

That surprised her. "*You* forgot something, Bigshot?"

His eyes were serious as he looked across at her. "More like there's something I don't want to forget."

What was that supposed to mean? "Okay. Are we going to make it to the airport in time or are you just going to stop the universe to suit you again?" She tried to keep up their familiar banter, to stay away from anything serious, afraid to lose it. But Pete wasn't playing, his face was serious, agitated maybe?

"We're not going to the airport."

"We're not? But I thought Em wants us there as early as we can."

"She does."

Holly looked at him. This wasn't making any sense. She could see that little pulse working in his jaw as he drove.

His voice was low when he spoke. He kept his eyes fixed on the road. "Em does want everyone there tonight, but I told Jack we'd be up in the morning." He reached over and took her hand, holding it on top of his thigh. "I can't go tonight, sweetheart. I want to stay here. With you." He squeezed her hand. "I'm sorry. I should have asked, I know."

Holly's throat closed up. For a moment she couldn't speak. He probably should have asked, but she didn't care. She had wished they were staying here tonight, too. She wasn't ready to say goodbye to what they'd shared this week. Then again, she never would be.

"I want to stay here with you, too, Pete." She managed to stop herself before she added, 'forever.'

# Chapter Seventeen

Pete pulled up in front of the house and jumped down from the truck. They hadn't talked much on the way back to his place. Just held hands. He didn't know what to say. He simply wanted to be with her. One more night. He opened the front door and let her enter ahead of him, glad they were home. Home. He'd loved this place since he'd bought it. He'd loved it even more these last few weeks. Now it did feel like home. Holly made it that way. Her purse on the counter, her few things in the bathroom. What would it feel like when she was gone? He didn't want to think about it. Tonight she was still here. She was quiet, subdued, but she was here. He followed her through the den and wrapped his arms around her, wanting, needing, to feel her close. She smiled up at him, but her eyes held a deep sadness. He closed his eyes and rested his head on top of hers. He hated knowing that he'd caused that sadness. Hated that he felt it too and there was nothing he could do about it.

He heard Jack's voice, *'Fuck the plan, Pete!'* He'd considered it, long and hard. He couldn't do it though. His whole life had been shaped by discipline, by determination, by damned hard work. By following the plan. He held her tight, his heart echoing Jack's words, his head trying desperately to cling to reason. The doorbell made her jump.

"I'll be back." He returned with bags full of takeout cartons. "I ordered us dinner from Mario's. That pasta you loved so much."

She smiled. "Thank you." She looked like she had so much more she wanted to say, but she busied herself with plates while he opened a bottle of wine. He carried everything through to the dining room.

She raised an eyebrow when he held out her chair. "Formal dining this evening, Mr. Bigshot?" Even the banter was tinged with sadness. It hurt his heart.

"We never got to eat in here." Damn, why had he said that? She lowered her eyes and said nothing. He'd wanted one last night together, one more night of all the fun and laughter they shared. One more memory. But this wasn't working. The end hung over them too clearly, too close.

She smiled now, making an effort. "Thanks for thinking of this, it's wonderful."

He put his fork down. The food *was* wonderful, and persuading the Chef at Mario's to allow his food to be placed in cartons and delivered beyond the walls of his restaurant had taken some doing. Pete couldn't taste it though. He reached across the table and took her hand. "I'm sorry, sweetheart."

She shook her head, forcing a smile. "Let's not go there, Pete. Please? We wanted one more night together, let's not waste it?" She squeezed his hand. "Tell me something fun?"

He nodded. It made sense. They both understood, already knew the truth of any words that could be spoken. He took a deep breath and launched into a funny story about a conference he'd attended a couple of months back. Soon she was laughing. They were back to their usual banter, the plates were empty, glasses refilled. The sadness lingered in her eyes though, and in his chest.

Pete stood and turned the music on. He offered her his hand. "Dance with me?"

She stood and stepped into his arms, "I suppose we should make sure we're up to scratch for our official duties."

It took him a moment to realize she was talking about the wedding. He just wanted to dance with her, hold her close and move to the music. He smiled. "I was thinking more along the lines of one of your CEO fantasies."

She met his gaze as he crushed her to his chest, "Surely there's one about dancing with the CEO?" He ran his hand down her back. "One where you dance with him before he makes love to you on the dining room table?"

"There is now."

Holly was struggling to hold back the tears. She was lying in his arms, in his bed, in his house, in his life. For the last time.

"Talk to me, sweetheart?"

She shook her head. He held her closer. She loved being surrounded by, enveloped in the warmth, the power, the presence that was Pete. She didn't want to step back out into the cold little world that was her life without him.

"Say you'll take the plaza project?"

Here it came. She'd hoped he wouldn't want to talk about that tonight. But she'd known he would. And she knew she couldn't do it. Not after seeing that Jade woman today. The thought of Pete with her....

"No."

She felt him tense. "No?"

"I can't do it, Pete. I have to make it a clean break." She turned over so they were lying face to face, naked bodies pressed together. His eyes were that deep violet color. She kissed his lips and melted against him as he held her tight.

"Isn't something better than nothing at all?"

"Not for me. I realized that today. It would be torture, Pete."

His brows came down. "What happened today?"

"I just realized I can't do it, that's all." He didn't look convinced, but he didn't need to know about her encounter with Jade and Mia, ugh! And their, *'We know what the boys like.'* She shuddered.

"Tell me what happened."

Damn, his eyes were boring into her, demanding the answer. How did he do that? "I saw something that made me understand just how hard it would be to be around you and not be with you. And I'm not prepared to do it, Pete. It would hurt me too much."

"What did you see?"

She took a deep breath, he obviously wasn't going to give up. "Jade."

His face clouded, eyes hard now. "I don't want Jade."

Holly shrugged.

He looked angry. "You've got to know I don't want her. I want you!"

Holly couldn't bite back the bitter little laugh. "Yeah and in your world, according to your plan, that means you can keep seeing her right? But not me."

"Sweetheart, I can't just see you."

"No, but you can see her!"

"I haven't seen her in months! What did she say?"

"Oh, Pete, it really doesn't matter. Let's not do this, Let's not spoil what we have left."

His eyes softened and his lips brushed hers, his mouth soft as he kissed her slow and sweet. He lifted his head. "I want you, Holly. That's why I can't do that with you. It's not enough. I can't offer you what we both want."

"I know, Pete. It wouldn't be enough for me either. So when we say goodbye, it'll be goodbye."

He rolled her onto her back and positioned himself between her legs, his eyes intense as he slid inside her, filling her. She brought her arms up around his neck as her body surrendered to him. His mouth came down on hers as they moved together. Tears filled her eyes even as the tension built inside her. He filled every part of her body and soul as he drove into her over and over again until he carried them both over the edge, bodies melding together as he found his release.

She wondered if she'd ever walk on the beach again without thinking of Pete. They'd woken early and made love again. One last time. They'd brought coffee mugs down to walk the beach as the sun came up. In a white T-shirt and denim shorts, he was as handsome as she'd ever seen him, chiseled features softened by a wistful look, tan skin glowing in the early morning light.

He'd stopped and turned to her. Reaching into his pocket, he smiled. "I got you something."

She raised an eyebrow.

"Promise me you'll wear it?"

"Perhaps I should see it before I make any promises?" she teased, but she knew whatever it was she would treasure it always.

He held out a flat, black velvet box. As she reached for it he snatched it away, laughing. "You have to promise."

She laughed with him. "Okay, I promise."

He put an arm around her shoulders and gave her the box. As she opened it, she swallowed hard. She could not cry. Would not cry. He was watching her closely. It was a bracelet, a much more delicate version of the one he wore himself. She knew what was engraved on it before she looked: 'Work.' She blinked away the tears as she looked up at him.

"Like you don't need the money, sweetheart."

She didn't dare try to speak around the lump in her throat while he fastened it onto her wrist.

"It's time for you to spread your wings, Holly. I just wish I could be around to see it. I hope that wearing this will help you, the way mine has helped me. To keep pushing. Keep your eye on the goal. To remember that it's about so much more than money. It's about building your life, not just your business, becoming all you can be." She bit her bottom lip as he wrapped his arms around her. "And I hope, maybe, sometimes, when you look at it you'll think of me, remember this. Remember us."

She felt the sob well up and buried her face in his chest, believing she'd never forget this, forget him. They stood that way for a long time before she trusted herself to look up at him. "I'll always remember you, Pete. Always remember us."

He held her eyes, searching them with his own, then nodded, saying nothing.

# Chapter Eighteen

It had been such a beautiful wedding. Emma looked sensational. She'd glowed as her Gramps walked her down to the little dock where the gorgeous Jack waited for her to say their vows. Pete stood by Jack's side, looking devastating in his tux. Devastated was how Holly felt and, from the way Pete looked at her, he felt the same.

Somehow she'd made it through the day, through her official duties. All that remained was the first dance. She could do this. She could hold it together for a few more hours. She watched as Jack led Emma onto the floor for their first dance as man and wife. She was so happy for her friend, that she'd found her happiness. She blinked back the tears, hey, she was allowed to cry at her best friend's wedding. They were happy tears for Emma, or so she tried to convince herself. She felt Pete behind her the moment before he slid his arms around her waist. When Emma and Jack's song ended, the wedding party would join them on the dance floor.

"You ready for this, sweetheart?" He spoke next to her ear, his warm breath fanning her neck. She'd never be ready for this. She nodded. He took her hand and led her out. Missy and

Dan, and Laura and Ben joined them. Four beautiful couples moving around the floor.

Pete held her close. She didn't dare meet his eyes, just rested her head against his shoulder, wishing she could melt into him. The song ended and she let go of him, still not brave enough to look up at him. All the bridesmaids and groomsmen were to trade partners at this point, opening the dancing for everyone. His hand lingered for a moment on the small of her back as she turned toward Dan. When she felt the warmth of his fingertips finally slip away, she felt as though all the warmth and light from her world went with them.

Dan stepped in as the song began. He led her beautifully. She looked up at him, surprised.

"You'll be okay, Holly." He was smiling at her reassuringly. She bit her lip, unable to reply. "What you and Pete have doesn't come along too often. And you know, with us guys, the smarter we are, the longer it can take us to see the obvious."

Holly gazed up at him. She hadn't expected anything like this from Dan. "Thanks, sweetie, but we're over."

Dan smiled as he led her around the floor. "You two are far from over. Just look at that face." He nodded his chin towards Pete, who held Missy stiffly as their paths crossed. He moved beautifully, but his face was set, his eyes fixed on Holly as they glided by.

~ ~ ~

Missy dug Pete in the ribs. "At least try to smile. You'll frighten everyone off the dance floor looking like that, not entice them onto it."

Pete dragged his eyes away from Holly and smiled at Missy. "How's that?"

She laughed. "We don't need the megawatt toothpaste commercial variety. Just try to look like you're enjoying yourself. It is Emma and Jack's big day."

"Sorry."

"So you should be, you're being a complete idiot, you know."

He could always rely on Missy. "Thanks, old friend. I thought I was doing a good job today."

"Well of course you are. You've been the perfect Best Man. No one would know, if they didn't know. But to those of us that do, it's obvious that you are being a great big idiot!"

He frowned down at her. "How so? What do you mean?"

"Don't give me that shit! I mean Holly, and you know it. If you let that woman get away, you're a fool."

He blew out his cheeks as the song came to an end, ready to get off the dance floor and go and get himself a drink. Missy tightened her grip on him. Despite how tiny and delicate she looked, she had some strength.

"Don't try to walk away from me, mister, just 'cause you don't want to hear it. You need to hear it!"

Pete gave in and led her into the next dance. "Don't give me a hard time, Miss. I'm doing well enough at that by myself. Aren't old friends supposed to help you through the tough times?" For a moment he let her see all the pain he was feeling.

Instead of easing up on him though, giving him the support he'd hoped for, she frowned at him. "I am trying to help you, stupid. It's only a tough time 'cause you're making it one."

"Dammit, Miss! It's not in the plan. I like her too much."

"You and your goddamned plan. Get over it, Pete."

"I can't, Miss!" Dammit, he didn't need this! He let go of her and stalked off the now crowded dance floor. He needed that drink.

~ ~ ~

Holly picked her way through the guests. Everyone seemed to be having a great time. If she kept moving, she could get away with a quick smile and hello here and there and not have to stop to talk to anyone for too long.

A beautiful, older woman sitting alone at one of the long tables smiled and beckoned to her. Holly made her way over and sat down beside her.

"You've done a wonderful job, dear."

Holly liked the woman immediately. She was incredibly elegant, yet laid back at the same time. "Thank you, I've had a lot of practice," she smiled back.

"Your time will come, and in the not too distant future, I'm thinking."

Holly shook her head. "Not for me. I have officially given up. You know what they say about always the bridesmaid? Well, after this weekend, I have to face the fact that I will never be the bride. Wouldn't even want to be."

The lady's face fell. "Oh, don't say that dear, that would make me very sad. I'm looking forward to getting to know you." She covered Holly's hand with her own. "Say you'll have lunch with us tomorrow?"

What a sweet lady! It seemed everyone up here was so friendly. "I'm sorry. I have to leave in the morning." She liked this woman, wished she'd be spending more time in Summer Lake and could get to know her.

"Then you must come back to see us soon. My husband will adore you."

Holly smiled sadly. "It's been lovely to meet you, but I don't think I'll be back here anytime soon."

The woman looked stunned. "But...."

"Mom?"

Holly looked over her shoulder to see Pete standing with an older man. If she wanted to know what Pete would look like in forty years, she need only to look to his left. His father was still a handsome man. Slowly her brain clicked. The woman she was talking to was the person he was calling Mom?

"Pete, dear. I was just getting to know Holly. You must bring her out to see us. We're going to be great friends." She patted Holly's hand.

Panic was starting to unfurl in Holly's chest as Pete looked between her and his mom. "I...I have to...." She scrambled to her feet and backed away. "It was lovely to meet you, Mrs., err.... Sorry." She turned and fled.

Pete stared at his Mom, who raised an elegant eyebrow. "Have you upset her, dear? She said she's leaving in the morning, but I thought you were coming for lunch?"

Pete could hear roaring in his ears. He wanted to go after Holly. She'd looked so hurt and confused. But he couldn't, his mom had taken hold of his hand. "I think you'd better sit down and tell me about it, Peter."

*Oh, shit!* Not what he needed to be doing right now.

"Peter, are you making a mess of things with that lovely girl?"

He sat down heavily in the chair next to his mom. Why had she said she was leaving in the morning? He'd arranged for Smoke to take them on the last trip back to LA in the evening.

"What's going on, son?" His dad was looking at him now, too. For God's sake, much as he loved them, he did not need a parental inquisition at this point. He looked at them both. "We dated for a while. We're done. Nothing more to it, okay?"

He couldn't believe it when his dad burst out laughing. "No way is *that* done, son. There's a lot more to it, even if you won't admit it yet." He turned to his wife. "Leave it, Anne. The boy's not seeing straight."

His mother patted his hand with an indulgent smile. "Off you go then, dear. Lunch at one tomorrow, if we don't catch you later."

Pete stood without a word. He scanned the guests, but couldn't see Holly anywhere. Screw it. He headed to the bar they'd set up down by the water's edge. Now he really needed that drink. He knocked back a whiskey, then took a long swig of cold beer. What the hell had his mom been playing at? He guessed that Holly had no idea who she was until he'd appeared. He couldn't forget the hurt he'd seen in her eyes. He took another drink of his beer as he swept his eyes over the party, searching for her. She wasn't on the dance floor. Where was she?

"Been a great day, huh Pete?" He turned to see Albert. The old guy had driven up from the city and brought some of the women from Phoenix who didn't want to fly.

Pete called for another whiskey and one for Albert. "Yeah, a great day." It really had been. He was happy for Jack and Emma. It was their day, after all, and he really was thrilled for them. He just wished he could focus on that and not on the heaviness in his chest or the hurt in Holly's eyes.

"If you had any sense, you'd be planning your own big day."

Pete's head snapped around to look at Albert. "What are you talking about?"

Albert didn't flinch. "I told you first time I met her, kid, she's a keeper."

Pete let out a deep sigh. "Yeah, but I can't keep her."

"Course you can. The girl is in love with you. For a smart ass, you can be pretty dumb sometimes."

Pete's heart was racing in his chest. Love? That's what Jack had said too.

Albert was going through his wallet. "Been meaning to give you a copy of these." He pulled out a photo. It was Holly. It must have been last weekend; she was wearing the slinky little black dress, standing outside his front door. She was unaware of the camera and had that faraway look in her eyes. "I don't know what you did to upset her, but she's riding home with me, Lexi, and the girls in the morning. I thought this might be a good time to give you these so you can ponder on however it is you've screwed up." He pulled out another photo. It was the same as the first, except in this one she was laughing, eyes shining, happy. Pete stared at it.

"Want to know what happened to make the difference between the first one and this?" asked Albert.

Pete waited, knowing he was going to find out, no matter what he said.

"Just the mention of your name. Don't be a fool, Pete. You're crazy if you let that one go." He emptied his glass and patted Pete's shoulder as he walked away.

Pete didn't know what to think. He stared at the two photos. The first one tugged at his heart. That faraway look, the one that made him feel so sad. Albert said she was in love with him? She couldn't be. She was cutting him out of her life. She was the one who wouldn't keep seeing him. He shook his head, only because there was no chance of a future in it. But he'd made it clear from the beginning he couldn't offer her that. He couldn't even think about what it might mean if she did love him. His heart was still pounding in his chest. Did he love her? Was that why all this was so goddamned difficult? Oh, who knew! Stick to the plan, that's what he had to do. He caught sight of Ben and raised his hand. Now there was a man who wouldn't give him any grief. He strode over to his old friend.

"What's happening, big guy?"

"Just trying to escape the old timers and their meddling. You know how they get at weddings."

Ben laughed. "Sure do, they've been trying to palm that little red haired chick off on me. Nice girl, but not my type. At least you've got Holly to keep 'em off your back. I'm guessing it won't be long until you go over to the dark side and get married yourself. Can't blame you for Holly though. She's quite something. When's she starting on the plaza?"

Not Ben too! "Listen, bud, can we not go there? There is no me and Holly. She's not going to do the plaza. Can we talk about something else?"

Ben rolled his eyes. "I didn't think there'd be any drama with you two. It was bad enough seeing the ride Jack had with Em."

"There is no drama. It's just how it is. We saw each other for a while. Now it's over. It happens, what's the big deal?"

Ben smirked. "Sure, Pete. Whatever you say."

"What the fuck is that supposed to mean?"

Ben laughed. "It means you've got some catching up to do. Get with the program."

Pete was about ready to explode. "There is no program. What I have is a plan. Remember? A plan that doesn't include a woman, yet. Not even Holly."

Ben just laughed again. "Work yourself up all you like, but even I can see that the two of you are in love with each other. You apparently still have some shit to deal with and can't see it yet. But you will. I just don't want to go through all that drama again before we reach the inevitable conclusion. I mean, I could understand it with Em. She was scared out of her wits, and hey, she's female. But you? I didn't expect you to be so clueless. Analyze the situation logically, like you would any other. You'll see I'm right."

Pete said nothing. Was he really missing something obvious, something that everyone else could see? And if so, why?

"Anyway," said Ben, checking his watch, "You still have Best Man duties to take care of. It's almost nine and Jack wanted to be out of here on time."

"Yeah, thanks bud." Pete left his friend and walked down to the edge of the stage where he waited for the band to finish their song. He shook hands with the lead singer, Chase, as he took the microphone from him.

"Ladies and gentlemen, we need to interrupt proceedings to send our bride and groom on their way."

Everyone gathered around Emma and Jack for one last toast. Pete watched as all the women crowded around Emma. He finally spotted Holly as she rounded up all the single ladies, ready for Emma to toss the bouquet. The look on her face slayed him, she looked so sad. She neatly dodged out of the crowd of giggling women before the bouquet flew through the air. Then she was hugging Em and Jack, wishing them well. Damn, he'd better get down there himself, say goodbye before they headed off. He worked his way through the crowd.

Emma hugged him. "We'll see you in a couple of weeks."

"Yeah, have a great time, Mouse."

Jack slapped his back. "Thanks, Pete. For everything."

"No problem, partner. You take it easy."

Jack pulled him into a man hug. "Don't worry about me. You get your head straightened out. Fuck the plan! And call me if you hit any snags, okay?"

"I'm not going to call you, asshole. You're going on your honeymoon. Get out of here."

Emma gave him another quick hug. "Then I'll have him call you. And watch who you're calling an asshole. That's my husband!" She laughed.

As Pete stepped back, more well-wishers crowded around to see them off. Jack caught his eye above the sea of people. "Fuck the plan," he mouthed, then winked as he ducked into the car.

Pete smiled to himself. He could always trust his partner to tell him what he thought. He looked around, searching for Holly again. He needed to talk to her, to hold her. He was starting to think that maybe he was missing something. Everyone was telling him he couldn't let her walk away, his heart certainly seemed to agree. He needed to find her.

He spotted the bridesmaids dress, the rich purple color, and his heart leapt, but no, as she appeared from behind the other guests it was Laura, not Holly. He surveyed the crowds. There! Down by the water. No. Right dress, wrong girl again. He'd bet Miss knew where she was though. He made his way down to the dock where Missy was talking with Dan.

"Hey guys. Have you seen Holly?"

Missy looked at him. "Have you come to your senses?"

He glowered at her, tired of everyone giving him a hard time. He wasn't used to feeling so clueless. "Do you know where she is?"

"No, but she asked me to give you this." She held out a little envelope that looked like it had been lifted from the front desk of the Lodge.

Pete took it and tore it open to read the note inside.

> *Pete*
> *I don't want to say goodbye to you, so I'm not going to.*
> *I hope your plan works out well for you.*
> *I wish you happiness always.*
> *Love*
> *Holly*
> *x*

He heard the roaring in his ears again, felt the pounding in his chest as looked around wildly. "Where is she?"

Missy put a hand on his arm. "She's gone, Pete."

~ ~ ~

Holly settled in the back of the taxi and let out a deep sigh. This was going to be a long ride and it was going to cost her a fortune, but it was a small price to pay. She couldn't say goodbye to Pete. His mom had been such a sweet lady, but when Holly had realized who she was, it had just been one hurt too many. His mom had wanted them to get to know each other. Holly would have loved to, but it was all over. She couldn't stick around for even more insight into a life that would never be hers. She didn't belong with Pete, with his parents in their beautiful home, or even at Summer Lake at all. Once she finally faced that fact, she had to get out. She couldn't torture herself by lingering, hoping for one more touch, one more kiss, one more moment with him.

She'd asked Albert earlier if she could ride back to LA with him. After seeing Pete's parents though, she couldn't stick around even until morning. She'd called the cab company that operated out of the resort and surprised them with a last minute booking for a one way ride all the way back to LA. Tonight.

Her phone buzzed in her pocket. A text from Pete.

*Where are you? We need to talk.*

As she read it, the tears came. There was no point in talking. It was over. Time to face it. She texted Missy.

*Pls let him know I'm OK.*

She didn't want him to worry, but she wasn't going to answer him. She thought for a moment, then texted Albert too.

*I left already. Thanks for the offer though.*

There. That was everything she needed to take care of.

"You okay, lady?" The driver looked at her in the rear view mirror.

"I will be. Thank you." She'd have to be.

# Chapter Nineteen

Pete shook Smoke's hand before he exited the plane. "Thanks, man. It's been a crazy weekend for you."

"No worries," Smoke smiled back to where Laura was still sitting in the cabin. "I enjoy it."

"Yeah, well. You should have a quiet couple of weeks now." He hadn't missed the exchange with Laura. "I won't need Papa Charlie for the next few days at least. You don't need to bring it back tonight, stay up there and catch your breath for a day or two if you want." Smoke had been flying wedding guests in and out of Summer Lake all weekend. He'd taken two trips back to LA and one to San Francisco already today. Pete and Nate were the stragglers getting back to LA, and Laura still had to get back to San Francisco. Pete had no problem if Smoke wanted to stay up there.

Smoke grinned. "I might just do that. Thanks Pete."

Pete walked back to the FBO building. Nate caught up with him at the door.

"You doing alright, boss man?"

Pete looked at him, he couldn't remember ever feeling this far from alright. "I'm beat," he said.

Nate nodded, "Some weekend, huh? Want to get a beer?"

Pete thought about it. He wasn't looking forward to going back to the house, he couldn't even think of it as home without Holly there. She hadn't answered any of his texts or calls. All he was going to do was wander around the place thinking about her. "Why not? Come on, I'll give you a ride."

They sat at the bar in a little place by the beach.

"Want to talk about it?" asked Nate.

Pete shook his head and took a long swig of his beer. There was nothing to say.

"You're not serious about ending it with her, are you?"

Pete snorted. "It's not up to me anymore. She left. Won't talk to me." He stared at Nate, trying to pull himself together, "And besides, I don't know what I was playing at. I don't have time for a woman in my life."

Nate laughed at him. Why did people keep doing that? He wasn't used to it! "You don't have time? And why's that, Pete?"

"You know damned well why!" Pete slammed his fist down on the bar.

Nate still smiled, unperturbed. He pointed his bottle at the chain on Pete's wrist. "'Cause of that, right?"

Pete looked at the silver bracelet and sighed. "Yeah, that's right. Work."

"But what does the other side say, boss man? What have you always preached to the rest of us mere mortals?"

Pete frowned. He didn't get where Nate was going with this. "Like you don't need the money?" he asked, confused.

Nate laughed again. "Yeah, you big old hypocrite! What have you always said? It's about so much more than money? It's about becoming all you can be? Building the best life you can, no?"

"What the fuck, Nate? That's what I do, it's what I am doing. What are you talking about?"

"I'm saying you are refusing to become all you could be and refusing to build the best life you could. When I first saw you with Holly, I couldn't believe it. I mean, not only did you have a woman with you at HQ, you had your arm around her no less! But watching the two of you together these last few weeks, I got it. You become something more when you're with her. The two of you could build a great life together, but you won't consider it because your only focus is on building a great business. Well, newsflash big guy, it's already built. It doesn't need you like it did in the early days. You've got a great staff, even if I do say so myself." He grinned. "We're capable of taking up any slack while you get a life, you know."

Pete looked at him, brows lowered, and unclenched his fist as he considered Nate's words.

"Don't give me the evil eye. I'm your friend as well as your employee, and since Jack isn't around to kick your ass for you, I see it as my duty."

Pete didn't know what to say. Was he really doing what Nate said? What he'd accused Holly of doing? Using the business as an excuse not to grow in a new direction? No! He was following his plan, like he'd always done. He looked at Nate.

"Take some time, think about it. Just don't take too long. I don't think a woman like Holly will be too short on offers if you don't get your act together."

~ ~ ~

Pete let himself into the house and stood in the hallway. His mind was still reeling from what Nate had said. That last part especially. She'd have other offers. Of course she would. But she couldn't. She was his! He was starting to understand how she'd felt about Jade. Just the thought that she might meet some faceless other guy made him want to throw something. How would he feel if he knew who she used to date and that she was seeing him again?

He unclenched his fist and walked into the den. Damn, how was he going to sit on that sofa without her feet in his lap? He slid open the doors and went out by the pool for some fresh air. So many memories out here too. Her first night here, falling into the pool together, making love, eating dinner as the sun set, indulging her CEO fantasies on the lounger, holding her close as they watched the stars.

He went back into the kitchen to get a beer from the fridge and leaned on the counter. One of her hair clips sat there. He closed his eyes as he remembered unfastening it so he could run his fingers through her hair as he kissed her. The way her eyes had glimmered up at him as her hair fell around her shoulders. The feel of her soft body as he'd held her to him. She was everywhere.

~ ~ ~

"Berto, no. Thanks for asking, sweetie, but I really don't want to."

"But, Holls, I don't want you staying home moping all weekend." He was getting that truculent look that she knew spelled trouble. Going toe to toe with Roberto was not a wise move, certainly not in her current fragile state. She decided to throw herself on his mercy.

"Please let me mope? I promise I'll let you help when I'm ready, but please, let me mourn for a while? It's what I need."

He came and hugged her. "Are you sure? You know you can spend the weekend with me and John. You don't have to be all alone."

"I know, but for now I need to be. You understand. Let me lick my wounds for a while?"

He gave a reluctant nod. "Alright, but I'm going to call you every evening."

"You don't need to do that."

"Perhaps not, but I want to. I just hate the way this is working out."

Holly was relieved he wasn't saying he hated Pete. Roberto could be quite aggressive in his dislike of those he thought had hurt his friends. "It turned out the way I knew it would, Berto. He was honest from the start."

"I know, but I thought he would come to his senses. I'm disappointed in him, Holls."

"Oh, Berto, don't be. He's a good man." She felt her throat close up. It had been almost a week, but she still felt as raw as she had when she left Summer Lake on Saturday night. She just needed time. The weekend loomed ahead, filled with nothing but time. "I'm going to get out of here, if you'll close up?"

Berto nodded. "At least we can thank him for that. He taught you that this place can survive without you."

She nodded as she grabbed her coat. "Have a good weekend, sweetie. I'll see you Monday."

"I'll call you later."

Holly took the bus home. Her old station wagon had been making some very strange noises. She needed to get it looked at, but she needed to make a bigger payment than usual this week on her grandmother's debt. She hated the fact that the loan sharks could ask for whatever they wanted, whenever they wanted and she had no choice. She'd gotten angry with their threats a couple of weeks ago, but they'd promised to pay the store a visit if she didn't shut up and pay up. Stupid men! The store was her source of income, how did they expect her to pay them anything if they smashed it up? She had to just bite her tongue and keep paying, there was no end in sight. She sat on the bus and looked around at her fellow passengers, a very different crew than the people she'd been spending her time with for the last few weeks. But still, she'd known all along that that was a short-lived fantasy life. This was her reality and she had to get on with it.

When she got home, all she wanted to do was soak in a hot bath with a glass of wine. And cry. She'd already cried so much this week. Her plan to deal with it all on Monday hadn't worked. Weren't you supposed to have a good cry and get it all out? It wasn't working that way though. Instead of getting any easier, it seemed the sadness grew heavier with every day that passed.

She sank into the bubbles and sipped her Cab. It wasn't nearly as good as the one from Pete's friend's winery. She sighed. Nothing in her cold little world was as good as anything in Pete's, she had to get used to it. Her cell phone buzzed. She dried her hands to check if it was anyone she wanted to talk to. It was Missy.

"Hey, Miss!"

"Hey, honey. How are you doing? I've been thinking about you all week."

"Aw. Thanks Miss. I'm alright. How are you?"

"Never mind me. I'm fine. How are you holding up? I can't believe Pete is being so stupid."

"Don't, Miss. He's not stupid." Even now she couldn't stand to hear a word against him. "He's just sticking to his plan. He never lied to me. I went in with my eyes wide open."

"Maybe so, but he's still being an idiot. He may be my oldest friend, but he doesn't get to hurt my new one."

"Thanks."

"Anyways, I also wanted to see what you're thinking about next weekend?"

"Not much." Holly could see her weekends stretching out into the future, filled with nothing but bubble baths, sad movies and tissues, lots and lots of tissues.

"Well, are you coming Friday or Saturday?"

Holly frowned. "I'm not coming at all!"

"Oh, yes, you are. Emma and Jack get back late Friday, and Gramps is having a BBQ for them at his place on Saturday afternoon. As the Maid of Honor, you don't have a choice. You have to be here."

"But I can't! I have to stay out of his way."

"You've got just as much right to be here as he has," Missy sounded pissed.

"I know I do. I'm talking about for my own sanity. Em will understand."

"I don't think so, she asked me to make sure you don't wiggle out of it."

"But, Miss…."

"But nothing. You don't have to be around him. You can stay at my house, but you do need to come, okay? At least think about it, honey?"

Holly nodded, "I'll think about it."

"He's a jerk with his stupid plan anyway. Sometimes life throws stuff at you and you need to make a new plan. You need…." Missy stopped abruptly.

"Hello?" Holly wondered if they'd been cut off, "Missy?"

"I'm still here," laughed Missy. "But I've got to go. I just remembered something. Something very important. I'll call you in the week, hon."

"Okay," Holly stared at her phone, trying to understand Missy's abrupt goodbye. Maybe Scot needed something? She couldn't go up there next weekend. She'd have to find an excuse. It'd have to be a good one too. She'd be letting Emma down, but it couldn't be helped. There was no way she was ready to see Pete again. She sighed. She wanted nothing more than to see him again, but she wanted to be *with* him. She couldn't simply be around him, one of the gang, just another friend. No. No way.

~ ~ ~

Missy hung up the phone and looked around her kitchen. She needed to knock some sense into Pete and he himself had given her the ammunition to do so; fifteen years ago. She dialed his number.

"Hey, Miss! S'up?"

"Hey, Hemming. Are you up here this weekend?"

"On my way now. Is everything alright?"

"It will be. I need to see you. What time are you getting in?"

"It'll be around eight."

"Good. You can buy me dinner at Ben's place. I'll be in the bar."

Pete sighed. "I don't suppose there's any point in my saying no? I was going to go crash at my folks place."

"You know there's no point, so hurry up and get your ass up here."

"Okay, but go easy on me, will you? I've had a miserable week." He sounded wrung out.

"Aw, poor baby! You know your poor Pete crap isn't going to wash with me. You're the one who made yourself miserable. I'm the one that's going to fix it. I'll see you at eight."

~ ~ ~

Pete found a spot in the square and parked the truck. He was dog tired. He'd been sleeping at the office all week, he couldn't stand being at the house. The pullout sofa in his office was comfortable enough, but he hadn't had much sleep. He worked his way through the crowded bar looking for Missy. What was she after anyway? If she wanted to give him a hard time, he wasn't going to stick around for it. He spotted her at one of the high top tables talking to Ben.

"Hey guys."

"Hey, bud." Ben looked him over. "You look like crap."

"Thanks. I was hoping to get some sleep, but bossy Melissa here demanded my company tonight." He gave Missy a rueful smile as he leaned in to peck her cheek. "Want to tell me why I've been summoned?"

Missy smiled back at him. "Take a seat, order a beer, we'll get to it. You look like you've had a rough day."

"Rough week." He pulled up a stool while Ben went for their drinks.

"Oh dear. Why was that, then?" she raised her eyebrows.

Pete wasn't in the mood to be messed with, not even by Missy. "Don't Miss. You know damned well why."

Missy's face softened and she touched his arm, "Sorry, hon, but why are you doing this to yourself, and to Holly?"

"Have you talked to her?" he felt his pulse race. He needed to know how she was doing.

"That's none of your business," said Missy. "Now answer the question. Why are you doing this to yourself?"

Pete heaved a frustrated sigh. "You know why. I've got to stick to the plan. Why are you doing this to *me*? That's what I don't get!"

Ben returned with their beers. "I've got to go upstairs for a while." He looked between them and grinned. "Give me a shout if you need a referee?"

Pete nodded. "I might be shouting for you to rescue me. She's got it in for me, bud."

Ben laughed. "Sorry, but you're on your own there. I'm no match for this one when she's pissed and it strikes me she's pissed."

"I am." Missy's smile was one of grim determination. "And leave your phone on, it's me that might be texting you for help to get this big, stubborn...."

Ben grinned. "I'm outta here. Good luck, Pete. I think you're gonna need it." He disappeared into the crowd.

"Can we at least order some food before you lay into me?" Apart from a lack of sleep, Pete hadn't managed to eat much since last weekend. His growling stomach was letting him know that now might be a good time to change that.

Missy smiled. "I took the liberty of ordering for us. We've got two big ole black and bleu burgers on the way. For old time's sake."

He smiled at that. "Wow! That's been a long time."

"Yeah," laughed Missy. "I realized when I ordered them that they must have been on the menu for fifteen years at least."

"That's right. We were way too young to order beer with them when we started that tradition."

"We've had some serious conversations over those burgers, huh Pete?" She was smiling at him.

He knew she was going to spring something on him, he just couldn't figure out what it was. "And you're spoiling for another one tonight, aren't you? So let me have it."

"What I really want to do is remind you about the most important conversation we ever had. And to thank you for it."

Pete smiled, he knew exactly what she meant. "You're welcome."

Missy's eyes sparkled with tears. "It was fifteen years ago, Pete, and I've been grateful to you every single day since."

"He's a great kid."

"He's the best kid in the world. I hate myself whenever I think what I might have done. What I thought was the right thing to do."

"Yeah, but Miss, you didn't do it."

"Only 'cause I talked to you that night." She reached out and took his hand. "Pete, I was seventeen years old and scared out of my wits. I honestly thought I had to have an abortion, even though I didn't want to. My family was going to go ape. I wasn't going to be able to go away to college. I was supposed to be the first in my family to go, you know. I'd had all these plans of how my life was going to be. Then there I was, pregnant with the father having left town before he even knew. You were there for me." She smiled at him through the tears that were running down her cheeks now. She made no attempt to wipe them away. "Do you remember what you told me, when I asked you what would happen to all my plans if I went ahead and had a baby?"

Pete nodded slowly, but she continued anyway.

"You told me sometimes life throws stuff at you and you need to make a new plan. You need to look at what's about to change in your life and ask yourself if you want the old plan

more than you want everything that comes with the new one."
She gripped his hand tight. "When you told me that it all
became so clear. The old plan made sense before I was
pregnant, but once Scotty was part of the equation, everything
that had seemed so important before meant nothing
anymore."

Pete swallowed around the lump in his throat. He loved Scot,
he was such a good kid. And although Missy never had gone
away to school or done many of the things she had hoped to,
he still envied her the life she had built in some respects. The
relationship she had with her son was something he hoped to
emulate some day with his own kids.

"Don't you see? I had to see you tonight to give you back your
own advice."

He ran his hand over his face and closed his eyes.

"Your plan has served you well until now, but, Pete, life just
threw something at you, something that means you need to
make a new plan. I'm scared that if you try to stick to your old
one, you'll always regret it, just like I would have if I'd stuck to
mine all those years ago. Can you imagine all the love and joy I
would never have known if I hadn't had Scot? You saved me
from making the worst mistake of my life. I'm trying to do the
same for you."

# Chapter Twenty

Pete leaned back against the tree and watched the sunlight sparkle on the lake. He'd slept late this morning. There was something about his old room that gave him a sense of peace. He always slept well here, and he'd been exhausted after the last week. Jack sometimes ribbed him about going home to Mommy and Daddy, but he didn't care. He loved his parents and he loved this house. He appreciated how lucky he was to have grown up here, with his family as his foundation. Thinking of his friends and their backgrounds, he had to admit he'd had it good. He'd known love and stability his whole life.

How many times in his life had he sat in this very spot? Underneath this tree. In good times and bad he'd been able to come here to figure things out. Even to mourn. He looked at the plaque laid into the ground where his dog was buried. Kipper. He'd been such a good dog. One of the gang. He'd been as good of a friend as Ben, Missy, and Emma. He'd died just before Pete graduated high school. He still missed him.

This morning he needed time to think. He'd had so much advice thrown at him this week, and he hadn't stopped to analyze any of it. He'd overridden it all with his need to stick to the plan. Missy had stopped him in his tracks last night.

She'd given him reason to question everything. The perfect advice. His lips quirked at that—of course it was, it was his own advice she'd just given back to him. Had his seventeen-year-old self been so much wiser than he was now?

As he ran through the conversations he'd had with the people closest to him, he was starting to think so. Jack had repeatedly told him to forget the plan. Albert had told him Holly was in love with him. Ben had told him to get with the program. Nate had called him a hypocrite. Last night, after dinner, Missy had left him with a parting shot—his own advice again from all those years ago. *'If sticking to your plan means making a decision you can't live with, then it's time for a new plan.'* But what would his new plan look like? It would include Holly, for sure. But in what capacity? He needed to give this some thought.

"There you are! I brought you some milk."

He looked up at his mom. "You brought me what?"

She smiled at him and held his gaze with her own. He'd never figured out how she could pin him down like that.

"You heard me, dear. Milk. Like when you were little." She handed him a travel mug and sat down on the ground next to him. She dug in the pocket of her shirt, pulled out a baggie of cookies and handed them to him.

He grinned at her. "Thanks."

She leaned back against the tree with a smile. "Sometimes you need your mom, and your mom knows what you need."

Pete munched on the cookies and drank the milk. They'd been the comfort food she'd given him whenever he was having a hard time as a kid. He couldn't remember the last time he'd had them.

"We'd hoped to see you last night."

"Yeah. Sorry. Missy called and we had dinner."

"Did she manage to talk any sense into you?"

He frowned.

"It's alright dear. It's just so easy to see that you're struggling. You haven't come to your senses yet. Missy's a good girl, with a lot of sense. I'm only guessing she was trying to help you."

Pete smiled, his mom never missed a trick. "She tried. I came out here to try to put it all together."

"I thought. I won't keep you. Just wanted contribute milk and cookies to the process." They sat in silence for a while. "He was a good dog, wasn't he?"

"The best."

"Do you remember the day you found him?"

"I'll never forget," smiled Pete. "He followed me home, all bedraggled and thin. I begged you to let me keep him."

His mom laughed. "You have no idea what it took to talk your father into it."

Pete laughed with her. "I can imagine. Dad ended up loving him as much as we did though."

"Well, Kipper became one of the family, because you loved him so much."

Pete smiled sadly. "He did."

His mom patted his arm. "All because you changed your plan so you could keep him. Do you remember?"

Pete raised his eyebrows at her. Apparently even his mom was climbing on the bandwagon. "Why don't you go ahead and remind me and make your point?"

She smiled at him, not at all deterred by the fact that he saw through her ploy. "Peter, dear, when you found Kipper, you were doing your paper route. Earning money to fund your other little business ventures. You planned to keep doing that job until you'd saved enough to buy a lawn mower for your yard service. When Dad said you couldn't keep Kipper because of the paper route, what did you do? You gave it up. You changed your plans because you loved that dog. Love changes everything Pete. You knew that all those years ago. I needed to make sure that you haven't forgotten. Now. I need to paint. Have you finished with that mug?"

He smiled and handed it back to her.

"I'll be in the studio if you need me." She stood and planted a kiss on the top of his head. "I love you, dear. I like to think your father and I taught you how important love is."

Once she'd gone, Pete sat smiling to himself. How he loved his mom! She was right, of course. He'd never known her not to be. She'd laid out for him what his heart had been trying to tell him all along. He'd known it as a kid, but somewhere down the line he'd gotten so caught up in building the business, he'd forgotten. Love was more important than anything else on Earth. And he loved Holly.

~ ~ ~

Holly got off the bus and walked the last few blocks to the store. Ugh. Monday morning bus rides were so depressing. Much as she disliked driving, she'd take it any day over standing huddled with the sleepy, smelly bodies on the bus. Her old car may not be much, but it was her own personal space with her music and her coffee. Hopefully she'd be able to get it fixed this week. The guys at the garage had said they'd call today and let her know what the problem was. And, most importantly, how much it would cost to fix. She entered the store and relaxed a little. She was grateful this place was doing so well. Roberto and the girls had it running like a well-oiled machine. She just had to hope that those horrible loan men wouldn't really smash it up like they kept threatening. It seemed they had some cash flow problems of their own and were passing the pressure on to her. At least that was a problem she could actively deal with. She could go to the bank, withdraw more money and take it to them. If only there was some way she could actively deal with her sadness over Pete. She'd do whatever it took to lighten the heaviness in her heart, to lessen the pain. But there was nothing she could do. She just had to live with it.

"Morning, Holls. How are you?" Roberto peeked out from behind the shoe rack.

"Hey, sweetie. I'm okay thanks. Not much has changed in the last twelve hours." He'd kept his word, calling her every evening, trying to draw her out and entertain her with tales of his weekend with John. She didn't need to tell him that he'd been her only contact with the outside world in a weekend full of tears and sappy movies.

"There's fresh coffee in the back. You can make me one too," he smiled.

She had their coffees fixed by the time he came in the back.

"Darling, what's with riding the bus? Where's the beater?"

"Still in the garage. It's going to get fixed." She avoided his eyes, but couldn't ignore the pointed silence. "It is! They're going to call me today and let me know what's wrong with it."

"And you have the money to get it done?" Berto knew the deal with the loan sharks. She'd had to tell him months ago when one of their lackeys had been hanging around the store.

"I should be fine."

"Should be? Want to tell me what's going on? You can't fool your Uncle Berto, you know. I've noticed the goons are back."

Holly sighed. There was no point trying to hide it and she didn't have any fight left in her. "Sorry. I didn't want to worry you. They keep wanting more and more money. I'm okay though. I just keep giving it to them. The car may have to wait a while, but it's no biggie. I've ridden the bus most of my life, it's not like I'm above it." She pursed her lips—so what that a couple of weeks ago she'd been flying around in a private jet?! Now she was back in her own world, which meant riding the bus when she had to.

"I don't like it, Holls."

"Oh, it's not so bad when you get used to it," she smiled.

Berto swatted the air in front of him in annoyance. "I don't mean the buses and you know it. I mean this whole debt thing. Those people are dangerous. There has to be a way out of it."

"I wish there was, sweetie. I tried for a bank loan, but they turned me down. This is just how it is, I'm handling it. It's not like I have a rich aunt or loaded friends I can borrow from."

Berto gave her a pointed look. "You do have one friend who would help you out in a heartbeat if he knew what you're going through."

Tears pricked her eyes at the mention of Pete. "No I don't. He's just a guy I used to know and I don't want to talk about him. I'm doing well holding it together, don't push me over the edge sweetie, please?"

Roberto nodded. "Okay, okay. I'll leave it alone. For now." He took his coffee and went back out into the store.

By mid-morning Holly had had enough of computer work and went out into the store. A huge bouquet of lilies was walking through the store behind a beaming Roberto. When they stopped in front of her she could see there was a tiny guy carrying them. He handed them to her and left.

"What's he got to say then?" Berto looked like he was about to burst at the seams with curiosity. He plucked out the card and gave it to her. Holly looked over his shoulder at a man lurking by the lingerie. Oh no. It was the same one who'd been coming the last few weeks. She gave the card back to Berto. "Be a sweetie and put them in the back for me would you?"

"But Holls! You...." He followed her gaze. "Oh. I see."

As Holly walked toward the man, Berto handed the flowers to Erin to take in the back. He moved close enough to hear Holly's conversation with the man.

"I don't have it yet. I said I'd bring it tonight. I have to get it from the bank."

The man smiled at her, running his gaze over her body. Ugh! Even his eyes felt slimy.

"That's alright. I came to let you know that when you do go to the bank you need to double the withdrawal."

"What?"

"You heard me. Two grand tonight. Not one."

"But that's crazy! I can't!"

"Sure you can."

"No, really. I can't!"

The man smiled a lazy smile and stepped closer. He smelled of cigarettes and garlic. "Maybe you and me can reach an agreement then. I'll make sure they go easy on you," he reached out and touched her cheek, "if you're easy for me." He took another step closer. Holly stepped back, repulsed.

Roberto dashed to her side. "Can you come quick, please Holly? We need you at the register." He smiled at the man and dragged her away. Once they were at the back of the store Roberto looked over his shoulder. "Phew! He's gone."

Holly fled into the office and sat down before her knees gave way. Roberto followed her and sat down himself. "Oh my God, Holly Hocks! What are we going to do?"

Despite her panic, she had to smile at him. He was fanning himself agitatedly with a brochure. "*We* aren't going to do anything, sweetie. *You* are going to forget everything you just saw and heard. I am going to get myself to the bank and hit what's left of my savings. I can cover it."

"But Holls, you're not going to be able to keep covering it are you? And that man!" He shuddered and made such a disgusted face that she laughed. Perhaps it was hysteria at the rising panic?

She took a deep breath. "I can cover it for now Berto. Let's get through today and its problems before we go looking for more. Will you hold the fort while I run to the bank?"

"Of course, but at least take my car. It'll be so much quicker than the bus."

"Thanks, sweetie."

As he handed her the keys, Roberto's eyes landed on the lilies Erin had placed on the desk. "He'd help you, you know."

Holly shook her head. She couldn't afford to think about Pete. Her every instinct was crying out for him. It wasn't that she wanted his money to dig her out. Oh no. When that man had leered at her, touched her face, all she'd wanted was Pete to protect her. To make her feel safe in his warmth. To be there for her, with her. "Leave it, Berto. I'll be okay."

Pete had to park a couple of blocks away from the store. She should have the flowers by now. His heart was racing. He couldn't wait to see her. He'd missed her so much. He was nervous though. She hadn't replied to any of his texts or voice-mails, but that was understandable. She'd made her decision and he admired her strength. But she'd made that decision based on the old plan. Everything had changed, and she needed to know. He loved her, he needed to tell her. Did she really love him? He was about to find out.

He opened the door and entered the store. One of the girls smiled and waved at him. Where was Holly? He couldn't see her. He spotted Roberto though and started towards him. Roberto straightened up from the mannequin he'd been dressing and saw Pete. His face broke into a huge grin. Pete was relieved; he hadn't been sure what kind of reception he'd get from Holly's overly protective friend.

"Pete, darling! You have no idea how pleased I am to see you!" Roberto actually hugged him. Pete hugged back, filled with gratitude that this, at least, was better than he'd hoped for.

"Hey, Roberto. It's good to see you too, man. Did the flowers arrive?"

Roberto's face fell. Hmm, maybe this wasn't so good?

"Yes they arrived, but not at the best moment."

Pete frowned, what did that mean? He looked at Roberto who, for the first time in Pete's experience, looked uncomfortable.

"Umm, she had another visitor and she had to go."

"Another visitor?" Nate's words rang in his head, *'A woman like Holly won't be short on offers.'* But so soon? She wouldn't? She couldn't be?

"No!" Roberto could see what he was thinking. "Not that kind of visitor, just some business she had to take care of right away."

"I see." Pete really didn't. He knew how hard it was to get her to leave the store. "Where did she go?"

"To the bank."

That was strange. She did her banking on Fridays. Something didn't feel right and Roberto was looking more uncomfortable by the minute.

"What's going on?"

"Um, I don't think it's my place to say."

"Can you at least give me a clue? Should I just give up and leave?" If she'd already found someone else, then perhaps that's what she'd want him to do? Roberto had said not, but he was giving off a weird vibe like he was hiding something.

"Oh no, Pete! Don't do that! *Please*, don't do that. It's not a man thing, it's a money thing. I think she's in a bit of trouble and I know she wouldn't want me to tell you about it."

"What kind of trouble?" he asked, but he suspected he already knew.

"I don't think I should say."

"It's alright, I know about the debt. I wanted to help her, but she wouldn't let me."

Roberto's face flooded with relief. "You know? Oh, Pete, it's been horrible! The man that came this morning was sleazing all over her! He scared me!"

"What did he say?" Pete's fist clenched at his side as a wave of anger coursed through him. Some guy was sleazing all over her? They were coming into her store? And she'd gone running straight to the bank? He had to make it stop. "Do you know who they are?" Roberto nodded. "Do you know how much she owes them?" He hesitated, but then nodded again. "Okay. You are going to help me to help her. I came here today to ask if she'll have me back, but more important than that, I'm going to pay off that debt. If she hates me for doing it, then so be it. At least she'll be safe. I shouldn't have let her talk me out of it before. I'm going to take care of it. Are you with me?" Roberto nodded once more. "Is she going straight to pay them once she's been to the bank?"

"No. She has to go see them tonight. She should be back soon, she took my car."

"Where's hers?"

"In the garage, she can't even pay to get it fixed."

Damn! She was in a mess. Why hadn't he pushed her to let him help? "Can you take a lunch break when she gets back?"

"Yes."

"Call me then and we'll go take care of this."

~ ~ ~

Holly paced the store. It was quiet this afternoon. Of course, it was always quiet when she wanted it to be busy. She wanted to be distracted, to make the time go faster. She wanted to go make the payment and go home. For all her bravado in front of Berto, that man this morning had scared her. It seemed he'd scared Berto too. He'd left for lunch as soon as she'd come back from the bank. He'd hardly said a word to her before he left and was gone for ages. Since he finally came back, she'd swear he was avoiding her. She felt bad. He'd been so supportive, but even Berto had his limits.

She had no idea how she would be able to keep up with the payments if they were going to pull stunts like today. Double the money, just like that? The store was doing well, but it wasn't a limitless source of money. She still had a few thousand left in her savings, but at this rate that would all be gone soon. She didn't dare think what might happen then. The guy from the garage had called a little while ago, but she'd let it go to voice-mail. The car would have to wait. She needed every penny to keep the loan men off her back. She shuddered at the memory of the guy this morning—she needed to keep *him* off her! She'd leave in half an hour and go give them the money. Then she could go home and figure out how she would cope next week. And the week after.

She looked up and saw the guy from this morning enter the store. *Oh, no. What now?*

The man walked through the store, heading for Holly. Her heart raced, wondering what crazy demands he was going to make this time. She went to meet him. She may be afraid, but he didn't have to know that. "What do you want now?"

"To give you this." He held out a manila envelope.

Holly looked at it, not sure that she wanted to take it. The man shifted from one foot to the other and thrust it toward her. Whereas this morning he'd been cocky and threatening, now he looked ill at ease and eager to be gone. She took the envelope and opened it.

"The boss sends his regards, and his assurance you won't be hearing from us again."

Holly stared at the sheet of paper in her hand. A receipt. PAID IN FULL.

She looked at the man, "What the...?"

"Look, lady. It's paid. We're done. You tell your friend we don't want no trouble. We leave you alone, he leaves us alone." He turned and scurried out of the store, leaving Holly still staring at the receipt in her hand.

She looked for Roberto, but he was talking on his cell phone. She went into the office and plonked herself down, stunned. Pete! It could only be Pete. Roberto peeked his head around the door.

"Is everything alright?"

She looked up at him, still lost for words. He came into the office, looking kind of shifty, fiddling with his cuff links and not meeting her eye. "Berto, what do you know about this?"

"About what?" He was a hopeless liar. His cheeks were pink and he was looking everywhere except at her.

She thrust the paper at him. "This! My debt has been paid off and those people are scared of my friend, whoever that may be! We both know it could only be one person. So what do you know about it?"

Roberto hung his head and said nothing. Holly's phone buzzed in her pocket. She automatically reached for it. It was a text from Pete.

*Go easy on Roberto. I'm the one you're mad at. I'm at home.*

Holly stared at the text, then at Roberto. "What did you do?"

"He came to the store, Holls. Just after you'd gone to the bank."

"And?"

"And I think you need to talk to him about it. Not me."

Holly drew in a deep breath. He was right. She did. Damn Pete! He'd promised her he'd leave it alone. Who the hell did he think he was?! She glared at Roberto. "Can you close up tonight?"

He nodded with a little smile.

"Don't you dare!" she yelled. "I'm madder than hell at you! I'm going to tell him what I think of him, too!"

Roberto grinned, now. "Do you want me to call you a cab?"

Damn! She'd have to. It wasn't like the buses ran to Pete's swanky neighborhood. "Yes. Thank you. We will talk about this tomorrow."

# Chapter Twenty-One

The cab pulled in to Pete's driveway. Holly focused on her anger. He was a Bigshot asshole! That's what he was. He had discarded her because she didn't fit his plan. He had no right to interfere in her life. She could handle her own problems! She paid the driver and watched the cab drive away. Well, here went nothing. She started up the steps to the front door, then stopped. Oh no. He had company. There was a blue BMW sitting outside the garage. Damn, she wished she hadn't let the cab leave. What had she been thinking? There was nothing for it now. She'd come to give him a piece of her mind. She was going to do just that, company or not. She continued up the steps.

The front door opened and there he was. He was even more gorgeous than she remembered, wearing a black shirt with gray pants and a gray tie. He leaned in the doorway, frowning down at her, blue eyes blazing. He looked...angry? What right did *he* have to be angry? She stomped up the steps and stood before him, glaring at him.

"What the hell have you done?" she demanded.

He raised an eyebrow. His face tight with anger. "Would you like to discuss this inside?"

"Not if you have company, no. I just want you to tell me what you think you're playing at!"

"I don't have company and I am not getting into this on the doorstep." He turned and went back into the house.

She stormed after him. "What do you think gives you the right to interfere in my life? I asked you to stay out of it, remember?"

"Oh, I remember, sweetheart." His voice was low and controlled. "I also remember that you made me a promise. You broke that promise, so I took matters into my own hands."

"What do you mean? I didn't break a promise!"

He took a step towards her, towering above her. His warmth permeated her anger. Even in these circumstances, she was grateful to be close to him again.

His eyes burned into her. "You promised me that if there was a problem, if it got ugly, you would tell me. You'd let me help."

She had promised that. "Yes, but...."

"No. No buts. I will not allow you to be in danger. I took care of it. End of story."

The arrogant pig! "You will not allow it?" She couldn't help the bitter laugh. "Excuse me, Mr. Bigshot, but you don't get to say what's allowed in my life. It's none of your goddamned business! You have your plan, remember? I'm not part of it and my problems are none of your concern!" He was so arrogant! She was not a charity case!

He caught hold of her arm. The pulse in his jaw was working overtime. "It *is* my business. *You* are my business."

She tried to pull away from him, but he held tight. "No I'm not, Pete." She could hear the tears in her voice. *No!* She could not show her weakness now. His warm hand closed around the back of her neck, forcing her to look up into his eyes. They burned into her own as he pulled her against him. Despite her anger, her body betrayed her as she melted against his hard chest.

"You are my business, sweetheart," he breathed. "You will always be my business, because I love you."

Holly froze and stared into his eyes. The truth stared back at her from the blue depths. "But what about the plan?"

The corners of his lips quirked up before they found hers. He kissed her so tenderly, deep and slow as he held her against him. She could feel his heart thundering in his chest as his strong arms encircled her. When he lifted his head, he still held her close. "It's time for a new plan. The old one doesn't work anymore because you're not in it."

She looked up at him, not quite believing she was hearing this. "But...but...."

"But what, Sweetheart? Don't you want me?"

She was shocked by the doubt and uncertainty on his face. Her arms came up around his neck. "I want you more than I want my next breath, Pete. I just don't know how it could work. How you could change your plan."

He smiled and kissed the tip of her nose. "I didn't know either. Until I tried to live without you. That made me realize that nothing is as important to me as you are. I need you in my life. The rest is just detail. We'll work it out. I love you, Holly."

She really wasn't imagining it. He'd said it twice now. He loved her!

"Tell me one thing, though. Why did you leave the wedding like that?" His eyes bored into hers until she had to tell him the truth.

"Because I didn't want to say goodbye to you." She lowered her eyes, but he hooked his thumb under her chin and raised her face to him.

"Why?"

*Oh, hell!* Here it came. "I couldn't stand to say goodbye to you, because I love you too, Pete."

His eyes were that deep violet color as his face relaxed and he held her close in the circle of his arms. She knew she was back where she belonged, safe and protected in his warmth and his love. She clung to him as he lifted her and carried her up to his bedroom. They peeled the clothes off each other and fell onto his bed. He pinned her underneath him, spreading her legs with his knees. She held on to his shoulders and pulled him down to kiss her as he thrust inside her already slick entrance. He was so hot and hard, filling her as she arched her body up to him. His lips left hers and he held her eyes as they moved together.

"I love you, sweetheart." His words took her to the edge.

"I love you, Pete," she cried as he exploded, taking her over the edge, flying away to a place where only they existed.

~ ~ ~

Pete pulled her closer to him as they recovered. She was his and he wasn't ever going to let her go. He would never be that stupid again. He wouldn't go back to a life that she wasn't a part of.

She wriggled around and looked up at him. "I do love you, but I'm still mad at you."

He tried to suppress a smile, but couldn't manage it. "You could consider it a gift."

She frowned. "No I couldn't. I don't get gifts like that."

He propped himself up on his elbow and smiled down at her, tracing her cheek with his finger. "You do now, sweetheart, you'd better get used to it." He couldn't wait to spoil her with gifts. There was one he was desperate to give her right now, but he knew she had to get this debt thing out of her system first.

"No, Pete, I'm serious. You can't just bail me out with that kind of money, it's not right. I need to pay you back."

He nodded. He'd known she wouldn't just accept it. "I thought you might see it that way. So, I've been thinking. The amount I paid today is actually less than I'd penciled into the budget for consulting on the plaza."

Her eyes were wide. "Seriously?"

"I told you it was a big fee. If you take the project, we'll still owe you some. Will you think about it?"

He watched her face as she considered it. She nodded slowly, but from the smile on her face he was hoping the answer would be yes.

~ ~ ~

Holly sat at the kitchen counter watching Pete pour the wine. She was still trying to take all this in. He loved her! She loved him. She didn't know what that might mean, or how they would work this. All that mattered was that they would work something out. They would keep seeing each other. That was all she wanted. As he said, the rest was just detail. Instead of bringing her drink over, he took both glasses and went to sit at the table in the nook off the kitchen. She followed and took a seat opposite him. They'd never sat in here, she liked it. It was a cozy little space with a window overlooking the garage. She looked down at the BMW out there.

"Do you know, I nearly turned tail and fled when I saw that car. I thought you had company."

Pete gave her a mysterious smile. "Come here. There's something I need to tell you about that car."

She frowned, wondering what he might mean. He held out his hand and she came around the table to sit in his lap. He wrapped his arms around her and held her close. She hooked her arms around his neck and kissed him. She'd missed his kisses and intended to make up for lost time.

He lifted his head. "Don't you want to know?"

"Know what?" She nuzzled into his neck and felt him shake underneath her as he chuckled.

"About the car."

"Oh. Yes. What?" She really didn't care, she just wanted to enjoy the feel of him. She snuggled closer and rested her head on his shoulder.

He kissed her neck then whispered in her ear, "It's yours."

She sat bolt upright, staring at him. "It's what?!"

His shoulders were shaking as he laughed his rich, deep laugh. "I said it's yours, sweetheart. For you. From me."

"Oh my God, Pete! You can't do that! I...."

He was still laughing as he pecked her lips. "I can and I have." His eyes were so full of love as he smiled down at her.

She clung to him. "Thank you!"

"There. Was that so hard? You are most welcome, my love. You want to take a look?"

They went down the back steps, and he handed her the key and opened the driver's door.

She sat inside and grinned—it was brand new! "Pete, I've never sat in a brand new car before, let alone owned one! Holy crap, Bigshot!" She got out of the car and jumped on him, laughing. "Thank you, thank you, thank you!"

He spun her around, then put her down. "No, sweetheart. Thank *you*." She pinched him and he laughed. "Yep, I'm for real."

She was struggling to believe it. "I need to check," she laughed. "I'd hate to wake up and find out you were just a dream." She pinched him again, just to make sure.

"Hey!" He laughed. "That tickles!"

"Nooo!" Her eyes grew wide and she tried to dodge him, but he was too fast. He had hold of her and was tickling her mercilessly. She couldn't stop laughing as she struggled to get away, but he held her fast. "Stop!" she begged, but he just kept on tickling and laughing. "Please, Pete, you've got to stop," she managed to get out through her laughter.

He turned her to face him and held her gaze, giving her a breather, but his hands were poised to continue. "You know there's only one way to make me stop. So, do you?"

She knew what he wanted. She brought her arms up around his neck and looked deep into his eyes. "I surrender."

~ ~ ~

"What do you think? Shall we have Smoke fly us up there tomorrow, or do you want to take your new car?"

They were sitting on the loungers by the pool. It had been such an amazing week. She'd stayed with him on Monday night and he'd talked her into taking the rest of the week off. They'd stopped by the store on Tuesday to thank Roberto for the part he'd played. Holly had tried to be cross with him, but hadn't been able to manage it. She was too grateful. They'd collected some of her things from her house and spent the rest of the week hiding out at Pete's, swimming in the pool, making love, walking on the beach, talking into the small hours, and making love some more. They'd gone out for dinner at Mario's and she'd driven. In her new car. She still couldn't quite believe it was hers, that he'd bought it for her. It drove like a dream.

"Let's take the car, can we? Road trips are a lot more appealing with my new wheels." She smiled at him. "Thank you, Pete. Thank you so much."

He reached across and took her hand. "As I have told you, you are more than welcome, my love. Do you want to leave at lunchtime? I have to take care of a couple of details in the morning, but then I'd like to get going. If you don't mind, I'd like us to stay at the cabin tomorrow night. Jack and Em won't get in 'til late and my parents are also coming in late. I'd like to see them Saturday morning before we go to the BBQ."

"That works for me. I should call Missy and let her know that I am coming after all, but I won't be staying with her."

Pete smirked. "She'd invited you to stay there?"

Holly nodded, "I didn't want to go at all."

His face was pained now. "Because you didn't want to be around me?"

She squeezed his hand. "I didn't want to be around you if I couldn't be with you."

"Well you're with me now, sweetheart, and you're never getting rid of me again."

She liked the sound of that.

"Do me a favor though?"

"What's that?"

"Don't call Missy. Let's just show up and surprise them?" He gave her a mischievous grin. "They'll forgive us anything once they know we're together."

She laughed, he was right. "Alright then, let's surprise them."

~ ~ ~

Pete worked the muscles in her neck. Man, she was tight. "We need to work this tension out of you, sweetheart."

She sighed and leaned back against him, giving him the perfect view over her shoulder of the steaming bubbles foaming around her breasts. He felt his desire stir, though how he had any energy left, he had no clue. He hadn't been able to keep his hands off her all week. Sitting here in the hot tub with her naked body between his legs, he wanted her again. He'd promised her a back rub though, and he intended to make good on his promise first.

"I don't see how I could have any tension left in me. This has been the best week ever." She turned around and knelt to face him. Putting her hands on his shoulders, she kissed him. Her lips were so soft. "Thank you, Pete. I love you. You make me so happy."

"That's the plan, sweetheart."

Her face clouded over, there were questions in her eyes, but she said nothing.

"What is it?"

"It's just. Well. I'm scared to ask, but what is the plan now? I mean, I'm glad you didn't stick to the old one, but I know you. I know you must have a new plan. I'm just scared to know what it might be." She hesitated. "But I think I need to know."

He drew her closer to him, lifting her so she straddled his lap. He smiled as he ran his hands down her back and pulled her closer so he was pushing at her opening. He tucked a strand of hair behind her ear. Holding her gaze, he said, "There is a new plan, and it goes like this." He held her hips as he thrust inside her, loving the way she grasped his shoulders, eyes wide as she began to ride him. The way her breasts dipped in and out of the steaming bubbles as she rocked her hips.

He reached down between them and coaxed her with his thumb. "I plan to have you." Feeling her tense, he let himself go and pulled her down against him, carrying them both through a shuddering orgasm. He kept his arms around her as she lay against his chest, breathing hard as they recovered. He kissed her neck. "And I plan to hold you."

She turned her head and met his eyes. He smiled, not sure if she understood, yet. He let go of her and climbed out of the hot tub. He toweled himself off then held out his hand. She stepped out and let him dry her down too. "I love you." He wrapped her in the towel and brushed her lips with his own. "And I plan to cherish you." He left her standing in the moonlight while he went inside the cabin. He returned with two glasses of champagne and a lump in his towel.

She was looking at him, confused. Maybe she wasn't getting this. He had to be sure. He set the glasses on the picnic table and turned to her, taking hold of her hand. "So, just to recap. I plan to have you, and to hold you. I plan to love you, and to cherish you." He smiled as he saw realization begin to dawn in her eyes. "For richer, for poorer, in good times and in bad. I plan to love you, for always. I've forsaken all others since the day I met you and I will until the day I die." He dropped down on one knee and held up the box he'd had hidden in his towel. "Holly, will you marry me?"

Her hands flew to her mouth and her eyes filled with tears. "Yes, Pete! Oh God yes!"

He stood up and wrapped her in his arms, kissing her with all the love he felt. "You just granted me everything I want in life, sweetheart. My plan is to do the same for you, for the rest of your days. Holly *you are* my new plan. You, me, and our kids when we have them."

Her eyes flew up to meet his. "Our kids? Oh, Pete, I want kids. I want your kids." She flung her arms around his neck. "I love you, Pete. I love you so much."

He'd thought this moment was supposed to be somber and serious, but he felt the laughter bubbling up. "And I love you, sweetheart. Now, do you want this ring?"

She loosened her grip on his neck and pecked his lips with a grin. "Oh. Yeah. Sorry!" She looked down at the open box in his hand and then back up at him in shock. "Holy shit, Bigshot! It's enormous!"

God, how he loved this woman! He shook with laughter as he pulled her against him so she could feel his arousal. "I like to think so."

She laughed and patted his bulging towel. "This guy is perfect for me. But that diamond? Geez, Pete! It's huge!"

"It has to be, it represents all my love for you." He took the ring from the box and took hold of her hand after she transferred her grandmother's wedding band to her right hand. He slid the diamond onto her finger, then looked into her eyes. "I love you, sweetheart."

Her arms came up around his neck and their towels fell to the ground as she pressed herself against him. "And I love you, Bigshot."

# Chapter Twenty-Two

Holly looked across at Pete, her fiancé! She was happy to let him drive her new car to Gramps', since she didn't know her way around Summer Lake, yet anyway. Though, as he'd told her this morning, she'd have the rest of her life to learn. He was making all her dreams come true. This beautiful place, their wonderful friends up here, he was sharing it all with her. It was her life too, now. Most of all though, *he* was her dream come true. He was hers, he only wanted her, and he wanted her enough to change his plan. They were getting married!

They'd gone to see his parents this morning to share the good news. She'd confessed to him before they went that she was a little nervous. They really were from a different world than she was.

"But sweetheart, you felt that way about me remember? And besides, you and Mom seemed to be getting along very well, until I showed up and spoiled it."

He'd been right of course. Anne had immediately put her at ease. Holly really did like her, and Graham, he was just like Pete! How lucky was she to get wonderful in-laws thrown in with her gorgeous fiancé? Everything about them, and their huge home, was grand, classy, and clearly very wealthy, but at the same time so warm, inviting—and fun! She could see that Pete's sense of fun was definitely a family trait. From Anne waggling her elegant eyebrows very suggestively, when she'd inquired how soon she could expect grandbabies, to Graham swatting his wife's backside as she'd bent over, everything about them was light-hearted and loving. She hoped Pete would like her family even half as much as she liked his. She felt a little bad that she hadn't even called them yet to tell them. She hoped her dad would forgive Pete for not following the old ways. Her family was quite traditional, both her brothers-in-law had sought his permission before proposing to her sisters. She was sure Pete would win him over though.

That beautiful smile was playing on his lips as he reached for her hand and held it on top of his thigh as he drove.

"What are you smirking at, Bigshot?"

"How happy I am. How lucky I am. How dumb I was being, and what great friends we have. Most of all, I'm smiling because I love you, sweetheart. I can't quite believe that you love me back. That we're going to get married, and that we have our whole lives ahead of us. Together."

Holly still couldn't quite believe it either. "I feel the same way, Pete. I keep wanting to pinch you. I'm scared I'll wake up and find it was all just a dream."

He squeezed her hand. "It's no dream. Welcome to our new reality." He turned the car onto the West Shore Road toward Gramps' place. "We need to figure out what this reality is going to look like, too."

"How do you mean?"

"Well, like we said, we're together, that's everything, the rest is just detail. But the details still need to be determined. Like whether you're going to do the plaza with me. How much time you want to spend at the store, or in LA at all. How much time we want to spend up here. What we're going to do with the house here." He grinned at her. "I told you in the beginning that you have impeccable timing. Well, you're in time to have your input on how we build our house. The basic plans are done, but I'm sure Jack can tweak it, if you want to change it. We can do whatever you like with the interior, finishes, appliances, flooring, all that stuff. I want you to have what you want."

Holly just stared at him. This wasn't like any reality she'd ever known. "Pete, that's so sweet of you, but I already have what I want, and that's you. I don't want you to change your life or how you build your house. I certainly don't want you spending more money on me. I know all that stuff is important to you, but it doesn't mean anything to me. All I want is to love you, and for you to love me."

He smiled across at her. "I do love you, sweetheart. The stuff is no more important to me than it is to you. If you can honestly tell me you'd be happier, we can go live in your townhouse. I don't care as long as we're together. But I don't think you would be happier...you're just not used to having options. I want you to get used to it. Remember my old plan was about holding off, until I had everything in place for the right woman and our family. Because of your impeccable timing, you came along sooner than I planned. It's so much better this way. You're not just stepping into the life I prepared, we get to build it together, to suit us both." He shook her hand so the bracelet jangled on her wrist. "Remember I said it's about building the best life you can? It took Nate to remind me what that really means. He also said I become something more when I'm with you. It's true. I don't want you to fit into my life, I want more than that. I want *us* to build *our* life, which will be something so much better than I could ever build alone. I want everything that you bring to the relationship. I'm happy to admit that you bring things I don't have, and I want you to share them with me. I hope you will accept and want to share what I bring. Does that make sense to you?"

She leaned across and kissed his cheek. "It does. I may struggle for a while though, to get used to it. Your world really is so very different from mine. You don't know where I come from, my family, my life, where I grew up. It's not like this." She loved her family, but her background was so different.

"We'll both have a lot of learning and adjusting to do as we figure this out, sweetheart. And," he shot her a sideways glance, "We can get started on it tomorrow afternoon." His lips were curving up at the corners.

What was he up to now? "What are we doing tomorrow afternoon, Bigshot?"

"Going to see your folks."

"Sunday afternoon? But everyone will be there. My sisters, the kids, everyone. It's a madhouse on Sundays. We could go in the week?" No way did she want his first encounter with her crazy clan to be the full-on Sunday experience. There would be kids running around screaming, television blaring, bothers-in-law in the back yard, drinking beer and working on motorcycles.

He was grinning at her. "Sorry, sweetheart, but they're expecting us tomorrow."

"They're what?!"

"That's where I went on Friday. To see your dad, and ask his permission. I promised that, if you said yes, we'd be over Sunday afternoon, just like the rest of the family. You might want to call them to let them know."

She stared at him in disbelief. "You did what?"

His grin grew even bigger. "Sweetheart, I couldn't ask you to marry me without seeing your dad first. I think he likes me. I think your mom does too. You're not ashamed of me, are you?"

She let go of his hand and pinched him, hard.

"Ouch!"

"You deserved that one! You know damned well I'm not ashamed of you. And Pete, you do know I'm not ashamed of my family either?" She didn't want him to think that. She just didn't know how to build a bridge between two such different worlds.

His eyes softened now, "Yes, sweetheart, I do. I just know you still have some hang-ups about our differences. I figured the quickest way to get over them is to let me into your life. I told you, you bring things to the table that I want. I can't wait to have sisters and brothers-in-law, nephews and nieces. To be part of a big rowdy family. You don't get any of that as an only child of older parents, you know."

"Be careful what you wish for, Bigshot. You have no idea." He was right of course. They were getting married, their different worlds would become one big mix. When she thought about it, her family would love him. He would love them. She could even imagine her mom with Anne. She smiled at him now. Then pinched him one more time. "Are you sure you're real? I'm starting to think this is all too good to be true."

"It's for real. I'm for real, *we* are for real." He squeezed her hand as he pulled off the road and into Gramps' driveway. "Now, are you ready for this?"

She smiled and nodded. She couldn't wait to see their friends' reactions when they told them. Emma was going to be so smug, and she didn't mind at all. There were quite a few cars along the driveway. She could see Missy's van and Jack's truck.

The whole gang was sitting at one of the long tables they'd used for the wedding reception. Gramps and Jack were working the grill.

Missy was the first to spot them as they walked down the path. "Yay!" she shouted. "You finally saw sense!"

Pete put his arm around Holly's shoulders and grinned. "Yeah. With a little help from my friends. Thanks, Miss."

Jack came over from the grill to shake Pete's hand and slap his back. "About time, bro!" He turned to Holly, hugged her, and clasped her hand. She watched his eyes grow big as he saw the ring. He looked at Pete with a huge grin. "New plan?"

Pete laughed and pulled her against him. "Yep. Thanks, partner. Meet my new plan."

"Em! Guys! You need to see this." Everyone crowded around them as Jack held her hand up to show off the ring.

"Yes!" cried Missy.

"Oh my goodness!" shouted Emma. "I was right! Congratulations! I'm so happy for you both!"

Dan came and hugged her. "Didn't I tell you?" He laughed.

Ben punched Pete's arm. "Told you, bud!"

Laura admired the ring, eyes wide. "That is sooo beautiful. Congratulations, girlfriend!"

Holly beamed at them all, this really was her life now. Pete stood behind her and wrapped his arms around her waist. She felt as though her world was filled with all the warmth and light he brought. She was back where she belonged, in his arms, in this place, with all these wonderful people who were her friends too; she really did belong here. Pete planted a kiss on the top of her head and looked around at everyone. "So, who wants to help plan a wedding?" he asked;

# A Note from SJ

I hope you enjoyed visiting Summer Lake and catching up with the gang. Please let your friends know about the books if you feel they would enjoy them as well. It would be wonderful if you would leave me a review, I'd very much appreciate it.

To come back to the lake and get to know more couples as they each find their happiness, you can check out the rest of the series on my website

www.SJMcCoy.com

Missy and Dan are next in Dance Like Nobody's Watching.

Additionally, you can take a trip to Montana and meet a whole new group of friends. Take a look at my Remington Ranch series. It focuses on four brothers and the sometimes rocky roads they take on the way to their Happily Ever Afters.

There are a few options to keep up with me and my imaginary friends:

The best way is to Join up on the website for my Newsletter. Don't worry I won't bombard you! I'll let you know about upcoming releases, share a sneak peek or two and keep you in the loop for a couple of fun giveaways I have coming up :0)
You can join my readers group to chat about the books on Facebook or just browse and like my Facebook Page

I occasionally attempt to say something in 140 characters or less(!) on Twitter

And I'm always in the process of updating my website at www.SJMcCoy.com with new book updates and even some videos. Plus, you'll find the latest news on new releases and giveaways in my blog.

I love to hear from readers, so feel free to email me at AuthorSJMcCoy@gmail.com.. I'm better at that! :0)

I hope our paths will cross again soon. Until then, take care, and thanks for your support—you are the reason I write!
Love
SJ

# PS Project Semicolon

You may have noticed that the final sentence of the story closed with a semi-colon. It isn't a typo. Project Semi Colon is a non-profit movement dedicated to presenting hope and love to those who are struggling with depression, suicide, addiction and self-injury. Project Semicolon exists to encourage, love and inspire. It's a movement I support with all my heart.

*"A semicolon represents a sentence the author could have ended, but chose not to. The sentence is your life and the author is you."*

\- Project Semicolon

This author started writing after her son was killed in a car crash. At the time I wanted my own story to be over, instead I chose to honour a promise to my son to write my 'silly stories' someday. I chose to escape into my fictional world. I know for many who struggle with depression, suicide can appear to be the only escape. The semicolon has become a symbol of support, and hopefully a reminder – Your story isn't over yet

# Also by SJ McCoy

## Summer Lake Series

Love Like You've Never Been Hurt (FREE in ebook form)
Work Like You Don't Need the Money
Dance Like Nobody's Watching
Fly Like You've Never Been Grounded
Laugh Like You've Never Cried
Sing Like Nobody's Listening
Smile Like You Mean It
The Wedding Dance
Chasing Tomorrow
Dream Like Nothing's Impossible

*Coming next*
### Ride Like You've Never Fallen

## Remington Ranch Series

Mason (FREE in ebook form)
Shane
Carter
Beau
Four Weddings and a Vendetta

*Coming next*
### Chance

# About the Author

I'm SJ, a coffee addict, lover of chocolate and drinker of good red wines. I'm a lost soul and a hopeless romantic. Reading and writing are necessary parts of who I am. Though perhaps not as necessary as coffee! I can drink coffee without writing, but I can't write without coffee.

I grew up loving romance novels, my first boyfriends were book boyfriends, but life intervened, as it tends to do, and I wandered down the paths of non-fiction for many years. My life changed completely a few years ago and I returned to Romance to find my escape.

I write 'Sweet n Steamy' stories because to me there is enough angst and darkness in real life. My favorite romances are happy escapes with a focus on fun, friendships and happily-ever-afters, just like the ones I write.

These days I live in beautiful Montana, the last best place. If I'm not reading or writing, you'll find me just down the road in the park - Yellowstone. I have deer, eagles and the occasional bear for company, and I like it that way :0)

JUL 2019

$19.95

50059071R00182

Made in the USA
Middletown, DE
23 June 2019